Below the Falls

Below the Falls
Rich Oliver

Dedication
To all my fellow nerds and those who love nature and the beauty of Texas and its wildflowers.

Acknowledgments
My thanks to all of my beta and final draft readers especially Clarise, Mary S., Mary T, Julia, and Sara for their help with reviewing and editing.

Published by: EquipU LLC
This is a work of fiction. Although based on the author's experience, all persons, events and names are fictional. Any resemblance to actual persons, living or dead, or actual events is purely coincidental.

ISBN: 978-0-9766569-4-4

NEW GIRL IN TOWN

JD leaned forward over the handlebars and pumped the pedals as fast as possible. The wind raced past, pulling on his shirt. He flew down the dirt road to town, imagining himself Clark Kent, aka Superboy. The bike frame vibrated as the tires ran over the rough gravel surface of the road, and a dust cloud followed the back tire. The road made it a rough, bumpy ride, but nothing could keep him from his appointed task of picking up groceries for his mom.

He looked up and applied full pressure to the brakes as a car turned in front of him. The bike skidded to a stop, tossing dirt into the air. Super-quick reactions kept him and his quest alive, and the use of his super abilities went unnoticed by the occupants. The vehicle pulled into Grandma Sullivan's house, a short distance from his mom's.

Grandma Sullivan was not his grandmother. The title of "Grandma" was a title of honor and respect given to her by the town. JD's paternal grandmother had passed away years ago when he was just a baby. It was shortly after his father was killed in the early days of the Korean War. His paternal grandfather passed away recently. His maternal grandparents lived back east in Virginia.

He rode past the driveway, stopped, and looked back at the car. It was Grandma Sullivan's car, alright, but Grandma Sullivan was not well. He knew this because he helped keep her garden and lawn looking trimmed. His mother went grocery shopping for her two weeks ago. "Who could be driving her car?" he thought. A woman and a girl got out of the vehicle. He didn't recognize the woman or the girl. The girl turned and smiled at him. She looked about his age.

JD frowned and continued down the road into town. None of his guy friends lived nearby. He wanted a guy friend to hang out with this summer, not a girl. He mulled the incident over and over in his mind. A stream of thoughts raced through his head. "Why God? Why another girl? Why? Why couldn't it have been a boy? Who are they? Why are they visiting Grandma Sullivan?"

He stopped at the highway intersection before riding across. The highway was the main road leading into and through the town. It was always busy with trucks. The crossing was just below a hill, so knowing if it was safe to cross was difficult. Taking the back way to town was longer, but that route avoided the traffic on the highway. It was also the "mom-approved" way to go. The first destination for this outing was around the square to Buckman's Newsstand and Bookstore in town. His mom always stopped at Buckman's on the way back from church to pick up a Sunday paper. Purchasing comics and science magazines with hard-earned money was permitted, but it had to be done under his mother's watchful eye during the Sunday visits to Buckman's. Today, he had free access to the bookstore and could browse freely without his mom scrutinizing his purchases.

"Hey, JD, running errands today?" Mr. Buckman said as JD walked into the store. "I just got in the new Superman comic and the latest issue of Scientific American."

The wooden plank floor creaked as he walked to the comic book racks. Tall, expansive windows let in enough light to preview the titles, and ceiling fans overhead slowly circulated the air through the store. He breathed deeply and smiled. Only a library could evoke a similar sensation in him, but the smell of freshly printed comic books and magazines in the bookstore beat the library hands down.

"Thanks, Mr. Buckman. I only have fifty cents. I want to get the comic and the Scientific American, but I can only buy the comic today."

"I'll tell you what, I'll spot you the comic, and you can owe me the twenty-five cents extra for the magazine."

"Oh, I couldn't do that. My mother wouldn't want me to accept any charity."

"Okay, I understand. While you are here, can you help me with this old desk fan? It's been making a squeaky noise. Think you can fix it?"

"I can try. Do you have any tools?"

"I have a toolbox full."

JD turned off the fan, removed the cage and the retaining nut from the fan blades, and then pulled off the fan. "Okay. Let me see. Yeah, just as I suspected, some twine got wrapped around the shaft. Here, let me see if I can remove it. Almost. It's wound tight. There, I got it!"

He reassembled the fan. "Let's turn it back on."

"Would you look at that. Blowing air and no squeaky sound. How did you learn so much about fixing things? Most kids your age don't know that stuff."

"I'll be a freshman when school starts in the fall. My granddad taught me most of what I know. He showed me how to fix the tractor and take my bike apart. I do read a lot, and I took one semester of shop class at school last year."

"Fixing that fan is worth the comic book and the extra twenty-five cents. How about you ask your mother if you can come to work part-time for me? I could use your special talents in the store. I'll pay you seventy-five cents an hour and throw in a few comic books and magazines. What do you say?"

"That sounds super. I'll ask my mom. Thanks, Mr. Buckman!"

JD carefully tucked his new treasures in the front wire basket and headed to the grocery store. He wanted his comics and science magazines to last forever, so he treated them like prized possessions. His mother wanted his comic books to disappear as soon as possible. His mother supported his curiosity and reading, but she wished he read the Bible more, or at least the classics. JD wanted to escape into the fantasy world that his comics created. The science magazines opened his eyes to the world's wonders.

He loved exploring everything he could on the ranch and in the city park. He brought back interesting rocks and bugs and even collected water samples to investigate with his microscope. Exploring the natural world excited him, but his comic books let him explore beyond reality. They opened his mind to new possibilities.

Besides being the Mom approved route, going through the park back home was worth the extra time. He considered the park a magical place. A river ran through the entire length of the park, and springs fed into the river along one side. The same river cut through part of his mom's land. A spring-fed creek ran behind both houses and fed into the river. Nature was everywhere, and it flowed in his blood despite his nerdy science brain. Growing up on a farm allowed him to acquire skills he would not have in a city, and having nature out the back door of his house provided him with a real-life natural laboratory.

A narrow road ran over a small concrete and stone dam in the park, creating a bridge across the river. The dam backed up the river enough to allow swimming in the summer or wading down the river below it. JD paused in the middle of the bridge and looked down the river as it disappeared around the bend. He imagined seeing the mouth of the long, steep canyon on his mom's land that used to belong to his granddad. The canyon had a hidden waterfall at one end.

His granddad had told him stories about the canyon. He said an outlaw gang once used the canyon as a hideout until ghosts scared them out. A legend said the waterfall was haunted. He wanted to explore and find out if the legend was true. His granddad had promised to take him down into the canyon, but he died before he could. He was determined to hike the canyon to the waterfall. The only thing keeping him from doing it was his mom. Somehow, he had to convince his mom to let him trek down into the canyon to the waterfall.

Once, his granddad took him in the truck to the canyon rim without his mom knowing. Granddad was adventurous and did not care much for restrictions. He told JD about a time when open ranges with no fences spread across Texas. He missed his granddad. His father died when he was just a baby, so he grew up not knowing much about his father. His granddad filled the father role and was his best friend. Losing him hurt and left a hole in his life. His uncle tried to step in, but granddad was his life teacher. He taught JD everything about the ranch, including how to fix almost anything. Taking things apart was a favorite activity. Most of the things he took apart were put back together. Some remained in a pile of parts and screws. Still, lessons were learned every time some disassembled item was added to that pile of screws.

JD thought. "I'm going to be a freshman in high school. Mom has to let me go to the canyon." He had to devise a plan so that his mom would allow him to explore the canyon and the hidden waterfall. It had to be a foolproof plan to convince his mom. "I bet Uncle Joe will help," he thought.

Back home, he grabbed the grocery sack and his prized possessions from the wire basket on the front of the bicycle and entered the kitchen from the back door. "Mom, I'm back."

"Did you remember the vanilla and almond extract?"

"Yes, Ma'am."

"Thank you, dear. Could you help me a little?"

"Sure, what do you need?"

"Grab that basket over there and put these finger sandwiches and biscuits in the middle with that jar of my peach preserves. I still need to put the glaze on the poppy seed bread."

"Mom, on the way to the store, Grandma Sullivan's car pulled into her driveway. She wasn't driving. A woman and a girl got out."

"That was probably Grandma Sullivan's daughter, Sheila, and granddaughter Kira. I told you about them before. They came from New Zealand to help out Grandma Sullivan. I want you to come with me to meet Kira and her mother. Kira will be here all summer, and I want you to be her friend."

Alarm bells went off in the brain. An entire summer with a girl tagging along! Nothing could be worse. His face scrunched up, and his feet went into automatic stomp-the-ground mode.

He had limited experience with girls. Sure, he had met girls. The Johnson twin girls lived nearby; he had played with them since he was a baby. The twins were more like sisters. They all went fishing, swimming, and exploring together. This past school year, something strange happened to the twins; they got all girly. They wanted to dress up, listen to records, and talk about boys and didn't want to do any of the fun stuff anymore.

JD considered girls to be boys with longer hair and mostly smaller bodies, all except Maria, who was twice his size, both in height and width. Maria was his first "fight" in school. It was more of a shoving match than a fight, with Maria doing the shoving and JD doing the falling down.

He, too, was changing. Girls made him feel funny inside and out. His speech got erratic and nonsensical when he tried to talk to a girl. The solution to him was to avoid all girls. Hanging with the guys and avoiding contact with girls was better.

The plan worked okay until his guy friends caught the same mysterious disease. When a girl walked by, his guy friends stopped talking to him. They whispered stuff and walked off to meet the girl, wanting to speak to her and carry her books. This weird behavior from his friends convinced him that aliens had put everyone in a trance. He didn't dislike girls but felt uneasy and nervous around them. Girls didn't like doing the stuff boys enjoyed, like exploring and fishing. Now, his mother wanted to put him in harm's way.

"What? Ah, Mom, do I have to!" JD whined. "All summer?"

"Yes, all summer! Grandma Sullivan is ill. Kira's mother will be busy caring for her. Kira has come all the way from New Zealand. She doesn't know anyone here, and she needs a friend. You're going to be that friend."

"But Mom, I had plans that did not include some stupid girl!" He kept the tone below the "pitching a fit" level.

"John David Jayson, what's got into you! Now listen here, mister, you're coming with me to welcome Kira and her mother with the same love Jesus gives us. You'll have to figure out how to include her in your plans.

"Besides, it won't be every day. She'll have other things to do while she's here. Oh, and remember, her mother is a dear friend of mine, so I expect you to treat them both with respect."

"Yes, Ma'am."

When mom used his full name, it was time to retreat to his room. Staying would mean having to listen to a long Bible lesson about how we needed to be more like Jesus and love our brethren. Then his mother launched the final salvo: "Now, go wash up and put on a clean shirt."

Washing was not a regular activity for a farm boy. Caked-on dirt, dried cow's milk, and sometimes gum lived on his shirt or jeans. Putting on a clean shirt, washing up, and combing his hair were activities about on par with taking out the trash. It had to be done, but you wished someone else had to do it.

At this particular moment, getting cleaned up was a surefire way to have his mother back on loving terms rather than judging terms. Devising a scheme to get out of being the chaperone for a girl the entire summer was next.

"Okay, Mom. I'm ready."

"Well, you look clean and handsome. Come give your mother a hug and a kiss."

JD smiled and thought to himself. "Works every time!"

"Can I drive to Grandma Sullivan's house? Please!"

"No, I told you before that I'll think about it when you have your learner's permit. Until then, you can practice using the tractor. Two pastures need preparation for planting. Driving the tractor around the pastures will give you plenty of practice."

Secretly, his uncle had been teaching him how to drive. Some of his friends already had their learner's permit. Handling the stick shift was still a challenge, but not as much on the dry dirt roads. JD hung his head and put on the "sad, hurt puppy look" that sometimes softened his mother enough for the second plea of "please, pretty please." But his mother did not buy it this time.

His mother looked into JD's eyes with one of those, "I'm sorry, I must be the mother now" looks. "Don't give me that puppy dog frown. This is not open for discussion. Put the basket on the floorboard so it doesn't flip over. And get into the car, now!"

That expended all options. The only recourse right now was to do as mom had commanded. But maybe some engaging conversation would help tone things down.

"Where's New Zealand?" JD asked as he got into the car.

"It's a long way from here. It's on the other side of the Pacific Ocean. You can look it up later in the encyclopedia. I wish you would read those encyclopedia books more often than those silly comic books. I want you to be on your best behavior when we arrive at Grandma Sullivan's. Remember, she is not well and needs to rest. I don't want any commotion from you, you hear?"

"Yeah, okay," JD mumbled. The engaging conversation idea was a complete disaster. He now stood on thin ice.

It only took a few minutes to travel to Grandma Sullivan's house. When they arrived, Sheila stood outside in the driveway. JD's mother leaped out of the car and ran to Sheila. Sheila hurried over and put her arms around JD's mom in an endearing embrace. His mom pulled back slightly and looked into Sheila's eyes. She wasn't crying, but she wasn't laughing either. The two stood there, smiling and staring at each other.

"I got your letter saying you were coming," JD's mom said. "I was so excited, but I know it has to have been so hard on you getting ready to come."

"Nana was doing so well. She and Kira spent days at the park. Then in February she started feeling ill. She didn't have the energy. She insisted on coming back to Texas. I couldn't stay there in New Zealand worrying about her. Getting everything ready to come just kept me so busy. I'm so sorry I dropped this all on you at the last minute."

"I am thankful you did. You will always have my love and support no matter. How's your mom? Is she up for visitors?"

"She's okay right now; she's taking a nap. We have an appointment with the doctor next week. Thank you for helping her until I got here. I should have come to see you when I arrived, but I've been so busy with mom and getting Kira sorted out."

"I understand. Your mother is your priority right now. We won't stay too long. I wanted to come to say hi and have JD meet Kira. JD come here and meet my dear friend. We grew up together before she moved to New Zealand."

From the car he weakly waved. "Hi."

"JD! Is that how I taught you to greet someone? You come here right now."

Greeting someone properly was not the problem. He was stalling, trying to avoid the inevitable. He did as his mother asked. He walked up to Sheila and reached out his hand. "Pleased to meet you, Ma'am."

Sheila turned toward JD, shook his hand, and smiled. "Hi, JD! Kira is looking forward to meeting you."

Sheila whispered to his mom. "Splitting image of his father."

"I know! Sometimes it's scary."

JD's mother turned to JD. "Please bring the basket in with you."

He stood there, trying to understand what was happening between his mother and Sheila. Sheila and his mother walked arm in arm toward the house.

JD went back to the car to retrieve the basket. He held the basket in one hand and shouted, "I've seen her–seen Kira already!"

He mumbled as Sheila and his mother entered the house. "I saw her this morning coming back from the store. I don't need to see her again."

"JD! Are you coming?" his mother called out from the doorway.

This was not a question but rather a command and warning not to make her come back out to repeat the command.

"Yes, ma'am, I'm comin'," JD muttered.

At the front door, he wiped his shoes on the doormat, opened the screen door, peeked inside, and scanned the room. The only people inside were his mother and Sheila. A smile grew on his face, and a calm came over his entire body. Maybe Kira was taking a nap or, hopefully, had just vanished and been taken back to the alien mothership.

"Have a seat, JD," Sheila said. "Kira went to get us some iced tea."

JD looked around and chose the bench near the door as his best option. He calculated it would be far enough from Kira's primary influence and close enough to the door for a quick escape.

"JD, please come sit next to me on the couch and bring the basket."

"I am fine right here," JD said, hoping that was the end of that request.

"What's the matter with you? Come here and sit next to me."

"He's a little shy around girls," JD's mother said softly to Sheila.

The red blush on his face showed he had heard what his mother said about being shy around girls. He handed the basket to his mother and plopped down on the far end of the couch.

He sat with a disgruntled face, nervously moving his feet back and forth, trying to hide his embarrassment. "I'm not shy. I prefer to hang out with the guys. Boys do fun stuff. Girls, well, they're girly and don't like doing stuff guys want to do."

JD's mom handed the basket to Sheila. "Here, I brought you some goodies for today and later."

"Thank you so much," Sheila said. "JD, you have nothing to worry about. Kira is more boy than girl. I wish it were the other way, but it's not."

The fact that two adult females tried to soothe away his inability to connect with girls just made it so much worse. If he had the superpower to vanish, he would have disappeared instantly. He thought. "Didn't anyone understand how life-threatening this was? At any moment, he could collapse from a coronary occlusion caused by the acute embarrassment."

It couldn't get any worse, could it? Then it did.

Kira entered the living room. She crept step-by-step into the room, face down, staring intensely at a tray with a pitcher and four glasses of iced tea. She walked like she expected to trip, sending the tray flying. JD stared at her intently, hoping precisely that would happen. That glorious event would move the focus of embarrassment from him to Kira.

JD focused his eyes on the tray, and it seemed to him his wish might come true. He could hear the ice cubes rattling about in the glasses. The tea splashed back and forth in the pitcher, almost spilling over the top. The tray vibrated. This was it! He was convinced that Kira was losing control of the tray, and it was about to crash into the center of the coffee table. JD moved as far back onto the couch as he could to move away from ground zero. His focus now moved up from the tray to Kira's face.

Still staring at the tray, Kira carefully put it down, stood up, and sighed. "Crikey, that was full on!"

JD's focus was not on Kira's words or her surprise at being able to deliver a tray of glasses and a pitcher of tea. It was on Kira's face and mostly on her eyes. Her steel-blue eyes sparkled like diamonds. Her hair was golden red. It was pulled back in a ponytail with bangs cut above her eyebrows. A weird sensation flowed through his body. He had never felt this way around a girl before. He couldn't stop staring. JD wondered how any creature could look so beautiful.

"Kira, this is JD. JD, this is Kira, my daughter. Please excuse her for her less-than-ladylike language."

Nothing happened. No one moved. JD was still staring at Kira's face. He was star-struck and couldn't move or speak. Nothing like this had ever happened to him before. He did not understand the feeling or the sensation flowing through his body. His nerdy mind was unable to process this new input.

"Well, JD, aren't you going to introduce yourself?" his mother urged. JD's mind was so absorbed in stargazing that it shut down his hearing.

"JD! Where are your manners!" his mother said in a noticeably louder and intense tone.

There's nothing like a mother's shrill, commanding voice to break any trance-like state. Complete control of his body had not returned, using his right hand to steady himself he was able to stand up. His eyes and attention were still focused on Kira's eyes. JD wiped his hand on his jeans and extended it to Kira. Kira moved towards him. She reached out with both hands and placed them on JD's shoulders. Her eyes, already glistening, seemed to beam a gleaming light towards him. With a bright, welcoming smile, she lowered her head to touch his forehead and said, "Kia Ora, JD!"

That did it. All the remaining strength JD needed to stand like a man vanished. He collapsed backward, nearly crashing over the arm of the couch and onto the end table.

"What was that?" JD thought. Only he said it aloud.

"That's a Kiwi greeting. It's called, the honji. What ja think eeet was?" Kira said with a giggle as she reached down and offered JD a hand.

"Oh, yeah...right...!" JD said. He didn't understand what that was or what a Kiwi was.

"Come here. Come close and touch your forehead and nose to mine. Don't worry, I won't bite you."

Nervously, he did as Kira instructed. JD's forehead and nose touched Kira's, and something strange happened. A sensation like an electric current flowed between the two of them, but it didn't feel like a static shock. The experience created a soothing calm, like breathing in and out slowly. The jitters and anxiety he usually felt around a girl faded away.

"Kia Ora, JD," Kira said.

"Kia Ora, Kira," JD replied with a stutter.

"How do you greet people in Texas?"

"Uhm…depends. If it's a grownup, then I'm supposed to shake hands and say, 'Pleased to meet you' or 'How do you do?'," JD said with a slight but noticeable glance towards his mother for approval. "But if it's some new kid or one of my friends, I just wave and say 'hey' or 'howdy' to them."

Kira raised her hand in a waving motion and said, "Howdy!"

JD smiled, laughed a little, and replied, "Howdy!"

"Mum, is it alright if JD comes and helps me with the bike?"

"Sure, if it's okay with JD and his mother. Susan, is it okay with you?"

"Well, I wasn't planning to stay long. I'm sure your mother needs her rest."

"Please stay. Nana's taking a nap. We can have some tea and chat a bit."

"Oh, all right. I guess we can stay a bit longer."

Sheila handed JD's mom some tea. "We can spend some time getting caught up."

"I would love that."

Kira grabbed JD's hand and pulled him through the kitchen, out the back door, and into the garage. "Come on, JD, I need your help."

There was little time to think about an answer, much less reply, but he blurted out, "What? Uh, okay, I guess!"

In the garage, in front of JD, was the girl's version of his bicycle. The bicycle had three speeds with handlebar brakes, a rack on the back, and a wire basket on the front.

"My mum got it used in town 'cause I'd need a bike. It would have cost too much to ship mine here and back again. Do you know much about bikes?"

JD understood bikes. He had completely disassembled his bicycle and put it back together several times. He loved to take things apart to figure out how they worked. Nothing assembled was safe alone in the same room as JD.

"Yeah, I work on my bike all the time. I didn't think girls did."

He stood staring at Kira, perplexed by this new sensation running through his body. He tried to summon up any machismo he had to take control of his body and the situation. It didn't work. He stood there staring, not knowing what to say or do. He couldn't get past her eyes and smile.

"Hello? The bike?"

"What? Right. Sorry. What does it need?"

"It needs better tires and tubes. My mum got some used ones. Here they are."

"First, let's check out the bike."

JD snapped out of his confusion and swung into his fix-and-repair mode. He checked the wheels, brake levers, pads, spokes, gears, and chain. "We gotta tighten the brake cables and the chain, and some spokes are loose."

"We should work on the tires first, right?"

"Yeah, sure," JD said, amazed this girl could work on a bike. He stole glances at her as she swiftly took action. Kira put the gears in the smallest chainring, disengaged the brakes, flipped the bike over, and pulled a socket wrench out of a toolbox. She then removed the front wheel while he looked on. His jaw dropped open, and his amazement maxed out. Still distracted by this beautiful yet not girly girl, JD sat silently, staring at Kira.

"You wanna do the rear wheel?"

"What?"

"I said, do you want to do the rear wheel?"

"Yeah, sure."

Kira tossed the wrench. "Okie dokie, here, catch."

JD grabbed the wrench out of the air and freed the rear wheel from the frame and chain. He was back in the fix-and-repair mode.

"You got any tire levers? And a spoke wrench?"

Kira searched through the toolbox. "Let me check. Yep…here ya go. Hey, do ya fancy a race?"

"You mean, who can finish installing their tire and tube first? Sure, what's the prize?"

"How about the winner buys spiders at the milk bar?"

"Buy the 'what?' at the 'what?'"

"Oh, right! I forgot you don't understand what that is. A spider is ice cream with a fizzy drink."

"You mean an ice cream float at the soda fountain. Deal! The first person to finish buys the floats tomorrow. Okay, Ready – set – go!"

"This was going to be breezy easy," JD thought. No girl could keep up with him. He could replace a bike tire with his eyes closed and half asleep. He glanced over at Kira. She had deflated the old tube and removed the retaining nut from the stem. He had to speed up! JD was determined not to let a girl beat him at anything. He had a trick that might knock off a couple seconds–by removing the tire without using a tire lever. Soon, he had removed the old tire and put the new one on. He only had to slip the new tube in, put the retaining nut back on the stem, and add the air.

Moments later, JD raised his hands. "DONE!"

"ME TOO!" Kira yelled a second later.

Kira looked over and inspected JD's work. "Nice work! How did you do it so fast?"

"I learned how to roll the old tire off and back on without using a tire lever," JD grinned.

"Well done, you!" Kira said with a smile and a slap on JD's shoulder. "Well, let's work on the rest of it."

Working together, the two put the front and back wheels back on, adjusted the chain, and tightened the spokes and brake cables. Grease and dirt dotted their faces and hands, but neither cared. They sat back and looked at each other with a satisfying smile.

"We did good, eh? Thanks so much for the help."

"Yeah, no problem. It was fun."

Kira was nothing like he expected. He was happy to be with a girl for the first time in a long time. "This is going to be a great summer," JD thought. It was like having the Johnson twins back as buddies only better. This girl was smart, beautiful and could fix a bike.

JD's mother walked into the garage. "JD, you ready? We need to go."

"Yes, Mom. We're finished."

Sheila walked in behind JD's mother. "JD, would you mind showing Kira where the college library is in the morning? Your mom said it was okay."

"Sure, no problem."

JD turned to Kira. "Why do you need to go to the library?"

"Stupid schoolwork." Kira groaned.

"Kira has to continue her coursework here through the summer, or she'll be too far behind in her studies," Sheila said.

"You have to go to summer school?"

"No, well, sorta," Kira said. "New Zealand is down under, so our winter is your summer, and your winter is our summer. Our second term began on the first of May."

"Kira's school agreed to let her come if she agreed to continue her coursework here," Sheila said. "The librarian will monitor her progress, give her the tests, and mail the results back to her school."

JD's heart sank to his knees. He had already started thinking of the cool things he and Kira could do this summer. This had to be another alien plot to destroy his happiness.

"Bummer!" JD groaned. "I was hoping to show Kira some cool things this summer."

He couldn't believe he just uttered those words. JD had gone from trying to avoid being with Kira to being disappointed he couldn't be with her. He thought. "What's happening?"

"No worries. I will only be at the library for a few hours in the morning on Mondays and Tuesdays. I got a bunch of stuff done before I came. We'll have plenty of time to do stuff!"

"Okay," JD said, trying to contain his excitement so Kira would not think he was a freak.

As Kira and JD headed out of the garage, JD's mother and Sheila gave each other a wink and a smile. This may not be an alien plan but a mother-to-mother plan. Either way, JD wondered how tomorrow would go. He was still skeptical but hopeful.

BECOMING FRIENDS

"Mom, I am going over to Kira's."

"Did you do all your chores? Did you milk the cow?"

"Yes, Ma'am!" JD said, heading into the kitchen.

"Come here and give me a hug."

His mother took one look at JD and did not like what she saw. "You need to go wash up. And put on a clean shirt. That shirt looks like your cow slept on it. It smells like dried milk."

"Ah, ma, do I have to? If I were to meet up with a guy, I wouldn't have to."

"Yes, you have to. I don't want my son going to anyone's house looking like part of the barn."

JD reluctantly stomped up the stairs to his room to get ready. He was interested in how Kira would be on a bike. She did impress him last night, but that might have been a ruse. Still, a girl who didn't act girly and didn't do stuff like all the other girls his age was the dream. He halfheartedly did as his mom requested.

Becoming Friends

"Okay, Mom. I'm ready to go!"

"Well, now, you look so handsome. You have fun! Be careful when riding your bikes into town, especially when crossing the highway. Some of those high school and college kids drive their cars like maniacs. And be back here by four. Kira, her mother, and Grandma Sullivan are coming over for dinner."

"Yes, Ma'am, I will," JD said, rushing out the back porch and hopping on his bike. JD had mastered the "slide on the bike without stopping move." It's a tricky move, but if it is done right, you can get going without even stopping to put the kickstand up.

JD made it in the same amount of time it took his mom to drive the car to Grandma Sullivan's house. When he got to the front porch, he did the "slide off the bike while laying it down dismount." At the front door, he rang the bell and knocked simultaneously.

Kira's mother answered the door and smiled. "Good morning, JD."

"Good morning, Mrs. Sheila, is…" JD stopped in mid-sentence after realizing his embarrassing mistake. "I mean. Good morning, Ma'am. Is Kira ready?"

"Yes, she is. You'll find her in the garage getting her bike. And you can call me Sheila."

"Oh, no, ma'am, my mom would not approve."

"Alright, how about this? Your mom and I are like sisters. How about you call me Aunt Sheila?"

"Yeah, I guess that would be okay," JD agreed, knowing he would have to clear it with his mother.

"Now go on, Kira is waiting for…"

He was already at the garage door before Kira's mother could finish her sentence. When he spotted Kira getting her bike, the doubts came back. He wondered if she had succumbed to the alien influence and become girly. Kira was a girl, and girls still made him feel weird and anxious, but last night she was more like a boy than a girl. He felt more at ease around her, but she was still a girl.

Kira's eyes brightened, and she smiled. "G'day, JD. Did ya have a good sleep?"

"Yeah, you ready to go?" JD said, not knowing what he should say now.

"Sweet as. I'm ready, Freddy, thanks to your help last night."

JD tried to act nonchalant. "Sure, whatever. Happy to help."

Kira's mother walked into the garage. "Kira, here's the packet. Be sure to speak with Mrs. Wilson. She's English and will help should you have any problems."

"No worries, Mum. I'll get by. I'm sure JD will help."

"Okay, smarty! You two be back here by four. We're going to JD's house for dinner."

"Choice! Bye, Mum!"

"Bye, Mrs. Sheila, uh, I mean Aunt Sheila!"

"Lead the way, JD!" Kira said.

"We'll take the back way to town," JD said. "I want to show you something on the way."

Going the back way through the park, it was over three miles to the college campus. It was safer, but JD wanted to show Kira the park along the river. He wanted to know if Kira liked the outdoors as much as he did.

"No worries. Where're we headed?"

"Down this road to the highway, we'll cross the highway to the road that runs through the park. I'll try not to go too fast for you," JD said as he zoomed ahead.

"Hey, wait up!" Kira yelled out.

When Kira reached the highway crossing, JD was waiting, straddling his bike, and looking back over his shoulder.

"No fair, you got the jump on me," Kira said.

"Oh yeah, I forgot you're a girl."

Kira straddled her bike and grimaced. "Oh, really, so that's how it will be. You think girls can't do what boys can do."

"Well, sorta. The girls I know do girly stuff like put on makeup and listen to records. Most wear dresses and can't ride bikes."

"You don't know me. I'm not like other girls."

JD pointed across the highway. "Okay, prove it. Once we cross the highway, how about a race? We'll do a proper 1-2-3 start this time. There's a steep hill up ahead. Can you bike up hills?"

Kira was not used to losing and did not take to being egged on with trash talk. "Ha! We have plenty of hills in New Zealand! You're on."

JD looked back at Kira and started to cross the highway. The sound of a truck's horn coming down the hill was the only alert of impending disaster. The truck was on a direct path to hit JD and drag him along with his bike down the highway. Without thinking, Kira waved her hand and whispered a few words. JD and his bike slid sideways into the intersection, missing the truck's back end. The truck sped past with the horn blasting.

The wind drag from the passing truck pulled up white caliche dirt from the side of the paved road and dusted the back of JD's head. The smell of diesel smoke filled his nose. He stopped for a moment and watched the truck speed away. JD shrugged, mumbled a curse word, and continued across the highway.

"Are you okay? You almost got run over!"

"Yeah, I'm fine. I have super-fast reactions. I was in total control."

"If you say so."

On the other side of the highway, JD pointed to a hill down the road. "You see that hill? After we pass it, it's mostly downhill to the river. We'll stop at the bridge."

"Aye, aye, sir!"

"Alright, ready?"

"Ready, Freddy!"

Without warning, JD shouted, "1-2-3 Go!" Off he went as fast as he could up the hill. JD yelled over his shoulder, "The last one at the bridge is a rotten egg!"

Given a fair chance, JD was fast on a bike, but so was Kira. Although JD was able to get a head start, she soon caught up. Going up a steep hill, even a small one like this one, was still challenging. You had to have leg strength and a bike with a chain that would not slip. JD was certain Kira would not be able to keep up. JD arrived at the top of the hill with Kira right behind him.

Going downhill was a different challenge, especially with the sharp turns and limited visibility. It was risky, but JD did not consider risk during a race, especially a boy–girl race.

Becoming Friends

Girls in Texas in the 1960s were taught to be ladylike and not to compete with boys in athletic skills challenges. Their mothers taught their young daughters to be diplomatic and let the boy think he won. Their mothers warned them. "No boy wants a girl who makes a boy look like a weakling. Girls should make the boys feel and look like they are their champions."

JD didn't care if Kira was a girl. He didn't like to lose. To him, losing to a girl was the worst. JD had one crucial advantage. He had traveled this road many times and could anticipate the turns. But this time, it was not enough. It was a close finish, but Kira reached the bridge just ahead of JD. JD thought. "Kira is not like the girls he knew. She was almost a boy."

"Come on, Sunday driver. Rattle your dags!" Kira said with a chuckle and a grin.

"What?"

"It means hurry up, slowpoke!" Kira laughed.

"Yeah, okay, you won fair and square."

"Hey, we say that too."

"Cool! Maybe you'll teach me some Kiwi Speak."

"Maybe, if you're nice."

"How did you get so good at bike racing?" JD asked, breathing heavily.

"Some of us back home race for the fun of it. We have an off-road route we use. I'm the only girl allowed to race."

Kira straddled her bike, looking around at the beautiful scenery in the park and along the river. "This park is wonderful. Is that a small dam? I can hear a waterfall. What kind of trees are those? They're so tall."

"Those are pecan and oak trees. And yeah, there's sorta like a waterfall below the dam."

Kira looked down the right side of the river. "What are those round stone areas?"

"Those stoned areas are springs. I thought after you're through at the library, we could come back here for a picnic lunch."

Kira smiled. "JD, is this a date? Are you asking me out on a date?"

"What? No, no! It's just a picnic lunch. My mom said to be your friend."

"Oh, I see. So, you don't think I am worthy of a date? I'm not pretty enough for you, eh?"

JD's hands slid back and forth across the handlebars. He stared straight ahead, avoiding eye contact with Kira. This was just the type of situation he hated. He didn't know what to do. JD unraveled into a chaotic confusion of thoughts racing through his brain. "What have I done, what do I do now, what? What? What?" Like some robot given a command that conflicts with its prime robot law, he was headed for overload.

"Relax, I'm just messing with ya," Kira chuckled. "I'd love to come back here and have a picnic lunch."

"Huh, okay, ah, yeah, I figured you were," JD blurted out with his brain still trying to find the anxiety off-button. "Great, okay, well, uh, that's super!"

JD mused about Kira's differences as they rode to the college library. Kira was more mature than any girl he had met. She was pretty, but not like a glamour model. She smiled with her eyes more than her mouth. Kira was open and friendly enough, but it seemed she was hiding some of her emotions. At times, JD felt like she was a sister, but back at the bridge, she elicited the same anxiety he felt around other girls. Last night, he was struck by her beauty and amazed by her ability to work on the bike.

31

JD pointed to the road across the dam. "Come on, we'll take that road to the college."

Kira followed riding along side of JD. "You sure are quiet. Is it what I said back at the bridge?"

"No, I was just thinking about stuff."

"What stuff?"

JD shrugged. "Nothing, okay? The library is just down this block."

Kira decided to let it drop for now. She didn't want to push it too far and potentially ruin the rest of the summer. After all, she was the visitor, and JD, at the moment, was the only other kid she knew here. Kira didn't like letting something drop.

"Look, I'm sorry."

"For what?"

"For teasing you back there. I guess it upset you."

JD knew the first rule at school: never let someone realize they had gotten to you. That would give them the green light to continue. Never show any sign of weakness. Being one of the most intelligent kids in school and president of the science club, he was already on the "prime target list" of the school bullies.

"Didn't bother me none." JD said, "Here's the library. Let's go find Mrs. Wilson."

They parked their bikes in front of the library. Kira grabbed the packet and silently walked alongside JD, looking around the college campus. She had never been to a college, not even in New Zealand.

"Wow, this is a huge college."

"It's a private school, but not even close to the size of the one in Austin. That's where I want to go."

"Oh yeah? What'd you want to study?"

"Not sure, probably something in science or engineering," JD said.

"Oh yeah?"

Kira was about to ask if JD was a science nerd but decided that might push JD right over the edge. This time, she just kept it to herself.

JD opened the library door and spotted Mrs. Wilson at the circulation desk. "There's Mrs. Wilson, come on."

At the circulation desk, JD said. "Mrs. Wilson, this is Kira. She's supposed to talk with you about her studies."

"Hello, JD!" Mrs. Wilson said. "And hello, Miss Kira - or should I say - Kia Ora Kira. Your mother said you would be coming. Do you have the packet?"

"Kia Ora, um, I mean – pleased to meet you, Mrs. Wilson. Yes, Ma'am, here is the packet."

"Thank you. First, come into my office. We'll go over the schedule and how this will work. Then I'll show you the table I have reserved for you over in the corner by the window. There should be plenty of light and few distractions."

"Mrs. Wilson, would it be okay if I checked on something in the reference section?" JD said.

"Sure, JD. Just be sure to put things back where they belong. I don't have anyone helping me today."

JD headed to the reference section to learn more about New Zealand. He never liked being uninformed, so he spent most of the next two hours reading about the country's history and geography, including the Māori people.

When Kira finished her schoolwork, she found JD in the reference section, reading and taking notes. "Hey, JD. I'm ready to go. Whatcha doing?"

"Just reading about some stuff," JD said while quickly trying to close and cover up the reference books about New Zealand.

"Ah...are you a bookworm?" Kira said, smiling as she caught a glimpse of the title of one book.

"Nah, I was just passing the time. So, you ready to buy me that ice cream float?"

"Yeah, that's right, I owe you one. So, where do we go?"

"There's a drugstore across the street. They have a soda fountain."

"Sweet as, let's go!"

Kira was carrying a couple of books and a notebook. He started to ask her if she needed help but decided against it. Yet, as if some inner force took over, he blurted out, "What do you have there?"

"Oh, just some books I need to read for my assignments."

With a girly smile, Kira turned to JD. "You want to carry my books for me?"

"What? Carry your books? Why would I want to carry your books? You can tie them to the back rack on your bike. We can leave the bikes here; no one will bother them."

Kira laughed. "You're too easy! I was teasing you."

JD looked bewildered and could not respond. Kira grabbed his arm and pulled him along.

"Come on, let's get those floats," Kira said.

As they walked along to the drugstore, JD was quiet and withdrawn. Once again, he feared he was entering the dangerous "girly" territory.

Kira nudged JD. "Hey, you do understand that if a girl teases you, she likes you."

"That's apocryphal and not scientific."

"Whatever, but I believe it's true," Kira said with a wink.

Somewhere deep inside, a new thought and feeling took hold and grew in JD. He liked that Kira cared about his feelings. It was okay, perhaps even better, that Kira was a girl.

"So, do you still want a picnic lunch by the park?" JD said.

"Sure, I'd like that,"

"Great!"

JD started to like this "girl" thing, then the worst thing that could happen happened. Right at the corner by the drugstore was Billy, one of the school bullies. He hoped Billy would just walk around the corner before they were seen. No such luck; Billy turned and saw JD coming across the street.

"Hey, nerd!" Billy shouted. "It's your lucky day. You get to buy me a soda!"

JD stood there, thinking. "What is it about bullies? They cannot pass up any opportunity to make fun of and belittle others."

He reached into his pocket for money to give to Billy but glanced at Kira. Normally, he would have just handed the money to Billy any other day. But not today, not with Kira watching. It was never about being physically hurt by Billy—well, maybe a little about that. JD was not physically weak, but emotionally, he was. The fear was more about confrontation, self-doubt, and humiliation. But being humiliated in front of Kira was much worse than getting beaten up. So today, the reaction was different.

JD stuffed the money back in his pocket and stood up straight. "Hey, Billy. Yeah, I'm not buying you a soda."

"What did you say, twirp?" Billy said, walking closer to JD.

JD walked closer to Billy. "I'm not buying you a soda today or any day."

Billy grabbed JD's shirt. "Listen, you little piss-ant. You're going to buy me that soda, or I'm going to beat the crap out of you right here."

Something inside JD came alive. It was similar to the assurance he felt yesterday while helping Kira with her bike. He still felt fear but countering that fear was self-confidence.

JD pulled his shirt out of Billy's grip. "No! Now, back off! Come on, Kira, let's go."

At first, Billy stood looking stunned by JD's rebuff, then he grabbed Kira's arm. "How about Red here buying me a soda?"

JD jumped between Kira and Billy. "Leave her alone!"

Billy swung at JD. JD stumbled back to avoid the swing, lost his balance, and fell to the ground. As Billy started to kick JD, Kira whispered something and poked Billy in the back of the neck right at the shoulder blade. Billy stopped and dropped to the ground in slow motion. He sat slumped over with his head down like he was taking a nap.

"What the hell just happened?" JD said, staring at Billy on the ground.

"I think he needed a timeout," Kira said with a sly grin. "Come on, help me get him up."

JD bent down and shook Billy. "Billy, Billy! Wake up!"

Groggy and disoriented, Billy said, "What? Where am I? What happened?"

JD and Kira helped Billy to his feet. He stood looking puzzled and a bit wobbly.

"You fell down and went to sleep!" JD said. "You, okay?"

"Yeah, I guess. I'm kinda tired. I gotta go home."

"You need help getting home?"

"No, it's just down the street," he said, walking around the corner.

Kira followed him and watched as he walked to his house. Billy stopped and turned around. He stood arms straight down and motionless. His eyes glowed. "You had no right to interfere. We have the right to test him!" It wasn't Billy speaking anymore.

Kira stepped back but stood firm. "Who do you follow?"

"We follow Abezethibou. You had no right to interfere."

"Leave this boy now."

"You will not save him. We will win. You do not have the power. You are but one and weak. We are many and powerful."

"My power does not come from me. You know that. Leave the boy now."

"We will be back."

Billy's eyes stopped glowing. "Why are you staring at me? I'm fine and don't need your help."

He walked off grumbling. "Stupid weird girl."

Kira turned and walked back to JD.

"Wow! That was strange!" JD said. "What was that eerie voice? Billy doesn't look okay."

"I think Billy was just groggy and mumbling something. He'll be okay. A long nap will probably help him. Come on, I still owe you an ice cream float."

"Oh yeah, that's right! You do! We should have them here. They'd probably melt by the time we got to the park. We can have the picnic another time."

"Sure, we've got all summer," Kira said while looking back to ensure Billy wasn't following.

"Better idea! Let's do the floats tomorrow. We'll buy bottled sodas and sandwiches for a picnic lunch today."

"Sweet as, that'll work."

JD and Kira walked inside the drugstore. College kids sat drinking sodas as rock and roll music mixed with the sound of the milk shake blenders. JD walked up to the counter and ordered sandwiches and sodas to go.

With sack lunches in hand, Kira and JD walked back to their bikes at the University.

Kira tapped JD on the shoulder. "Hey, thanks for standing up to Billy back there. You were brave."

"Normally, I'm not. But I wasn't going to let him hurt you."

JD and Kira leisurely rode their bikes down the back road to the park. They stopped on the hill before the bridge. Kira straddled her bike and surveyed the scene. "This is great. I love the trees along the shore and the sound of water flowing over that small dam. Where can we have our picnic?"

"Come on, I have a favorite spot. It's across the bridge on the other side."

JD led Kira to a picnic table under a pecan tree along the river's edge. Kira sat at the table facing the river, and JD sat beside her.

Kira closed her eyes and held her head up. "The breeze feels so refreshing on my face."

"Yeah, this is my favorite picnic spot. I come here often."

"I can understand why. It's so beautiful and peaceful. Hey, you got something to open the soda bottles?"

"I sure do! I have a bottle opener on my pocketknife."

"Well, aren't you the Boy Scout!"

"Ha! Me a boy scout? I wasn't even a Cub Scout. So, that was strange about Billy today. Did you see his eyes? They opened wide and glowed. Kinda freaked me out."

"I wouldn't worry about it. Probably just a reflection or something caused his eyes to look funny. He was just mad, that's all. Probably embarrassed too. I'm sure he'll be fine."

"I'm sorry it happened. My friends are not like that. Billy's just a mean bully. No one likes him, not even his brother, who is also a bully. Funny how bullies don't seem to have many friends."

"No worries, you handled it well. Billy probably has some inner demons."

"Yeah, whatever, I didn't like how he treated you."

"Don't worry; I can take care of myself, but I appreciate what you did."

Kira looked down the long stretch of the park running along the river. "Hey, when we're finished eating, let's check out those springs."

"Sure. They're pretty neat. When I come during the week, I'm usually the only one. I can go exploring up and down the river."

Kira took a sip from her bottle of soda. "Thanks for getting lunch."

"No worries. Hey, try this. I got a bag of peanuts. Put some in your soda. You're not allergic to peanuts, are you?"

"No, I'm not."

Kira slipped a few peanuts into her soda bottle. "Hey, this is cool. It fizzes a little when you do that."

"It's a Texas tradition. Actually, I think it's a southern tradition."

The two sat eating lunch and enjoying the fresh air and scenery.

"I love this," Kira said. "It's so peaceful. You can hear the fish jumping, the bees buzzing. I can even see butterflies visiting the flowers. So much life energy here."

"Yeah, the park is one of my favorite places to explore."

"One of? If the others are anything like this, they have to be awesome. Will you show me the others?"

"Sure. Say, can I ask you something?"

"Ask away," Kira said.

"What does 'sweet as' mean?"

"Hmmm…it's just an expression like something is cool,"

"Okay, so what does 'crikey' mean? And why didn't your mom like you saying it?"

"It's also an expression, but like a curse word. My mum doesn't like me to curse. She wants me to be girly, all prim and proper. Boring! I want to explore stuff and be what I want to be."

"So, you like to explore stuff?"

"Oh, yeah. I love to explore. Why do you ask?"

"See down the river over there? Way down the river beyond the bridge, there's the opening of a long canyon on the far side of the river. I want to hike the canyon."

"SWEET AS! Can I come with you?"

"Yeah, if you want. There's a waterfall at the far end of the canyon. My granddad said outlaws used to use the canyon as a hideout."

"Choice as! Oh, that means something's great. Maybe there's hidden treasure there."

JD's eyes perked up. He smiled. He could not believe the turn of events. The girl he did not want to tag along said she didn't want to be girly, and she wanted to explore. He couldn't believe it.

Uncontrollably, he blurted out. "That's super!" Realizing he went a bit too far with his elation, he countered with. "Are you finished with your lunch?"

"Yeah, all done!"

"Okay, let's clear the table. There's a trash can over there."

"So, are you a clean freak?" Kira teased with a smile.

JD looked startled and embarrassed. Kids never like being told they are anything their parents want them to be.

"Hey, relax!" Kira said, trying to ease the tension. "I think it is a good thing! Especially keeping our garbage out of nature. I hate going hiking and finding someone's trash on the trail."

"It's just the way I was taught. Come on, I think you'll like the springs. They've been used for thousands of years by Native American Indians."

"Wow, that's so cool!"

JD led the way to a round stone area near the picnic table. Due to the geology, springs dotted the entire region. It was well known throughout the county that Native American Indians had hunted in the area and camped near the springs.

At the springs, Kira looked down at the clear water bubbling up from the ground. "Wow, the water is so clear! Is it safe to drink?"

"I wouldn't drink it. I took a sample from the pool's edge, examined it using my microscope at home, and found several amoebas and paramecia."

"Yeah? You mean one-cell critters? That's super cool! I want to see that sometime."

This was a first for JD. Here was a girl who not only didn't laugh at the fact that he had a microscope but was also interested in what he found using it.

"Yeah, but there are other critters here, too. Come down here along the stream. Look, do you see the minnows and tadpoles?"

"Wow, yeah, I do," Kira said. "There are hundreds of them."

JD got a stick and lightly tapped the tall grass along the bank of the stream coming out of the spring-fed pool. Hundreds of tiny frogs jumped out of the grass.

"Wow! That's a lot of frogs!"

JD turned over a rock. "There! Look! See that?"

"What? Where?"

A crawdad scurried out into the spring with its tail, stirring up the water.

"Koura! We have those in New Zealand too!"

"Here, we call them crawdads."

"Māori call them Koura," Kira said. "But the Pakeha Kiwis call them crayfish."

"I read about the Māori. What is Pakeha?"

"Pakeha is the Māori word for New Zealanders who are not Māori," Kira said.

"So, I guess I'm Pakeha?"

"No, silly, you're an American. You would have to live in New Zealand to be considered Pakeha. If you visited New Zealand, you would be a Tauiwi or foreigner."

"Hmmm...interesting. I want to learn more about New Zealand."

"I'll make you a deal. We'll explore where you live this summer, and I'll tell you more about New Zealand."

"Deal! I know some neat places, but I'm not sure you'd be interested in all of them."

"Try me. I like anything outdoors."

JD smiled. "Cool!"

"We'd best head back," Kira said. "I have some home-work to do and some chores before we come to dinner at your house."

"Yeah, I have some chores, too."

Kira touched JD's arm and smiled. "Hey, I had such a fun time today,"

"Me too," JD said, blushing a little.

There was no racing going back, just two friends riding their bikes home. JD's mind was still trying to process all that had happened today–this morning, going to the library, the incident with Billy, and the picnic lunch with Kira. Kira was not like the other girls. He felt different around her than he did with anyone else. When JD faced Billy, he felt confident and more assertive. Sure, Kira produced some of that same anxiety he felt around other girls, but it was not the same. He was not afraid to be himself around Kira.

At Grandma Sullivan's, JD stopped and straddled his bike. "I guess I'll see ya later?"

"Yeah, see ya later, and thanks again for the fun time today."

"Sure, no problem," JD said as he rode away. "I had fun, too!"

THERE'S A GIRL IN MY ROOM

"Mom, I'm home!" JD said as he entered the back door. "Mom?"

JD heard sobbing coming from the living room. He walked down the hall and found his mother on the couch, bent over, crying into a handkerchief.

"Mom, are you okay?"

JD's mother sat straight up and wiped the tears from her eyes. She was a strong woman with an immovable faith, and it was rare for JD to find his mother like this.

He sat down next to his mom and put his arm around her. "It's about dad, isn't it?"

"I'm sorry. Seeing Sheila today just brought back so many memories. I wish your dad were here. Growing up, your dad, Uncle Joe, Sheila, and I were all friends. We were more like brothers and sisters. Your dad was the explorer, always pushing us to go somewhere new. I miss him so much."

"Are you sure you are up for visitors tonight?"

"Yes, I'll be fine. Mothers are human too, and we have our weak moments."

"I understand. I miss granddad. Sometimes I wish he were here to help me with stuff. He always had an answer, and I could tell him anything."

"Your grandfather was a unique person. I might not always have an answer you will like, but I will always be here to listen. Now, let's get this house ready for guests."

"I'll help. Just tell me what you need me to do."

"Thank you. Yes, you can help with a few things. Did you have a fun time today with Kira?"

"Yeah, I did."

JD started to say more. He wanted to ask about girls and tell his mother how Kira made him feel. But he didn't want to ask his mother about things that seemed okay in his brain but might not be if said out loud.

"So, what do you think about Kira?"

"She's nice."

"Nice? Is that all?"

"Yeah, well, she's different. She's not like other girls. We had a picnic lunch at the park, and she liked exploring the springs."

"That sounds like a good thing, right?"

"Yeah, sure, I guess."

"She's certainly an adorable girl. And her mother said she's smart and gets excellent grades in school. She's been through some difficult times recently, so treat her nicely."

"Yeah sure, but what do you mean? Is it because her grandmother is sick?"

"You'll have to ask her for the details. It's not just about her grandmother feeling ill. Just be respectful – like I always want you to be."

"Okay, I will. Kira's mom said I should call her Aunt Sheila. Is that okay?"

"I think that's okay. Sheila and I grew up together. We were best friends from the start and as close as sisters. Yes, Aunt Sheila is proper if it's okay with her. Now, can you help me clean a bit? I need you to dust and sweep the living and dining rooms. And straighten things up. You know."

"Sure, Mom. After that, I need to do something."

"I might need help in the kitchen. What do you need to do?"

JD didn't want to tell his mother what he needed to do. He was sure it would reveal too much, so he tried the soft, quick mumbling trick, hoping she would not hear the real thing he was saying.

"I need to clean my room," JD said softly.

"What did you say? Did I hear you say you would clean up your room?"

"Yes, I mean, Kira's coming over, and I wanted to show her some stuff."

Cleaning his room was right up there with removing the manure from his cow's stall. It had to be done, but he hoped someone else could do it. He couldn't let any of the ranch hands clean the stall, because his cow was a 4-H project. He had to do it all himself.

He never went to any trouble to clean his room if some of his guy friends were coming over, not even if it was the Johnson girls. JD's mother was shocked and amazed that JD wanted to present a clean room for Kira, whom he had only met yesterday.

"Well, I might have to lie down for a bit after that news. You must like Kira. Is she someone special?"

"No, Mom, I don't want her to think I am a slob. That's all—nothing special."

"Okay...okay..." JD's mother smiled. Her baby boy was growing up.

JD cleaned and straightened the living and dining rooms and then went to clean and tidy his room. After dusting and sweeping, he tried to figure out what would be best to have on display. Should he keep his microscope out? What about his rock and mineral collection? He wanted to keep his shortwave radio and his telescope out. Since Kira said she liked the outdoors, he left the National Geographic magazines out and stacked the Scientific American magazines underneath them. The comic books had to go.

"JD?" JD's mother shouted up the stairs. "JD..."

"I'm in my room," JD responded.

"Ah, there you are. When you finish with your room, please prepare the dining room table. Use the best silverware and dishes."

"Okay, I'm just about finished."

"Thank you!"

As his mother walked away, she mumbled to herself. "We certainly don't want to look bad for Kira."

JD finished up with this room and hurried downstairs to set the table. It was almost time for them to arrive, and he still needed to wash up and put on a clean shirt. He thought to himself. "Wow, that's three clean shirts in three days! That had to be a record!"

"Mom, I'm done with the table," JD said as he headed for the stairs. "I'm going to wash up and put on a clean shirt."

JD's mother stopped what she was doing. "What? You're going to wash up and put on a clean shirt without being told? Oh my, I sure hope that won't bring on a storm."

JD didn't hear what his mother said. He was too focused on getting ready. He didn't even stop to think that his current behavior was much like all the other guys who had fallen under the alien "girly" spell. Using a washcloth, he got himself nearly as clean as bathing. He brushed his teeth and combed his hair, parting it on one side. He finished putting on his clean shirt when he heard the doorbell ring. The reality of the entire evening slammed right into his brain. The typical self-doubt crept back up. What if she laughed when she saw his room? Would she like how he looked? Luckily, he heard his mom yell out before he went into a complete meltdown. "JD, please come answer the door and welcome our guests!"

His mother's voice always seemed to have a reversing effect. If he felt calm, it would make him anxious–if he felt nervous, it would calm him down. One exception to that rule was when he had done something wrong. That always produced guilt. This time, his mother's voice snapped him out of his anxiety tailspin. He was calm and ready for anything— that is, until he opened the door.

Kira stood in the doorway, wearing a dress, her hair flowing in front past her shoulders. This was the first time he had seen her in a dress and without her hair in a ponytail. During the school year, girls always wore dresses unless they were in PE class. Many continued to wear summer dresses or the new wrap-around skirts during the summer. Some girls wore shorts or jeans. The real "girly" girls always wore dresses. Even the tomboyish Johnson twins had gone over to the girly side and now wore a dress or skirt.

Kira stood before him in a dress. Her steel-blue eyes glowed brighter than the porch light, which was casting a halo around her golden red hair as it flowed down her shoulders almost to her waist. He could feel his heart beating in his chest. His legs twitched and bent at the knees. He had to breathe. Why couldn't he breathe? Once again, he was in a conflict of emotions. His brain was worried Kira had gone over to the girly side. Still, simultaneously, his heart beat a different rhythm. He stood in the doorway holding onto the door to steady himself and blurted out. "You're, you're, you're wearing a dress!"

"Yeah, sorry, my mum made me," Kira whispered.

Gripping the door and hoping not to faint, once again, he blurted out. "And the hair, hair, your hair, it's, it's!"

"Yeah, mum again," Kira whispered. "She wanted me to brush it out and wear it long. So, are you going to invite us in?"

"What? Oh, yeah, sorry! Please come in!"

Right behind Kira was her grandmother, walking with a cane and being helped by Kira's mother. "Evening, JD. It's been a while since I've seen you."

"Hello, Grandma Sullivan. May I help you?"

"No, no, we're doing fine. But thank you!"

JD's mother walked into the living room carrying a tray with a pitcher of iced tea and glasses. "Y'all come on in, sit and have some tea. Dinner is almost ready."

"It certainly smells delicious," Kira's mother said. "Can I help you with anything?"

"I can always use the company," JD's mother said.

"Kira, would you help Nana to the couch?" Kira's mother said. "And pour her some iced tea?"

"Absolutely! Come on, Nana, let's get you sorted."

JD's mother telepathically looked at JD, suggesting he should offer to help Kira. It took him a few seconds to receive and decode the message, but he got the hint.

JD walked over to Kira. "Here, let me help you."

Kira smiled. "Thank you, JD, but I think I got it."

JD reached for the pitcher. "I'll pour Grandma Sullivan some iced tea. Kira, would you like a glass too?"

Kira smiled. "Yes, please."

Grandma Sullivan settled down on the couch. This was not the Grandma Sullivan who was always up before dawn, being both ranch foreman and manager of her sheep ranch. This was a much more mellow and diminished person than she was before. She had always been this cheerful but tough, rough rider of the ranch for ten years since her husband had died. Last year, she sold most of the ranch to her husband's brothers. She planned to spend time with her daughter and granddaughter in New Zealand. Originally from New Zealand, she was native Māori by birth. She met her husband, who was from Texas, while he was on assignment in Auckland. Her tribe identified as Māori, but they were from an ancient people who were said to possess supernatural powers. She was the last remaining elder from her tribe. Her daughter and granddaughter were her only living relatives by blood.

Last November, she headed to New Zealand to spend New Zealand's school Christmas break there. She returned in March of this year to sell the rest of the ranch, with plans to move back to New Zealand. But soon after arriving back home, her health declined. Her doctor could not determine the cause of her illness. He wanted her to get more tests done in the city. Her daughter Sheila came to help her sell the rest of the ranch and get the medical tests done. Despite her illness, Grandma Sullivan still had the spirit of a ranch foreman and rough rider.

JD poured and served Grandma Sullivan a glass of iced tea. He poured another for Kira. Several times, he stole a peek at Kira. He felt strangely attracted to her physically and emotionally. In the span of only a couple days, he had gone from not wanting a girl around to wanting her around. He felt it but did not understand it.

"JD, I haven't been able to thank you for caring for my yard and garden," Grandma Sullivan said. "And I believe I still owe you some money."

JD stood holding the glass of iced tea, staring at Kira.

"JD, are you okay?" Grandma Sullivan said. "Did you hear what I said?"

JD handed the glass of iced tea to Kira and replied to Grandma Sullivan, still looking at Kira. "You've already paid me for the time you were gone."

Kira took the glass of tea and smiled at JD. "Thank you, JD."

"Yes, but this is for the times since I've returned."

"Oh, I can't take your money for that. That was to help you while you're not feeling well."

"Okay, how about I put it in a fund for fun? I'm sure you and Kira will have expenses this summer."

It was not the norm to accept any form of outright charity. JD did not want someone else to cover the costs of being Kira's summer guide. Kira looked at JD and realized he was not comfortable accepting the money.

"I have an idea, Nana. You can pay me for any extra chores around the ranch. And I'll have some spending money. I certainly want to be able to pay my fair share of the fun."

"Alright, I guess. I do have some orphaned lambs that need to be cared for. You'll need to help feed them and clean their pen. Sam's in charge of the orphan lambs. Check with him and he'll show you what needs to be done. The lambs need special care, so I expect your best."

"I'll do it. That'll be great!" Kira said.

Kira walked over to JD and whispered, "I hope you have experience caring for sheep, 'cause I don't!"

JD considered that a strange comment since New Zealand was known for its sheep ranches. Being in 4-H and with his granddad's training, he could care for any farm animal.

JD's mother entered the living room and announced, "Dinner is ready. JD, please help me put the food on the table."

"I'll help too," Kira said.

JD's mother looked at him and nodded toward Grandma Sullivan on the couch.

He received the message and offered. "Grandma Sullivan, can Kira and I help you to the table?"

"No, but thank you. You know, I am quite able to get around on my own. Just hand me my cane."

Kira handed the cane to Grandma Sullivan. "Here you go, Nana. JD and I will be ready if you need us."

Dinner went reasonably well, except JD was asked to say grace. Since he was the "man" of the house, he was expected to be the spiritual leader. But his mother was the true spiritual leader. JD was more of a spiritual laborer whose spiritual labors were directed by his mother.

In rural Texas, religious training was part of every kid's life. Church was as much a part of community life as Friday night football. JD believed in God but only participated in religious activities because his mother and the church instructed him to do so. Saying grace at dinner was not the highlight of the meal for him. He was happy when dinner ended because he wanted to invite Kira to his room.

"Susan, thank you so much for the dinner," Sheila said. "It was delicious. You'll have to give me the recipe for that squash casserole."

"Yes, yes. It was delicious," Grandma Sullivan said. "And the company was most enjoyable."

"Thank you both; I'm glad you enjoyed it. But I have tasted Grandma Sullivan's dishes; mine do not compare."

"Oh, poppycock, my dishes are for hungry ranch hands to fill their stomachs. Yours are delicate and fill the soul."

"Why, Grandma Sullivan, you're making me blush," JD's mother said. "You're much too kind. Now, who wants coffee?"

"Uh, Mom, may Kira and I be excused?"

"Yes, please. I want to check out JD's room!" Kira said. "If that's okay with you, JD?"

JD was surprised by Kira's request. He was about to suggest that, but she beat him to it. Kira wanted to learn more about JD, and she figured one way was to check out his room. What we keep close to us in our private rooms says much about who we are and what we value.

"Sure, but please help clear the table before you go."

"We'll do better than that," Kira said. "We'll wash the dishes. Won't we, JD?"

"Wait. What? Yeah, okay, we'll wash the dishes." Washing dishes was not part of the plan, but JD felt he had to agree.

53

"Just clear the table and scrape the food off the plates," Kira's mother said. "I'll help Aunt Susan with the rest."

"Great! Thanks, Mum!"

Kira and JD hurriedly cleared the table and got the plates ready to wash.

"Okay, JD, where's that room of yours?" Kira said with a Cheshire cat smile.

After seeing Kira's Cheshire cat smile, he no longer thought this was a good idea. The Johnson twins had seen his room many times, but that was before they went through the "girly transformation." Kira oscillated between being a "sister-like" friend and a "girly" friend in JD's mind. The real-world concept of a girlfriend had not yet reached his brain. This mental oscillation was uncomfortable, so he went with the sister-like friend. Yet, he had this strange and new attraction to Kira that he had never felt before with any girl.

"Mom, we're finished in the kitchen," JD reported.

"Please come here." JD's mother said.

He walked over to his mother in the hallway to the living room. "Yes, Ma'am?"

JD's mother drew him close. "When you were little and had the Johnson twins over, I did not worry much. But now you are a young man inviting a young woman to your room. So please keep the door to your room open."

JD was puzzled why his mother would even ask that. "Sure, Mom, but why?"

"It is the proper thing to do when entertaining a young lady in your room."

"Okay, no problem," JD said, still puzzled by the request.

"Thank you. I'll bring up some cookies and milk in a bit."

JD gave his mother a quick hug. "Thanks, Mom!"

He walked back over to Kira.

"What did your mum want?"

"Not important, come on!"

Up in JD's room, Kira stood in the doorway and scanned the room. She saw books and magazines, a baseball glove and a tennis racket, some rocks, a microscope, a telescope, and some electronics. She walked around the room, sometimes stopping to look closer at something. When she came to the bed, she sat down, leaned back on her elbows, and said, "You are such a nerd!"

JD was surprised to receive that response. Did this mean she viewed him just as Billy did? He stood by his desk for a minute, looking confused and hurt. He swayed back and forth, looking at the floor while his finger traced an outline on the top of the desk.

"I'm not a nerd. Just because I like to study and explore stuff doesn't make me a nerd."

"Easy, don't be so sensitive! I like to explore stuff too. Some of my friends call me a nerd. I ignore it. If they don't want to learn, that's their loss. What's that thing on your desk with the dials?"

"It's a shortwave radio," JD said. "I built it from a kit."

"You built it?"

"Yep, I just finished it last week."

"Cool! Can you get any music stations?"

"Yeah, there's a station from Mexico. I'll try to pick it up."

He turned on the radio and tuned it to the Mexican station. Rock and roll music blared out of the kit's tiny speaker. Kira got up and started dancing to the music.

"Come on, dance with me!"

"Nah, I can't dance!"

"Come here, I'll show you. Let your body feel the beat and your feet do the rest."

"Okay, but be warned – I have two left feet."

"No worries, just keep both of them moving to the beat and away from my feet!"

Kira showed JD several dance moves, including some swing moves. It was initially slow for JD, but it wasn't long before the two danced and laughed through several songs. One of the dance moves brought them together face to face. They stood looking into each other's eyes, moving closer and closer to each other. Their lips were almost close enough to touch. JD was not freaking out. This was going to be his first real kiss. But his mother's footsteps and voice caused JD to step back several feet.

"Are you ready for some milk and cookies?" JD's mother said as she walked into JD's room. There was no response from the two shocked teenagers in the room.

"Oh my, please turn off that noise!" JD's mother said.

JD nervously walked over and turned off the radio. He had come within seconds of being caught kissing a girl in his room.

"So, are you two ready for some cookies and milk?"

JD, still frozen in place by shock, stood motionless in silence. Kira quickly stepped up to save the moment from disaster.

"Thank you, Mrs. Jayson," Kira said, faking excitement. "Are those chocolate chip cookies? They're my favorite!"

With the help of Kira's interjection, JD finally regained composure. "Yeah, thanks, Mom!"

"Okay, enjoy the cookies, but please keep the volume down," JD's mother said.

"Yes, ma'am, we will," JD said.

As JD's mother left the room, she paused at the door, looked directly at JD, and said, "And behave."

Both Kira and JD responded at the same time with. "Yes, ma'am!"

After JD's mother had left the room, Kira and JD looked at each other with eyebrows raised and a muffled laugh.

"Wow! That was close!" Kira said.

"Yeah, too close!" JD said with a concerned look.

"You've never kissed a girl before, have you?" Kira said, smiling.

"What? Yeah, I have lots of times!"

That was a lie. He hadn't kissed a girl yet. One of the Johnson twins had kissed him. It happened when he and the Johnson girls were four years old. Photographic proof of this was the only reason he learned about the kiss. Technically, JD was still a virgin when it came to kissing girls or any other physical interactions with girls. Kira created the desire in him to find out what it would be like.

"Okay, if you say so," Kira said as she scoped out the room. She stopped at the desk and picked up a photo. "Who is this?"

"That's my dad. He's dead."

"How did he die?"

"He was killed in the Korean War," JD said without any emotion. "He went over to join a MASH unit. It's like a mobile hospital."

"Was your dad, a doctor? How did he die?"

"Yeah, he was. It happened before the war actually started. They had just set up the mobile hospital and a mortar round hit the tent he was in. He and two other people were killed."

"I'm sorry. How old were you when he died?"

"That's okay, I was born on the day he died, so I don't remember him. My uncle got the telegram from the War Office. He gave it to my mom after she came home from giving birth to me."

"That must have been rough on your mum."

"Well, yeah, but she did have my uncle. And my granddad until he passed away last year."

"That's a lot of loss to overcome," Kira said. "It must be hard growing up without a dad."

"It was alright. My mom's been great, and my Uncle Joe. My granddad was like a father and my best pal until he died."

Kira picked up another photo from the desk. "Do you have a dog?"

"I did, but she died."

"Oh, I'm sorry. I've never had a dog or any pet."

"It's fine, it happened several years ago. Her name was Dolly. Dolly was the best. She was part rat terrier and part beagle. She kept the greenhouse clear of rats and helped me in the garden."

Kira held up a piece of paper. "Is this a map?"

"Yes, that's what I wanted to show you!"

Kira's interest was certainly piqued. "Yeah? What's it a map of?"

"It's a map of the canyon I told you about when we had the picnic. The one with a creek and a hidden waterfall!"

"Choice!" Kira said with growing excitement. "Where is it? Can we go there?"

"Only a few people have seen it! Well, at least only a few people who are living today."

"Who owns it?"

"It's mine! It will be when I'm eighteen. My granddad left it to me. It was supposed to be my dad's."

"Have you ever been there?"

"My grandad took me in his truck to the canyon rim. My mom doesn't know about that, so don't blab. She doesn't want me to go down into the canyon. She says it's too dangerous. Granddad promised to take me down to the canyon floor when I was older, but he died before he could. The waterfall is at the far end. It's supposed to be haunted."

"Haunted? You mean like ghosts?"

"Well, yeah. Granddad said outlaws saw ghosts there and stopped using the canyon as a hideout. They went to a cave in the hill country. Texas Rangers surrounded the cave and arrested the outlaws as they came out to go rob someplace."

"Wow! We have to go to the canyon! Where is it?"

"It's a long way off. The canyon is long and narrow. It has steep walls. It's over two hundred feet to the bottom in some spots. We would have to find a way to hike down to the canyon floor."

"Do you have any other maps? Like the ones surveyors use with lines that show the hills and stuff. Are there any maps like that?"

"I don't know, but my Uncle Joe works in the land office for the county. I bet he does. He's smart and has a college degree in geology."

"Alright! Let's go visit Uncle Joe!"

"Okay, we can do that. How do you know about surveyor maps?"

"You're not the only one who's smart. Those maps are used in New Zealand when people go tramping."

"Tramping? You mean like tramps who ride the railroads?"

"No, silly. Tramping is the Kiwi term for hiking. Some make a sport of it. They use compasses and maps to track where they are going, find clues, and write in a logbook that they have made it to a certain point."

"So, we could go tramping through the canyon!"

Kira stood like a professor teaching a class and said, "Precisely, my good man!"

JD muttered. "Cute, smart, and funny!"

"What did you say?"

"What? Uh, nothing."

"Say, you wanna meet at the drugstore tomorrow at noon?" Kira said. "I owe you a float! Afterward, we can visit your Uncle Joe. Is his office in town?"

"Sounds like a plan to me! And yeah, Uncle Joe's office is at the county courthouse in the town square. That's not too far from the campus and the drugstore. Oh, wait. I have to finish plowing the back pasture in the morning. That shouldn't take too long. I don't have much left to do."

"And I need to start caring for the orphaned lambs. How about we postpone visiting your uncle until the day after tomorrow?"

"Sounds like a plan! I'll finish the plowing, then come help you with the lambs."

"Wow, thanks," Kira said. "This is going to be a great summer of adventure!"

JD handed Kira a glass of milk. "Say, you know… you're a fun person."

"Yeah? Well, you are, too," Kira said. "We should make a list of the stuff we'll need."

"Like what?"

"You know, hiking stuff. Hey, do you think we could camp out too?"

"I don't think my mom would go for that. Maybe Uncle Joe can convince her."

"Awesome. Let's get started. Got a notebook and pen? And pass me one of those cookies, please, sir."

JD passed the plate of cookies. "At your service, Ma'am. What should we call our plan?"

"What about –Trek to the Waterfall?"

"Yeah, I like that!"

JD and Kira worked on their plan for fifteen minutes. Between the joking around with funny names for stuff and the giggles, they barely made it through the first page before JD's mother came to the door.

"What are you two working on that has made you so giddy?"

JD quickly put away the notebook before his mom could figure out what it was about. It was too early to present the idea to his mother. "Uhm, nothing, Mom. We're just making a list of what we want to do this summer."

That was not the whole truth, but technically, it was not a lie. JD had been instructed to be Kira's friend and show her around. JD's idea and main goal for the summer was to go to the canyon.

"Okay, but it's time for Kira to head home. Kira, your mom, and grandmother are waiting at the door downstairs. Have you got everything?"

"Yes, Ma'am," Kira said. "Thank you so much for having me over this evening. The meal was lovely!"

"Thank you, Kira. That's sweet. I'm glad you enjoyed it. You are always welcome here. Your mom and I were best friends when we were your age. I guess we are still best friends."

"Yes, Ma'am, I know," Kira said as they approached the door. "My mum has spoken about you many times."

"What's this, I hear? Are you telling stories about me?" Kira's mom said.

"She told me that you spoke often of me," JD's mother said.

"And that is true. Now, I have the pleasure of speaking with you often. But right now, I need to take Kira and Nana home!"

Kira turned to JD, embraced him, and said, "I had a fun time. Thanks for offering to help me feed the orphan lambs in the morning."

JD uttered. "Sure, I'll come right over after plowing in the morning. Say about nine?"

"That's cool. I'll be waiting for you at the barn. See ya!"

"Great, see ya!" JD said, trying not to show too much emotion. He did not want his mom to interrogate him late at night about his potential feelings for Kira.

"So, you and Kira," JD's mother said as she waved goodbye to her guests. "You and Kira seemed to be getting on well, huh?"

"And here it comes," JD thought. Somehow, JD needed to escape before the full-frontal assault on his deep-seated emotions began. JD thought. "Why do moms insist on knowing more about you than you know about yourself?"

"She's cool," JD said, trying to lower the excitement. "You know, for a girl. Wow, look at the time. I'd best get to bed if I am going to finish plowing that pasture early in the morning."

"Before you go to bed, please bring down the glasses and the plate from your room."

"Oh, no!" JD thought. He had forgotten about the glasses and the plate. He needed to sneak back downstairs without confronting his mother again. Luckily, when JD returned with the dishes, his mother was in the living room.

"Mom, I put the dishes in the sink," JD shouted. "I'm off to bed."

"Come here and give me a hug first."

"Rats!" he thought. He had almost escaped to the safety of his room. Now, he had to re-enter his mother's domain and scrutiny zone. Resisting now would result in a further inquiry into why he was too old to hug his mother. He rushed into the living room to hug his mother.

"Thanks for your help today."

"Sure, Mom. You're welcome."

"Please remember what I said about Kira. She's been through a lot and needs a trustworthy friend."

He looked perplexed. JD's mother was not someone to overact or exaggerate something.

"Sure, Mom. You can count on me," JD said as he hugged her.

"I am counting on that," JD's mother said, teary-eyed. "Love you. Now go to bed!"

"Love you too, Mom. Mom, I'm going to help Kira tomorrow with the orphaned lambs. I'm surprised she has no experience with sheep and lives in New Zealand."

"Kira and her mom live in Auckland. There aren't many sheep in the city. Don't forget to do your chores before you go."

"Yes, ma'am. Will do. Oh, I almost forgot. Mr. Buckman asked if I could come to work for him part-time. You know when I don't have school or chores."

"Yes, I think that would be a great experience for you. Be sure to do a good job."

"Thanks, Mom, I will."

A LAMB IS SICK

JD got up before sunrise, had breakfast, and finished the plowing. He got to the sheep barn early in the morning to help Kira. He planned to examine the lambs to check if any needed immediate attention. Ewes sometimes stopped nursing their newborn lambs. These lambs were considered orphaned and would die if not cared for. Most ranchers consider orphaned lambs too much trouble. Grandma Sullivan figured it was worth the effort if the lamb could survive with human care long enough to rejoin the flock.

The young ones had to be given a bottle containing a mixture with the same nutrition as the mother's milk. It was easy to spot a sickly lamb. The healthy ones crowded around, wanting to be the next one to nurse. The sickly ones held back. Some were too weak to stand. Not all the orphaned lambs would survive. JD had had a few lambs die in his lap while trying to make them take the bottle.

He entered the barn and saw Kira sitting on the barn floor with a lamb in her lap. The lamb wasn't moving. Kira was crying and screaming, "No! This is not how it's supposed to happen. This is wrong!"

"Kira, what's wrong?"

Kira was sobbing so hard that it was difficult for her to speak. She looked up at JD. Tears were streaming down her cheeks. She was shaking and quivering. JD sat down next to her.

"The lamb is…is…is…is…it's dead!" Kira sobbed. "I couldn't save it. I failed! This is wrong!"

"Kira, it's okay. Some lambs don't make it. They are just not strong enough. It's not your fault."

"You don't understand. This is not supposed to happen. Not to me!"

"Well, explain it to me. I want to help."

Kira put the dead lamb in JD's lap, stood up, and shouted at JD. "I can't explain it, and you can't help!"

"Where are you going?"

Kira ran out of the barn and back to the house. JD sat, confused, looking at the dead lamb in his lap. He wasn't sure what to do next. In the past, he would just go home. He would escape to his room to work on some science thing or read comics. This time, it was different. Kira was too important. To JD, she was more important than his confusion and anxiety. JD set the lamb down, stood up, and walked out of the barn.

From the barn, he watched Kira and her mom talking on the back porch. Kira was agitated and shouting. Kira's mom bent down, looked Kira in the eyes, and then put her arms around her. She whispered something to Kira. Kira calmed down and went inside. He approached Kira's mom to explain what happened with the lamb. He wanted to make sure Kira was okay.

"Aunt Sheila, is Kira okay? One of the lambs died in her lap. This happens. It has happened to me. She was upset about it."

"She's still upset, but she'll be fine," Kira's mom said.

"May I speak to her?"

"You can try. She's in her room."

"Can I take her a glass of water?"

"Sure, but don't be upset if she doesn't want to talk right now."

"That's okay. I know how it feels to lose a lamb."

JD knocked on the door to Kira's room. "Are you okay? Can we talk?"

"I'm okay, but I don't want to talk right now."

"I brought you a glass of water. Crying always makes me thirsty."

"Go away! I said I don't want to talk!"

JD sat down next to Kira's door. He didn't want to leave until he determined that Kira was okay, but he did not know how to make her feel better.

"I get it. You feel bad. I have had lambs die in my lap while getting them to take a bottle. It broke my heart when they died. I felt like I failed them. The first time it happened; I ran to my granddad crying. He hugged me and told me something that helped me. It didn't take away the pain but helped me understand why it was there."

Kira opened the door to her room and sat down next to JD.

"So, what did your granddad tell you?"

JD was surprised that Kira had sat down beside him. He was even more surprised that she wanted to talk. He was nervous and unsure of what to do or say next. It was like giving someone a shot of adrenaline. One slip with the injection, and the patient is dead instead of being revived. He hoped what he had to say would cheer up Kira. He and his granddad had a special place where only the two of them would go. When JD was upset, granddad knew where to find him.

"He told me that storms are a part of life," JD said nervously. "He said if all days were sunny without storms, we would never appreciate the sunny days. You know, stuff happens. Sometimes, we can't do anything about it. Part of life is figuring out how to deal with it and go on."

Kira turned, put her arms around JD, and hugged him. "I'll be fine. Your grandfather was a wise person. I need some time. Thanks for caring. Sorry for yelling at you."

"Okay, how about I leave you alone today. But I want to show you something. It's where I would go when I was upset. Granddad would come and tell me stories and help me calm down. Do you think you can be up early?"

"Sure, I guess."

"Cool, can you be up before sunrise tomorrow?"

Kira grinned. "Hmm, well, I like my beauty sleep in the morning."

"Ah, you're already pretty enough."

"Ha! So, you think I'm pretty."

"Well, yeah, I guess. So, what do you say, Miss 'I gotta have my beauty sleep?' Can you be up that early?"

"Tell you what. Bring me hot chocolate and breakfast buns, and we have a deal!"

A Lamb Is Sick

"Done!" JD said with a confident smile.

Back home, JD found his mom in the kitchen fixing lunch. He was entering dangerous territory by even talking with her about Kira. This was too important. Kira was too important. He pushed aside his reservations. "Mom, I need to tell you something."

He told his mother about what happened with Kira and the lamb. "Mom, she was upset, even crying. I want to take her to see the sunrise at the bluff, where Granddad and I used to go. I already told her. I promised to bring her some breakfast buns. I don't even know what she likes."

"Thank you for coming to me for help. I'll call her mom and ask her what Kira's favorite breakfast pastry is."

"Could you please help me make them?"

"Yes, but you need to tell me what's going on?"

"Here it comes. The talk about girls!" JD thought.

"Nothing's going on. I want to cheer her up."

"Sounds to me, you have feelings for her."

"Aw, Mom, why do we have to talk about feelings? She's just a friend, and I enjoy being around her. I don't want her to feel bad and not enjoy her time here."

"Do you remember how you felt when Dolly died?"

"Mom, Kira's not a dog!"

"No, but Dolly was your best friend. She went everywhere with you. She was always happy when you came home from school. How did you feel when she was gone? How did you feel when your granddad died?"

"It hurt. It hurt bad inside."

"Kira is a wonderful girl but is only here for the summer. I want you to be her friend, but I don't want you to get hurt when she has to leave. Sheila and I were more than just friends. She was the sister I never had. When she went to live in New Zealand, it hurt. I missed her so much. Sure, we wrote, but it wasn't the same as having her here with me. Her leaving hurt deep inside for a long time. We were all surprised. All of us were hurt, especially Uncle Joe. Getting feelings for someone is not bad; it is a positive thing. The loss of someone close to you hurts, but that is part of it, too. Do you have feelings for Kira?"

"I don't know. She's not like anyone. She's smart. She's fun to be with. She likes stuff I like. Yeah, I guess I like her. What do I do? Do I stop liking her?"

"I'm not telling you to stop. I want you to understand the risk. And I always want you to be kind and caring. I think the breakfast plan is a great idea. I'll call Sheila right now, and we can start on the baking."

JD walked over and put his arms around his mother. "Thank you, Mom. I love you."

JD's mom wiped the tears from her cheek. "I love you, too." Her little boy was growing up too fast.

Good Morning Sunflowers

JD was up before the rooster was able to even think about crowing. The sun was still sleeping. With the help of his mother the night before, he had baked sticky cinnamon buns for the morning surprise. His mother did the baking while JD watched and, at times, aided. Nearly as fast as a superhero, he made his bed, dressed, and washed up.

He went downstairs and started preparing the breakfast box. He poured the hot chocolate into the thermos and packed it with two cups in his backpack. Lastly, he added the sticky buns, carefully wrapped in an old bread bag.

"Good morning, early bird," JD's mother said as she entered the kitchen. "Did you remember to pack some napkins?"

"Good morning, Mom. Thanks, I almost forgot them."

"Do you have your flashlight?"

JD was confident that he had remembered everything, but his mother kept bringing up things he had forgotten.

"No, I forgot. What else?"

"How about these two kitchen towels. And grab that picnic blanket from the hall closet. You can sit on that."

"Thanks, Mom," JD said as he hugged his mother.

"Be careful along that trail. It's going to be dark. That trail is rocky. And you two behave yourselves."

JD was already heading out the door. "We will, Mom, I promise."

The setting moon provided some light, so it wasn't totally dark outside. JD's bike light also helped light the way. He arrived at Grandma Sullivan's well before sunrise. Kira was sitting outside on the porch.

"Morning, Nerd Boy," Kira said. "So, where are we going?"

"You'll see. Come on. It's not far. It's behind my house by the creek."

"First, did you bring the goods?"

JD pointed to his backpack. "All in here!"

"Sweet as. Let's go! My tummy's hungry for some brekkie."

JD turned down a small dirt road just before his house. He stopped a short distance down the road.

"Leave your bike here. We need to walk the rest of the way. Follow me."

A full moon hung close to the western horizon. Morning sounds filled the air, including the soft cooing from mourning doves mixed with the percussive sounds of crickets and even a few cicadas. In the distance, water rushed over rocks in the creek.

Kira stopped, closed her eyes, and took a slow, deep breath. "Listen to those sounds. Feel that cool breeze. There's so much energy everywhere! Thanks for doing this."

"Wait till you see the main event. Come on. Watch your step. It's uphill some and rocky."

The two walked up the trail running along the side of a bluff. JD led with his flashlight, barely illuminating the way up the path. The first light of the blue hour had slipped across the horizon. It was still too dark to make out much except large shapes. You could make out the outline of a tree next to where the moon was setting. JD used the flashlight to find the right spot.

"Over here. There's a flat rock we can sit on to watch the show."

JD laid down the picnic blanket, and Kira helped straighten it out. She sat down, kneeling back on her legs, and looked out from the hill, but could barely discern features in the landscape. The moon slowly descended towards the horizon in the west as the sun began its ascent.

"Where are we?" Kira said as she strained to see any landmarks. Lights in the distance to the south flicked dimly. She figured the lights to be from the town. She could also tell they were sitting on a bluff higher than the landscape below or on either side. The sky filled with blue, and some sunlight slipped over the horizon through clouds. It was easy to see a few feet around on the top of the bluff, but the ground below and behind the bluff was still in shadows.

"All will be revealed soon. Can you hold the flashlight, and I will pour the hot chocolate."

"Sure, I'm glad I brought a sweater; it's chilly here. I thought Texas was always hot. I did not expect this."

"Here, this hot chocolate will help."

"Thanks. And the pastry?"

JD pulled one of the sticky buns out of the bag and handed it to Kira on a napkin. "Here you go."

"Wow! A sticky bun! My favorite!"

"Yeah," JD said with a smile. "I know. I helped my mom bake them! She did most of the baking, but I did help."

Kira licked her fingers and wiped crumbs from the edge of her mouth. "They're super sticky. Do you have any more napkins?"

"Yes, and here's a kitchen towel to put in your lap."

"I need it to wipe my sticky hands!"

At the beginning of twilight, the sky had already turned a dark blue. Light leaked over the horizon, dimly lighting the ground as it bounced around through the clouds. Rays of light shot through clouds in the east, and the blue sky retreated toward the west. The dark gray clouds now took on the hues of the rainbow. The moon hovered over the horizon in the west.

Kira turned and stared at the rising sun in the east. "Wow! Look at those colors!"

Kira sat with her mouth partially open and her eyes wide open. "This is so spectacular!"

"Turn around and look to the west."

"Oh my! The moon is so full. I don't have any words."

JD had been there with his granddad and the Johnson girls several times. But seeing it with Kira through her expressions, he was seeing it again for the first time.

"I'm glad you like it," JD said with a satisfying smile.

Kira reached over and squeezed JD's arm. "I love it. Well done, you! Thank you for putting this all together. You have lifted my spirit."

JD smiled, happy that Kira was enjoying the sunrise and moonset with him. "You haven't seen the main event yet!"

Kira and JD had a clear view of the horizon from the top of the bluff. Sunlight created long shadows as the sun rose from behind the tree line. The eastern sky was now filled with color. A shade of light blue rapidly replaced the dark blue.

"Come over here. Stand facing the west."

Kira pointed back to the east. "But the sunrise. It's not over."

"You'll see."

The top of the bluff was still in a dim light without harsh shadows. Kira saw JD and most objects near her but was not casting a shadow.

"Hold my right hand and stretch out your right arm."

"Is this a sneaky way to get me to hold your hand?"

"No, silly, watch!"

JD moved closer to Kira and held her left hand. The dim light was gone in a flash, and the bright sunlight streaked across the top of the bluff.

"Look, our shadows."

"Wow!" Kira said as she clasped JD's hand. "Choice as!"

JD gently pulled Kira toward the edge of the bluff. "Look down there."

Kira could make out a field of tall flowers in the shadows. "What's that?"

"Wait, and you'll see."

As the sun rose, the shadows below retreated, revealing a multi-acre field of tall sunflowers. The sunflowers stood like the terracotta army of Qin Shi Huang. Their thin, green, spiny stems were topped by round yellow blooms that shone brightly in the morning sunlight.

"Putirā! So beautiful."

"What does putirā mean?"

"Sunflower in Māori. The Māori have a saying, "Turn your face to the sun and the shadows fall behind you.""

"I love that. Look closely at the flower tops. They're all facing the sun in the east."

"Sweet as. They're like an audience, and we are the actors on the stage. We should take a bow!"

Still holding hands, Kira and JD stretched out their free arms and bowed to the audience of sunflowers. Kira turned, put her arms around JD, and gave him a long, tender hug. She whispered in his ear. "This has been the best morning of my life. Thank you so much."

That warm energy he had felt before flowed up and down JD's body. This energy soothed his spirit but also activated something in his body. Kira was awakening something inside of him.

JD whispered back. "This is the best summer of my life."

Kira kissed him on the cheek. "Me too. And the summer has just begun! Where to now, my fellow explorer?"

"Let's grab our stuff. There's a path down to the sunflower field and back to where our bikes are. That path is an easier way up here, but I didn't want to give away the surprise."

"Super, I want to look at those sunflowers up close. We need to head back soon. I have some schoolwork and chores to do."

"Yeah, I got some chores, too. How about we meet at the drugstore tomorrow for lunch? We can visit my uncle after lunch. Like one o'clock?"

"Works for me!"

Later that morning, JD's mind was not entirely focused. He was always thinking and daydreaming about something while doing anything.

Today, his mind was even further away from executing his chores. Perhaps this absent-mindedness made the time go by faster. Maybe it was the excitement of seeing Kira for lunch the next day. Whatever the reason, JD finished well ahead of schedule and daydreamed through lunch.

"How was the sunrise breakfast?"

There was no answer from JD, for he was there in body, but not in mind or spirit.

"JD! I asked you a question."

JD was still not fully back in the present, but his better-respond-to-mom alarm had gone off in his head.

"What?" JD said, but he quickly corrected his obvious protocol mistake. "I'm sorry. I didn't hear you. I was thinking about something."

"I asked how the sunrise breakfast went."

The excitement and thrill of the sunrise with Kira had been rushing around in JD's head all morning. It poured out of him like a gushing fountain.

"Mom, it was great! Everything was perfect. The clouds were exactly right, so the sky filled with color. You should have seen Kira's face. Her eyes opened up wide, and she squeezed my arm! And when she saw the sunflowers, she was super happy. We bowed to the sunflowers. She is so cool. Thank you so much for helping bake the sticky buns. Kira loved them. She's really something. She, uh, she thanked me for everything."

He almost told his mom about the tender hug and kiss, but no boy would blab to his mom about something like that. That might start the lengthy talk again about girls, how you have to be a gentleman, and on and on it would go.

"And then?"

"We took the trail down by the sunflower field. Kira wanted to see the sunflowers up close. We also found some other wildflowers. Kira likes nature stuff. She is so much fun to be with."

"What do y'all have planned for tomorrow?"

JD had not told his mother about the plan to visit his uncle for fear that it might result in a probe into the reason for the visit.

"I want to show Kira the town square. First, we'll have ice cream floats at the drugstore by the college."

"That's nice. You should stop in and say hi to your uncle."

"Sure," JD said, thinking what a break that was. "If he is not busy."

"I will give him a call. I'm sure he can find a few minutes to say hi."

"Wow, this is perfect!" JD thought. He was amazed at how well he had pulled this off. He avoided talking to his mom about girls and got his mother to help set up the visit to Uncle Joe's office.

THERE'S A SNAKE IN THE GRASS

Getting up before the rooster has time to crow is not something any boy wants to do unless they are going to do something fun, like fishing or taking a trip to the state fair. This morning, JD was motivated to wake up early. Before sunrise, he was starting his chores. Nellie, his cow, was surprised he came so early to milk her. Soon, he finished all his chores and got ready for his "rendezvous" with Kira at noon. He was combing his hair when he heard his mother walking down the hall.

JD's mother knocked on the bathroom door and said, "JD, do you want some lunch before you go?"

"No, Mom, but thanks. We'll get something at the drugstore."

"Remember to go by your uncle's office. I called him, and he's expecting you after lunch. And properly introduce Kira."

"Yes, Mom, I will," said as he came out of the bathroom and presented himself to his mother. "How do I look?"

JD's mother brushed back his hair with her hand. "Very handsome and too grown-up. You two have fun and behave yourselves!"

JD hugged his mother and rushed down the stairs. "Okay, Mom. We will."

In less than one week, JD had gone from a boy who did not want to hang out with a girl to a young man rushing to do just that. He was head-over-heels excited about this girl. She wasn't like the girly girls at school. She was like the Johnson twins used to be. She was ready for adventure. As he raced down the road on his bike, his mind was busy going over everything he and Kira needed to do to prepare for the trek.

It was not the trek that excited him; it was Kira. There was something unique and amazing about her. She boosted his spirit while challenging him at the same time. Kira was fun like the Johnson twins but was a better version of them. He and the Johnson girls had gone on many adventures, including a few on the dangerous side. The Johnson twins were "pals" even though they were girls. Kira was a girl despite also being a "pal." Even now, as JD biked down the road towards the university and the drugstore, a mix of emotions was swirling around in his brain. He was excited with anticipation.

As he approached the drugstore, that excited enthusiasm was quickly muted. At the side of the drugstore, he saw Kira talking to an older boy leaning against the building. The boy looked old enough to be one of the college kids. He was smoking a cigarette. Kira was laughing as the boy recounted and gestured a humorous story. The boy said something, looking straight into Kira's eyes. Kira reached out and hugged the boy. The boy motioned to the drugstore door, inviting Kira inside. Kira followed the boy inside the drugstore.

A sudden surge of negative images churned around in his head. What did he see? Kira was supposed to be waiting for him. Why was she talking and laughing with this guy? Why did she hug the guy? What was this fearful, gut-wrenching feeling he had? The fear froze him in place. He could not go forward to the drugstore. How could he face this unknown? He stood in the middle of the street straddling his bike, staring at the drugstore door.

JD felt a hand on his shoulder. "Hey, kid! You, okay?"

He turned. A college kid mouthed something. He did not understand at first, then the silence broke.

"Hey, kid! You should get off the street," the college kid said. "You're going to get run over."

The words from the kid's mouth didn't register, but somehow, they tipped the scales of JD's emotional stability. He turned the bike around and headed back home. The fear turned to hurt. The girl he wanted to be with was with some other guy. Tears were trying to come out of his eyes, but he was now in a state of emotional superposition. He was hurt, angry, shocked, and confused all at the same time. His body had not yet responded to the confusion. A stew of emotions churned together in his brain.

Back at home, JD let his bike fall to the ground as he dismounted. He stormed up the stairs to his room, entered, and slammed the door behind him. Luckily, JD's mom was not there, or he would have received a stern lecture about not slamming doors. Then his mom would start the probe to determine why he was angry. As he lay on his bed for over an hour, staring at the ceiling, he tried to figure out what had happened. What exactly had he seen? What did it mean?

He did not like unknowns. Once, when he was only five, he awoke during the night. In the dark, it looked like someone, or something, was sitting in his chair. Rather than cowering under the covers in fear, he got out of bed, turned on the lights, and confronted the pile of folded clothes his mom had placed on the chair. He attacked problems by facing them and submitting them to a complete investigation. He gathered the facts and gave them a careful analysis.

But in this instance, with Kira and the older guy, the hurt kept him from further investigating the situation and removed sound logic from his analysis. He could not confront Kira and ask her what had happened. He was irrational and confused. He couldn't avoid Kira for the rest of the summer. Now, with ill-prepared logic, he decided on a different approach. There was a knock at the front door. From his bedroom window, he could tell it was Kira. Kira knocked a few more times and left. After Kira left, JD put his "plan" into action.

It only took him a little time to acquire the necessary props for his plan. He headed over to Grandma Sullivan's. He was ready to confront Kira and show her he was not some girl-crazy kid. He was a man, not a boy.

He knocked firmly on Grandma Sullivan's door with new confidence in his spirit. "This was going to work," he thought.

Kira's mother opened the door. "Hi, JD! Kira was looking for you. Didn't you two have plans for this afternoon?"

"Yeah, something came up. Is Kira home?"

"She came home a little upset and worried."

"Yeah? Well, I'd like to explain to her what happened."

"Okay, you can find her by the creek. She went exploring."

"Oh, okay. Thanks!"

"JD, is everything okay?"

"Uh, yeah, I mean, yes, Ma'am. Everything is going to be fine."

"Alright, you go on then. You two come back here to the house, and I will have some lemonade for you."

"Okay, sure, will do!" JD said as he turned to head down to the creek.

The creek was a little over a hundred yards from the back of the house. It ran behind Granma Sullivan's house and his house. JD had explored nearly every trail through the meadows to the creek. Most of the trails were made by animals (wild and domesticated ones) as they headed down to the creek to water. The creek cut through several small hills, leaving behind bluffs. From these bluffs, you had a panoramic view of the creek and could even catch a glimpse of some wild animals or birds. He figured correctly that Kira would be on one of those bluffs overlooking the creek.

Kira was crouched down low, watching something by the creek. It was time to put his plan into action. He took out the pack of cigarettes he had swiped from one of the ranch hand's lockers. He pulled out one of the cigarettes and lit it. This was only the second time he had experimented with smoking. He and the Johnson twins had tried it once before. But he still had not mastered the inhaling and the exhaling. Quietly, he approached Kira's location and sat down nearby.

There's something about tobacco smoke. It does not matter whether there is any wind or what direction the wind is blowing. Tobacco smoke, especially cigarette smoke, somehow finds its way through the air to the nostrils of anyone nearby. Before he could take more than one puff, the smoke had traveled to Kira's nose. She turned around and saw him sitting with a cigarette in one hand. "What the hell are you doing?"

JD coughed. "I'm smoking."

"I know. Why on earth would you do that? That's a stupid thing to do."

"Really? You only think so 'cause you can't do it." JD said mockingly.

Kira crawled over to JD, yanked the cigarette from his hand, and took one long drag. She rolled the smoke around in the back of her mouth, blowing some out in a smoke ring and the rest through her nose. Like a seasoned Marine, she field-stripped the cigarette.

JD sat staring in shock and awe. "What...wait...how... you...when did you?"

"Now, what's this all about?" Kira said as she sat next to JD. "And where were you at noon? I waited at the drugstore for an hour for you to show up. Speak up and stop stuttering."

"I, uhm...you were...uh," JD said as he tried to hold back the tears. Kira was noticeably upset, which forced his emotional superposition to collapse. The tears were coming.

Tears dripped down JD's cheek. "I saw you with that guy."

"So?"

"You were laughing, and you hugged him."

"Yeah, so what?"

"I figured you found someone you liked better than me."

"You're an idiot. That boy is a distant cousin of mine."

"What? But you hugged him! I don't understand."

"First of all, I can hug anyone I darn well please. But if you let me, I will explain."

JD wiped the tears from his eyes and face. "Okay, I'm listening."

"Before you got there, I saw Billy on the side of the drugstore. I stopped to check how he was doing. Billy began teasing me and grabbing me."

Anger replaced the tears. "What the? I'll beat the crap out of him if he tries that again."

"Calm down, tiger. Let me finish."

"Okay, go on."

"Well, about that time, this older guy came up, yanked Billy away, and told Billy to back off. It turns out this guy is a cousin of mine. I gave him a thank-you hug. He offered to sit with me until you showed up, so no one else bugged me. Now tell me, what the hell is up with the cig?"

"I saw that guy smoking. And he looked cool, so I figured you would like me more if I smoked."

"Well, you figured wrong! I thought you were different and not like the other boys back home. When my grandmother told me about you, I was excited. For the first time, I hoped to meet someone as nerdy as me."

"But...you...uh...you!" JD uttered.

"But what?"

"You took that cigarette and smoked it like it was not your first time! Do you smoke?"

"I used to, but not now."

"But you're my age. When did you start? When you were twelve? When did you quit?"

"I quit last year. Do we have to talk about this now? It is not something I want to talk about – not something I'm proud about."

"Well, yeah, I think we need to talk about it!"

"Fine, I'll tell you about it if you promise not to act like an ass again around me. And never smoke around me again."

"Okay, I promise."

"You lost your dad when you were little, right?"

"Yeah."

"Well, my father abandoned my mother. He took all the money he could find and left without even saying good-bye to my mom."

Tears welled up at the edges of Kira's eyes. She was trying to hold them back. JD looked at her, not knowing what to say or to do.

"I'm sorry," JD mumbled. "That had to be tough. Why did he leave?"

Kira wiped the tears at the corners of her eyes and took a deep breath. "He was a bum who just used my mom to get what he wanted and left. He left before I was born, so it didn't matter. My great-uncle filled the dad role when I was growing up. He took me exploring and taught me a bunch of stuff. I learned so much from him. He was like a dad and my best friend. And the letters from my grandmother also helped a lot. I guess I managed okay, but I always had problems making friends in school. Then my great-uncle died."

The tears were back, and Kira could not hold them back. "When he died, I felt...I...bloody hell. I hate crying."

Kira bent over, sobbing. JD reached over, put his arm around Kira, and hugged her tenderly. "It's okay. You don't have to tell me anymore."

Kira wiped the tears from her face and sat back up. "I'm fine. I want to tell you this. When my great-uncle died, I felt lost. I was angry and hated that I was now alone."

"But you had your mother, right?"

"Yeah, but she was always working. She did what she could. But every day after school, I was alone. My best friend was gone, and I had no one else. My mum got me a bike. I rode my bike to school. After school, I went exploring."

"That sounds like fun. The Johnson twins and I loved exploring with our bikes until they got all boy crazy."

Kira smiled. "Boys can make a girl crazy in many ways. In a way, that's what happened to me. I was out exploring one day after school and ran into this group of boys. They were racing each other on their bikes. I asked if I could have a go at it. At first, they all laughed and said girls were not allowed to race. I challenged them to a race. I said if I won, they had to let me join."

"What happened? Did you win?"

"Yeah, I did. I beat the entire group, every one of them, and all by a long stretch. They let me join their group. For the first time in my life, I belonged."

Tears were returning to Kira's eyes. "I didn't feel alone anymore."

"That sounds like a good thing."

"It was good in the beginning. We had weekly races. We went exploring on our bikes. But some of the guys wanted to do other stuff like drinking and smoking. Soon, we were all doing it and more. We didn't have any money, and even if we did, we couldn't buy the cigs and booze, so we stole them. And we bullied any kids who challenged us."

"Oh, I see."

"At first, it was exciting and fun. We did what we wanted to do. No one told us what to do – well, that is until one day, we got caught stealing some cigs."

"Oh Wow! What happened?"

"I got suspended from school and grounded. I also had to do community service work during the past school holiday. That was this past November when my grandmother came to visit."

"Yeah, she asked me to take care of her garden and mow the yard while she was gone."

"Nana helped me get back on track. Most of my community service work was helping in a national park near our home. Nana would take me to the park in the morning for my community service. We would have a picnic lunch when I finished my community service tasks for that day. Afterward, we went on hikes. She taught me so much about plants and animals. We talked about all sorts of stuff. It turned out to be the best school holiday of my life. Even the community service work wasn't that bad."

"That sounds awesome to me. It sounds like some of the times I had with my granddad. My interest in science comes from my uncle, but my desire to explore comes from my granddad."

"I know. My grandmother told me all about you. That was the reason I was so excited about coming here."

"Really? You wanted to meet me?"

"Yeah, I wanted to meet the nerd boy from Texas," Kira laughed.

JD frowned and hung his head down. "I'm not a nerd. No one likes a nerd!"

Kira reached out and lifted JD's head. She warmly gazed into his eyes and kissed him on the cheek. "Well, I like this nerd. And if loving to explore and to learn is being a nerd, I am proud to be one too!"

JD looked at Kira. "I'm sorry I upset you today. I freaked out, and I shouldn't have."

"You're forgiven, but if we're going to be friends, we must trust each other and talk it out. Deal?"

"Deal. I'm glad you came to Texas. My mom mentioned she and your mom were friends, as close as sisters. She said you were coming to visit. I wasn't excited about having a girl around, but I'm glad you came. I don't even know your last name."

"It's Sullivan. My mom and dad were not married. He was a sailor. They met while my mom was working at the USO after the war. He led her on and said they would get married, but once my mom was pregnant, he shipped out and never came back. My great-uncle tried to track him down but couldn't. I guess that makes me a bastard child."

"I don't care about that. I think you're awesome. I'm super glad you came. You and I are similar. I grew up without my dad; my granddad was my best friend. What was it like growing up in New Zealand? You said you like to explore? What do you like to explore the most?"

"It was alright. My uncle got me interested in nature. There're some cool parks in Auckland. He took me to a few parks near where we lived. After he died, I would ride my bike to one of the parks just to be close to him. That's where I ran into the gang. When my Nana came, she got me interested in nature again. She knows lots about plants and animals. I love hiking on trails and finding new bugs and critters. I think they are cool and interesting."

JD smiled, stood up, and offered Kira a hand. "I think we have some planning to do!"

"I agree," Kira said as she stood up.

Just as they turned to head back to the house, a rattle-snake crawled out from the grass beside the trail. JD stepped forward without seeing the snake right in front of him. As the snake began to strike, Kira spoke two words and reached out her hand. JD froze in mid-step. He was stiff as a board, caught with one foot up and one foot down. The snake stretched like a pole in mid-air, with its fangs less than an inch from JD's leg. Kira walked around JD, bent down, and looked at the snake. She shook her head in disapproval.

She securely grabbed the snake behind the head. When Kira touched the snake, it moved as if awakened from a deep sleep. She carried it a few yards towards the creek.

Before she set it go, she looked the snake straight in its eyes. "This was your unlucky day. You have listened to the wrong voice. Come on, you'll find a better meal down by the creek. And be careful about whom you obey in the future! Remember, your kind has a history of listening to the wrong voices."

Deep, eerie voices shouted from the mouth of the snake. "We have the right to test him! You must not interfere!"

"Wrong, I am not interfering. I'm here to stay. Tell your friends that I have awakened."

"We are many. You are but one."

"I stand with many more than you can count. Leave the snake now, or I will show you who I am."

"This is not over. We will be back."

"I'll be ready."

The snake slithered off towards the creek. Kira walked back to JD and lightly touched him on the shoulder. He took his next step. Everything ran again in real-time. The two strolled back to the house.

"So, is our plan back on then?" JD said, unaware that anything strange had happened.

"You mean for the trek? Yes, I am looking forward to it!"

"We need to talk about how we should approach my uncle."

"I think it is best to come clean and tell him the truth," Kira said.

"I wasn't suggesting we lie to him. Perhaps, we don't tell him everything at once."

"I vote for dumping the entire bloody plan at his feet. We need his 100 percent support. He is either going to say no or support the idea. But if he found out we held back details, that support will be more like zero percent."

"I suppose you're right. We can only convince our moms to let us do the trek if we have my uncle's complete support."

"Without your uncle's support, neither of our mothers will agree," Kira said. "This I know."

"How about we meet after your studies tomorrow?"

"No studies tomorrow. Remember, I only go on Mondays and Tuesdays. On Mondays, I take the tests for the previous week's assignments. On Tuesdays, we review the test results and the new material, and I'm given homework assignments. So, I have homework that I have to do before I visit Mrs. Wilson again on Monday. I should be able to finish that anytime this week. But I do have to take care of the lambs in the morning."

"Do you need help with the lambs?"

"Thanks, but I think I need to do this by myself. You helped me yesterday with the sunrise breakfast. I'm much more confident today. You're a great friend."

JD smiled. "I'm glad you are feeling better. How about we meet after lunch tomorrow? We can go visit my uncle."

"Okay, see ya tomorrow after lunch. Don't stand me up again."

"I won't. I promise."

Back home, JD knew he would be cross-examined about why he didn't go by Uncle Joe's office.

"Your uncle called and said you did not come by," JD's mom said. "What happened?"

"Something came up, we're going to go tomorrow."

"Is everything okay? Why do I smell cigarette smoke?"

"Some college kid was smoking outside the drugstore. Everything is fine now. Do you need me to do anything?" That was true, but not the reason his mother smelled cigarette smoke. His mother did not know all the things he had done or experienced. One of his friends had brought a magazine to 4-H camp last year. It had pictures of nude women in it. His mother would have had a heart attack if she knew that. Then there was the time he and some friends rode their bikes to the county airport and raced down the runway until they were chased off. It was better for his mother that she did not know everything. It was better that way, especially for him.

"Do you need me to do anything?" JD asked. Offering to help always diverted his mother's attention away from what he had done to what he could do.

"I wish they would stop letting people smoke at the drugstore. You could check to see if anything needs to be harvested in the garden. I bet the strawberries are ready. I need some more to make my strawberry preserves."

JD grinned. "Sure, mom, I'd be happy to." Crisis of discovery averted.

UNCLE JOE AND THE FOUR AMIGOS

"Mom, I'm off to Kira's," JD said as he hurriedly finished his lunch.

"Wait, just a minute. You wash your face and brush your teeth first. No girl wants to see and smell lunch on a boy's face.

"Good point!" JD said as he rushed up to his bathroom. Usually, he would complain about having to delay important afternoon exploration. However, things were back on track with Kira, and he did not want to derail his progress with an unattractive appearance.

"All done, Mom! I'm off to Kira's."

He zoomed out the door before his mom could respond. The trip to Kira's seemed even shorter as JD raced down the road. Kira was waiting with her bike in the driveway next to the road.

"I'm ready, Freddy! Which way to your uncle's office?"

"My uncle's office is downtown in the County Court-house. We'll go through the park. There's a road before the university that we can take. On the way, I can show you where I go to school. It's a combined junior high and high school."

"Sweet as! I can find out where you get all nerdy."

"Hahaha, I'm nerdy everywhere."

By now, He brushed off Kira's teasing about him being a nerd. JD was what he was. He didn't care what others thought about him, but he did care what Kira thought.

It was a sweltering summer afternoon that made you wish you were swimming. The blistering sun and hot wind made you want to do that even more. Summer in Texas could be brutal and deadly, but kids found a way to play through it.

Summer was freedom. It was freedom from school, where you were told to do this and do that. JD enjoyed school, where he had access to the school library. He enjoyed everything about school except the endless, boring homework. Exploring was his first choice either on his bike or in a book. He had many future dreams. He wanted to be an astronaut and explore space, a photographer for National Geographic, a scientist, or maybe a journalist. The list of things JD wanted to do seemed endless, but the common aspect was exploration.

The two stopped next to a two-story red brick building. "Is that your school?"

"Yep, over that way is the track and field area. Tennis courts are on the side of the building. The high school football team practices here, but the official stadium is in the park."

"That's American football, right?"

"Is there another type of football?"

"Well, in New Zealand, we have rugby. It's like American football, only without the helmets and pads."

"That sounds rough and dangerous,"

"It's not for the weak, that's for sure."

"Come on, we will use this side street to get to the town square. It's safer than riding bikes down the highway into town.

JD and Kira biked down the street. Old Southern-style houses with wraparound porches and tall oak trees lined both sides of the street. People were on their porches enjoying the shade and iced tea. A few waved at JD as they passed by. As a farm boy, he didn't have many friends in town, but people from his church remember him as the kid who read books during the pastor's sermon. That is when his mom wasn't looking.

"These are beautiful homes, and I love the tall trees."

"They're oak trees. Some could be two hundred years or more old."

"Wow! Can you imagine the stories they could tell?"

As they approached the County Courthouse, JD pointed to the bike racks. "We can park the bikes over there."

"So, your mum phoned your Uncle Joe? That's brilliant. How did you get her to do that?"

"It was weird how that worked. Before I could say anything, she suggested it."

Kira got off her bike and looked around the square. The county courthouse was a near duplicate of the one in Austin, only smaller.

"I love this building. Those tall columns and the dome are cool. What's the statue on the top?"

"That's lady justice."

"Why's she wearing a blindfold?"

"From what I have read, the blindfold means she judges without regard to the person."

"Cool," Kira said and mumbled. "If only people did the same."

"What?"

"Nothing...doesn't matter. Let's go to your uncle's office. But first, I need a drink of water. Is there a water fountain inside?"

"Yeah, there's one on the second floor near my uncle's office."

Kira and JD silently walked up the winding staircase to the second floor. There were two water fountains just across from the top of the stairs. One had a sign that read "White," and the other had one that read "Colored." Kira walked straight to the one marked "Colored." Just as Kira took a drink from the fountain, she heard a voice from behind her.

"Young lady, you're drinking from the wrong fountain," the voice said.

Kira stood up and turned around. Standing before her was an older man dressed just like you would picture a "southern gentleman," who might be someone's grandfather, a county judge, or both.

"Why is this the wrong fountain?" Kira said. "Is it broken?"

"That fountain is for colored people only," the older man said. "You need to use the fountain for white people."

Kira pressed her hand against the white backstop of the fountain.

"Sir, as you can see, my skin is not white."

The older gentleman was now agitated. "Look, missy, I can see you are not Negro, and that is what is meant by 'colored.'"

"Sir, with all due respect, I am not white like you are."

JD looked at Kira and saw that her skin color was darker than his would be at the end of the summer. He never even realized it before.

Kira turned and took a long drink of water from the fountain marked "Colored." The old man mumbled and grumbled something ungentlemanly, then walked toward the fountain marked "White."

Just as the older man bent down to take a drink, Kira said, "Oh, by the way, I wouldn't drink from that fountain. It's broken."

The older man mumbled something about "damn hippies" and "the younger generation" as he turned the faucet handle on the fountain. Water shot straight up into his face. When he tried to turn off the water, the faucet handle kept spinning around. Water sprayed over the fountain basin onto the floor. The older man walked away, yelling obscenities at the top of his voice.

Kira grinned and held her head back as she turned to walk away. "I did try to warn you, sir. Now you're white and all wet,"

All this time, JD stood bewildered, his mouth open in shock, trying to understand what had just happened. He wondered how Kira knew that the fountain marked White was broken.

"Close your mouth, JD; you'll catch a fly. Let's go find your uncle."

That was not difficult because JD's uncle was standing by the door to his office, trying to figure out what had just happened.

"What was that all about, JD?" JD's uncle said.

JD described what had happened, including the details of Kira's "I'm not white" demonstration and the older man's "not-so-gentlemanly" words.

JD's uncle laughed and said to Kira, "I must say, I don't think I have met anyone quite like you, except perhaps your mom. JD, aren't you going to introduce your friend?"

"Uncle Joe, this is Kira. She's from New Zealand."

Kira smiled, offered her hand, and said, "Pleased to meet you, Mr. Jayson. JD speaks highly of you."

"It's Hayden, not Jayson. I'm the older brother of Susan, JD's mom."

"Sorry, I just assumed."

"Not a problem! I'm pleased to meet you, Kira. And please call me Joe or Uncle Joe. Mr. Hayden makes me sound too old. JD's mom called and filled me in. And given your mom and grandmother, you are exactly how I pictured you. Your mom, JD's mom, dad, and I were childhood friends long ago. We were the Four Amigos."

"Really?" Kira said. "Did you go on any adventures together?"

"We sure did! We were always out exploring, much to our parents' chagrin. We got into more trouble than we should have. But don't tell your mom, I said that. So, what are you two up to today besides upsetting old white men?"

"It was not my intention to upset that gentleman. I just wanted a drink of water."

Uncle Joe smirked. "Some old white men need to be upset at times. Too many are living in the past."

JD quickly interjected. "We came for your advice and help on something."

"Yes, we need your knowledge and help," Kira said with a twinkle in her eyes.

"Uh…hmmm, and just what is it you need?" Uncle Joe asked with suspicion in his voice.

"I wanted to show Kira the geographic layout of the canyon and the hidden waterfall on the property. I only have that hand-drawn map. We wondered if you might have a topographical map of the area."

"The canyon and hidden waterfall, I haven't thought about that area for some time. Hmm…are you two planning to go there? Your mother will not approve of that."

"Mr. Hayden, I mean Uncle Joe. Did the Four Amigos ever go there?"

"Well, yeah, we went many times until the cave-in."

This was news to JD. No one, not even his granddad, had said anything about the Four Amigos and their adventures to the hidden waterfall. He wanted to challenge his uncle about this historical revisionism; instead, his first thought was about the cave-in.

"Cave-in?" JD said. "What cave-in? I don't remember Granddad saying anything about that. I wasn't aware of any cave. And what's this about the Four Amigos?"

It was unsettling to JD to think that this massive block of historical information had been kept from him.

"Well, sure, caves are all over this region. Most of the caves on the property are small and not easy to explore. But the cave-in was not a real cave. You know, I should not be telling you this story."

"Why is that?" JD said.

"Your mom wanted to keep it a secret until you were older. She didn't want to encourage you to go there."

Kira smiled at Uncle Joe and batted her eyes. "Please, Uncle Joe, tell us. We promise not to snitch on you to JD's mum."

"Hahaha! I'm not worried about that too much. That's not accurate. I am a little worried. JD's mom can be fiery at times as well."

JD had never heard his uncle refer to his mother as "fiery" or anything like that. To JD, his mother was calm, relaxed, and collected. Sure, she was very passionate about some things, but never fiery. This was one of those moments when one's view of one's parent was stretched.

"Please, Uncle Joe. We promise not to tell on you." JD pleaded.

"Okay, I think it is time you learned the whole story. I will deal with your mother later."

Uncle Joe went to a tall filing cabinet. "Ah, here it is. Here is the topographic map of the ranch. And I also have recent aerial photographs too."

"Wow, that's impressive!" Kira said. "So, where is the hidden waterfall on the map?"

"Right over here in the southeast section of the ranch. Observe how the lines are close together. That shows a steep area of topography."

"How steep is it?" Kira said.

"Some canyon sections are nearly vertical, but most are at a sixty-to-eighty-degree inclination. Over here by the river is where the cave-in happened."

JD stood investigating the map and aerial photographs. "Uncle Joe, how was the canyon created?"

"Excellent question. The canyon is the result of the collapse of a huge underground cavern. At one point long ago, the river cut a river basin canyon through this area. The sides of the canyon along the river were nearly vertical. But above that river area was more land higher up with a spring that fed into a small creek...hmm...is this getting too geeky and detailed for the two of you?"

Kira glanced at JD and smiled. "Uh, not likely."

"Okay, just stop me when it is. Let me back up a bit. All of the topography in this region is what is called karst topography. This means the dissolution or dissolving of soluble rock by water. In our area, the soluble rock is mostly limestone laid down in layers. Rain falls and becomes slightly acidic. The rainwater seeps through cracks and dissolves the limestone rock."

"So, that can create caves?" JD said.

"Yes. These underground caves can be of various shapes, sizes, and lengths. The canyon where the hidden waterfall was most likely caused by the collapse of a long cavern carved out by the spring creek as it disappeared below ground through some crack or crevice. The roof of the cavern was close to ground level. The softer soils above that roof eroded away due to flash flooding. The exposed rock went through weathering that eventually resulted in the collapse of the cavern ceiling."

"So, was that the cave-in?" Kira said.

"No, that was just the creation of the long, narrow canyon. Normally, a canyon with the spring creek at one end would eventually open at the river's edge. But this canyon was a blind or box canyon. At the end, near the river's edge, the spring creek had gone down further under harder rock above. It found a shortcut to the river. When the cavern caved in, the end near the river was blocked by the rock falling in from the cavern roof. But over time, and due to flash flooding, an opening like a narrow tunnel was created. The bottom of this opening eventually exposed the spring creek to the river."

"So, that was like a natural bridge over the spring creek?" Kira said.

"It was more like a tunnel than the opening below a bridge," Uncle Joe said. "Like dominoes falling on each other. There is always a crack or crevice between the dominoes. The rock layers from the cavern roof that collapsed on each other were not one solid mass but a pile of slabs with cracks filled in by rocky debris. The water eventually eroded the rocky debris and created the narrow tunnel from the river into the canyon."

"What about the cave-in?" JD said.

"Hang on, I'm getting to that part. When the Four Amigos would go to the hidden waterfall, we would wade or swim across the river to the island before the tunnel opening."

"Wait, whoa!" JD said. "There's an island there? Why hasn't anyone told me about this?"

"That was part of the secret."

"Is the island part of the property?"

"Yes, and no, it is within the property since the property line extends across the river on both sides. However, state law says that any such island along a navigable river is public land. This means anyone can boat or float down the river and stop on that island without trespassing."

"Oh, okay, please continue," JD said.

"As I was saying, we would head for the island first. The island was the Land of the Four Amigos. It was easy to wade across from the island to the tunnel's opening along the river's edge. We used the tunnel to access the canyon and hike the creek to the falls. One day, when we returned from the waterfall, our dog, Junie, went back through the tunnel to chase a rabbit. Rocks started splintering off the sides of the top of the tunnel. I ran back to find our dog and was caught in the rockslide. JD's mom pulled me out before the rest of the rock fell.

"Wow! Were you hurt?" Kira said.

"The big toe on my right foot was crushed badly, and I had a long gash in my leg above the ankle. JD's mom freaked out thinking she was going to lose her brother. We were over an hour from the house, and I was losing blood fast. Kira's mom helped stop the bleeding. JD's dad and mom made a makeshift stretcher. Getting me across the river was tricky. Luckily, we had inner tubes that we had used to float our gear across. They strapped the inner tubes under the stretcher and floated me across the river. Kira's mom rode ahead to tell our parents. JD, your mother, and dad stayed with me. By the time help came, I was barely conscious."

"Wow, so you nearly died that day?" JD said, reaching over to hug his uncle. "I am glad you didn't die, Uncle Joe."

"Me too, sport! Junie eventually found his way home, so all was well. I lost most of my big toe, so I wear a special shoe on that foot."

"Uncle Joe, Kira, and I want to hike the canyon and go to the waterfall. Will you help us persuade Mom to let us go?"

"Hmmm…that is not going to be easy. Almost losing her brother was painful enough, but losing your dad in the war was the worst. I doubt she will be open to exposing her only child to a risky adventure. Especially one with a painful memory."

"Oh, please, Uncle Joe," Kira said. "Could you please try to convince her to let us go? I've been on many treks in New Zealand and know all sorts of survival stuff."

"Yeah, and I have an achievement award for camping and safety in 4-H," JD said. "I know how to read a map, make fire and administer first aid."

"Alright, enough, I'll come over after work today. But I'm not promising anything. JD, your mother can be stubborn at times. Let me get the intern to get a copy of the map printed. I will bring the copy with me later."

"Thanks, Uncle Joe," JD said. "That's all we can expect."

Uncle Joe stepped out of his office. "Kele, come meet my nephew and his friend."

"Sure, but you promised to call me Jack. Kele is my Comanche name."

"Okay, I prefer Kele, but sure, Jack, whatever you want."

Uncle Joe introduced Kele. "Kids, this is my summer intern, Kele, who prefers to be called Jack."

Kira walked up to Kele and held out her hand. "Pleased to meet you, Jack. Did I hear you say you had a Comanche name, too? Isn't that a Native American Indian tribe?"

"Yes, it is. My people hunted in this area along with other tribes."

Uncle Joe held out the map of the canyon. "Jack, please go by the printing office and get a copy of this map made."

Jack looked at the map. "Is this the canyon with the waterfall?"

"Yes, it is, why?"

"My father, who was a member of the tribal council, told me a legend about this canyon. My people would not enter the canyon. They believe the waterfall is a door to the spirit world. Good and bad spirits come and go through the door."

JD stepped forward. "Is the waterfall haunted or dangerous? Should we not go there?"

"It's just a legend. I doubt there is any truth to it."

"That's good to hear, but I was hoping it was true," JD said. "I mean, how cool would that be, right?"

Kira didn't say anything. She remembered her Grandma telling her about a waterfall her ancestors also believed was a door to the spirit world. That waterfall was on the South Island of New Zealand. Kira tugged on JD's arm. "Come on, JD, let's let your uncle work. Remember, I owe you a float!"

"Hey, yeah, that's right!"

Kira turned and embraced Uncle Joe. "Thank you, Uncle Joe, for the story and the information. I learned a lot today."

"Yeah, thanks, Uncle Joe," JD said. "That was helpful!"

"You're both quite welcome. Go on, I'll see you two later."

As Kira and JD walked out of Uncle Joe's office, Kira whispered to JD. "Uncle Joe is super smart and handsome! But not as handsome as you."

JD didn't know how to respond to the handsome comment. Things were going well with Kira; he did not want that to change by saying something stupid.

"Yeah, Uncle Joe is cool. He's always been there for me, especially after my granddad died. He's a smart guy. I hope he can convince my mom to let us go on our trek."

"Me too. So, where can we buy those ice cream floats?"

"There's a five and dime store with a soda fountain next to the bookstore. They'll have them there."

"Bookstore? Can we stop at the bookstore first?"

"Sure, it's your treat, so it is your plan." JD was not going to mention that the bookstore was where he bought his comics and science magazines.

"Cool, I hope they have comics and science magazines," Kira said with a wink.

"Oh, they have that and more."

JD walked into Buckman's store and approached Mr. Buckman. "Hey, Mr. Buckman, this is my friend, Kira. She's from New Zealand."

Mr. Buckman looked at Kira. "It's nice to meet you, Miss Kira. Welcome to Texas. JD is a fine young man and smart, too. He fixed this old fan for me."

Kira bumped JD with her elbow. "Thank you, Mr. Buckman. Yes, I agree, JD is special. He's showing me around."

JD, trying not to blush, changed the subject. "Mr. Buckman, my mom said it's okay for me to work part-time for you. It has to be after chores and schoolwork, of course."

"That's great. Come back when you have time. We'll fill out the paperwork and work out a schedule."

"Thanks, Mr. Buckman. I'll do that. I have to go right now. This Kiwi owes me an ice cream float."

As the two walked into the five and dime store next door, Kira nudged JD again. "Going to be a working man, eh?"

"It's just part-time, like after school and weekends."

"Maybe you should buy the floats today," Kira teased.

"You wish, but a bet is a bet."

"Wow, strong, confident, and he has money. This is getting better and better."

JD turned to Kira as they walked to the counter to order. "I'm going to order a root beer float and have them blend it in the milkshake blender. What do you want?"

"Yes, a black cow sounds yummy to me."

"A what?"

"Black cow, same as root beer float in New Zealand," Kira explained. "Your way sounds even better."

"Done," JD reported after he ordered the floats. "Do you want to sit at the counter or in a booth?"

"Booth, please, and remember, I am buying."

"Oh yeah, that's right."

JD and Kira sat down in a booth across from the counter. Only a few people were in the store, which was a discount store with a soda fountain in the back. A large ceiling fan revolved around, barely moving the air inside the store. A light hung from the fan, providing soft, dim light over the booths, illuminating the dust suspended in the air by the motion of the fan.

The wooden floorboards creaked as the soda jerk brought the root beer floats to the booth. "Here you go, enjoy. You can pay at the front."

JD pulled napkins from the dispenser. "You might need these. I have it blended so I can suck it through a straw like a milkshake."

"Mmm, this is so good. There's a chemist near my school where we go and get spiders. These are better."

"Chemist? Why would a chemist serve floats?"

"Chemist is the Kiwi word for drugstore. Do you like any other floats"?

"Root beer is my favorite, but I like strawberry too. I also get them to use the mixer like a milkshake. I like it better than a strawberry milkshake. It is so good."

JD sipped on his straw and stole looks at Kira.

"What? What are you looking at?"

"You, I just can't get over that you are a girl and like the same things I like."

"Well, stop staring at me all the time. It's freaking me out."

"Okay, I'll try. So, what did you think about the meeting with Uncle Joe and what Jack said? Do you believe the waterfall could be haunted? I don't believe in ghosts."

"I think we need to talk to my grandmother. Her people have stories about waterfalls. We have to go by there on the way to your house anyway."

"Okay, we can go now if you're finished."

"Yes, let's go."

The man at the register in the front of the store looked at JD when Kira paid for the root beer floats. JD stared back and shrugged his shoulders. Kira smiled, batted her eyes, and curtseyed.

Outside Kira remarked. "That was weird how that man looked at you when I paid the bill. He couldn't believe a girl was paying. I guess he is still stuck in the past. The times they are a-changin'."

"This entire town, except the university, is stuck in the past. It will take a major change across the country before this town changes its ways. From what I see on the news, that is starting to happen. I don't let it bother me much. I shrug it off. Let's go see your grandmother."

Grandma Sullivan was in the parlor having afternoon tea when JD and Kira arrived. "Ah, there you are. JD, would you like a cookie, or are you too full after your root beer floats?"

"How did you know we had root beer floats?

Grandma Sullivan smiled. "So, you two want to go to the canyon, don't you?"

JD looked at Kira and looked back at Grandma Sullivan. "What, how? How did you know that?"

"Yes, well, what is more impressive is how I knew to put out your favorite cookies? But now, let's discuss what you called the 'Trek to the Waterfall.' You know your mother will not like it, but Uncle Joe was a good choice to help convince her."

"Nana, you told me stories about your people and waterfalls."

"Kira, they are your people, too. And yes, my people believed waterfalls were portals to other worlds and the afterlife."

"Do you believe that?" JD said. "Seems like the Bible Stories my mother tells me."

"JD, the boy who has a scientific answer for everything. Yes, I do believe that. My people have believed that for thousands of years. It brings comfort to those who pass on. The home of my tribe is on the South Island of New Zealand. Waterfalls flow down a cliff on one side of a large lake, and from the shore of the lake, people fish. The water falls into a mist before it gently touches the water below. It's a beautiful place."

"Nana, why would you leave such a beautiful place?" Kira said. "Why would you come so far away from it?"

"For love. I met your grandfather and fell in love. He had this ranch back in Texas and asked me to accompany him. I followed my love to Texas."

"Why did my mum go back to New Zealand? Why didn't she stay here? The Four Amigos were such close friends. Why would she give that up?"

"Your mother said she went back to help with the post-war recovery, but I think love scared her. Her father had died, and she saw how much that hurt me. I think she was afraid of falling in love and being hurt. Your mother is a free spirit who loves exploring like you two. The Four Amigos were all like that. They were never satisfied with exploring near home. That is why they went to the canyon. It was far from home, and in their imagination, it took them away from home. After the accident, they awoke from their dream world. Well, enough reminiscing the past, you two had better get over to JD's house. They are waiting for you."

Grandma Sullivan motioned to Kira to stay behind.

"Hey, JD, I'll meet you outside."

"Sure, I will wait for you outside."

"What did you want, Nana?"

"You are going to have to show him. Do you remember how to invoke the dream walk?"

"I think so, but when do I do it? Why?"

"You know how this works. You must walk the path. What you need to know will be revealed when you need to know it. He is important. You are important. The two of you together is more important. That is all I can share right now. Be alert and on your guard. The enemy never sleeps."

"I will."

Kira found JD outside straddling his bike. "I'm ready, Freddy. Let's go face the storm together."

"My uncle is probably not there yet. That is when the storm will come. I hope he can convince my mom. I want to hike the canyon, haunted waterfall, and all."

"Me too."

THE PLAN

Later that evening at JD's house, Kira and JD listened carefully from the living room. In the kitchen, Uncle Joe tried convincing JD's mother to let them go to the canyon. They could only hear bits and pieces, but JD's mother was unhappy. Uncle Joe kept arguing that JD was old enough and that his dad would have approved. JD's mom did not accept that premise and reminded Uncle Joe how much pain she endured that time, long ago, during the cave-in and afterwards. Uncle Joe reminded her of their wonderful memories of visiting the hidden waterfall. The loud back-and-forth discussion went on for what seemed like forever. After a silence of several minutes, Uncle Joe offered a compromise idea. Uncle Joe and JD's mom came into the living room a minute later.

"Okay, Sport. Your mother has agreed to a trial trek."

"A trial trek?" JD said. "What does that mean?"

"You and Kira can do a day trip to the island. You can also explore and investigate any paths into the canyon. However, you may not go down into the canyon at this time."

JD and Kira looked at each other with a confused and worried look.

Uncle Joe continued, "If this trek goes okay and you can find a safe way to enter the canyon, then your mother has agreed to listen to a well-thought-out proposal for a trek down into the canyon."

They both jumped up and down enthusiastically and happily, shouting. "Wow-wee! We're going to the canyon!"

"Whoa, wait! Calm down. Do you accept these terms?"

Kira and JD gave each other a quick nod of approval, stood at attention, saluted, and said simultaneously, "Yes, sir!"

"Okay then. Oh, I almost forgot. Here is a copy of the topographical map of the river and canyon."

JD took the map. "Super! Thanks, Uncle Joe!"

"Mom, can Kira stay for supper? We've got lots of planning to do."

"Sure, if her mother approves. I'll give her a call. I need to explain all this to her anyway. You two start planning, I'll tell you what Kira's mother says."

"Can Uncle Joe stay too?" Kira said. "I want to hear more about your treks to the island and the canyon."

"Sure, if he wants to,"

"Yeah, sure, I'm not one to turn down a free meal. Especially, one cooked by my sister."

"Come on, JD. Let's list the supplies we will need for the trek."

"Don't you think that is overkill for a short trek?"

Kira whispered to JD. "Yes, but it might impress your mum and Uncle."

JD gave Kira the thumbs-up sign. Their main goal was the trek to the hidden waterfall, which was in the canyon beyond the island. For now, they had to settle on exploring the island and finding a safe way down into the canyon.

Kira called out items to bring. "First, we will need a first aid kit, insect repellent, flashlights, canteens for water, a pocketknife, rope, lunchboxes, a map, a compass, and a notebook with pencils."

"Yeah, and I have that old Army backpack my grandpa gave me to put all that stuff in."

"Can we stuff an extra change of clothes in it? And what about hiking sticks? They might come in handy if we plan to climb up the side of the canyon."

"I don't have any. But we can make some out of sotol cactus stalks if we find some or use some branches."

"That's so cool! How can we bring all this stuff down the river without getting it soaked?"

"That's easy. We do what the Four Amigos did, we use an inner tube covered with a net."

JD's mother came in to check on them. "How's the planning going?"

JD said. "We are almost done. We need to make out a list."

"When you are done, please set the table for dinner. Kira, your mom, said it was okay for you to stay for dinner and go with JD to the island. She's a bit concerned about you going into the canyon, but she agreed to the deal. Prove yourselves on this trip, and we'll consider the trek down into the canyon."

"Understood. Thanks, Mrs. Jayson."

"You're welcome, Kira. And please call me Aunt Susan. Mrs. Jayson reminds me that I am a widow. Besides, your mother and I are more like sisters than just friends.

"Dinner will be ready in about 20 minutes, so you two finish what you're doing and get the table ready."

"Yes, ma'am," JD said.

"Okay, have we missed anything? Hey, how about a camera?" Kira said. "We could use it to prove the trail is safe into the canyon."

"Great idea. I have a Brownie 127 camera. My uncle gave it to me."

"That should work. Let's come up with a schedule."

"What do you mean?" JD said.

"Well, when we go tramping in New Zealand, we devise a schedule drawn on a map. That way, we figure out how long it will take to hike to where we need to go."

JD's jaw dropped, and his heart skipped a few beats. "Wow! This girl is beautiful, smart, and organized," he thought to himself.

"What did you say?" Kira said.

JD's face blushed, and he swallowed a couple of times as he realized he had muttered those thoughts out loud. He tried to do a quick cover-up. "Uh, hmm, nothing. I agree with you. We need to be organized."

"No, no, no, I heard you. You said I was smart and beautiful."

"No, I didn't! You must be hearing things. Come on, we don't have much time. Let's write down the list."

Kira approached JD and tugged gently on his shirt, pulling him closer. Eye to eye and nearly nose to nose, she smiled. "Okay, but I heard what I heard."

JD swallowed a couple more times, stood up, stepped back a couple of steps and almost tripped over his feet. "I'll grab a notebook and a pencil. I think one is right over here."

Kira chuckled. "Be careful with that sharp pencil; you might hurt yourself."

"Hahaha, very funny. Can we work on the plan now?"

"Sure, let's check the map from Uncle Joe."

The two kept working on the plan with more teasing and giggling. That all ended quickly as they heard JD's mother's footsteps coming up the stairs.

"JD, your twenty minutes are up. Please come down. I want to serve dinner and need help setting the table."

"Okay, we're coming," JD said.

Uncle Joe shared more adventures of the Four Amigos during dinner, much to Susan's dismay. After dinner, JD and Kira presented their plan for the day-long trek to the island.

"Okay, here's our plan," JD said. We will bring the supplies on this list, including safety items like a first aid kit, insect repellent, and suntan lotion." He hoped the suntan lotion would show how serious he was, since he never used it until his mother nagged him to do so. JD's skin was a walking summer calendar. Early in the summer, he was pale-looking, but by August, he was a golden reddish brown.

"We will start early in the morning," Kira added. "Based on our estimates, it will take close to an hour and a half to get there by bike."

JD continued. "We'll take the dirt ranch road to the low water crossing Granddad made. We will wade down to the island. We'll use the idea you guys used to float your gear to the island using inner tubes."

"As soon as we are on the island, we'll set up our base camp," Kira said. "We'll spend some time exploring the island. Then we'll check for a safe way into the canyon."

"JD, what about snakes? How will you deal with them?" JD's mother said. "I know you explore all around the ranch and have never had a problem with snakes, but you will be so far away. What happens, God forbid, if one of you gets snakebit?"

"We'll use our hiking sticks and beat the grass and rocks before approaching an area. Mom, I go camping every year with 4-H, I can do this."

"Susan, the boy has taken First Aid in school and is certified in 4-H. He is well prepared." Uncle Joe said.

"I know, I know, but it's so far. They could be hurt, and no one will get to them for hours."

"Okay, I have an idea," Uncle Joe said. "Let's plan this trial trek for this coming Saturday. That way, I will be off work. I can take them in the station wagon to the low water crossing early in the morning and check up on them around noon. You can see the island from the low-water crossing. How about that, Susan?"

"Yeah, okay, that would make me feel better."

"You two set up your 'base camp' on the island where you can see the low water crossing. Plant a pole where I can see it from the crossing. Use a green bandana if everything is okay. Use a red bandana if you need help. Susan, do you have any old scarves?"

"Uncle Joe, I have a green and red one," Kira said. "If we settle on a time, we can be sure to be where you can see us. Say, around noon? We will hang a green flag for okay and a red flag if we need help."

"I will bring my binoculars, so I will have no problem being able to observe that flag or you two from the crossing," Uncle Joe said.

JD and Kira instantly turned to each other and said, "Binoculars! We forgot binoculars!"

"No problem," JD said. "I have some."

"Good, because I wasn't going to let you use mine," Uncle Joe said. "But I am working on a surprise for the canyon trek. Uh, if it happens, that is."

"Let's not rush things," JD's mother said. "Now, what time will you all head back? I want you back here well before sunset."

"Uhm, how about we head back about six?" JD said. "We should be back here at the house about seven. Sunset is not until around eight thirty,"

"Let's make that six for you all being back here. That means you should return to the low water crossing by five."

JD and Kira glanced at each other and nodded. They both decided it was best not to try to negotiate for one hour with JD's mother.

"Six it is!" Kira said. "Well, I best be getting home. I don't want to be on the bad side of Mum before our big day. And I have homework and chores to do before then."

"Uncle Joe, can you pick us up at Grandma Sullivan's at 6 am Saturday? Let's start early, if we have to be back at the crossing by five," JD said.

"Well, I like to sleep in on my day off, but yeah, what the hell!"

Kira rushed over and hugged Uncle Joe. "Thank you, Uncle Joe."

"I just remembered something," JD said. "Do you have any shorts and old tennis shoes? We're going to be wading upriver to the island. Shorts would be best, and old tennis shoes. It'll be deep enough to float most of the way. We'll need the tennis shoes when we are on the island and hiking up to the top of the canyon."

"I have shorts and tennis shoes," Kira said.

"Okay, it's getting late. Kira, Uncle Joe will drop you off at your house. I'll call your mother and tell her you are coming. I will also give her an update on the plans."

"Come on, Red," Uncle Joe said. "Let's take you home."

"Coming, Uncle Joe."

Kira rushed over to JD, hugged him, kissed him on the cheek, and whispered in his ear, "I had a wonderful time today. See you Saturday morning."

JD turned an August color of red. He was still not that comfortable with a girl becoming touchy-feely, but strangely, he liked it coming from Kira.

THE INVISIBLE ISLAND

Saturday morning, JD was up before the rooster opened his eyes. He packed his backpack and headed downstairs for breakfast. He could smell something cooking in the kitchen. His mom had cooked bacon and eggs with toast.

"Mom, it's five o'clock, you didn't need to get up. "I can fix my breakfast. I do it during school days."

"Yes, but I wanted to see you off on your adventure day."

JD walked over and embraced his mom. "Thank you, Mom. I love you."

JD and his mom sat down to have breakfast. JD said grace, and JD's mom added. "Please keep them safe today."

"You and Kira have fun today, but please be careful."

"We will, I promise. We will go slow and not take any chances."

"Thank you, I appreciate that very much."

JD finished breakfast, hugged his mom goodbye, and headed to Grandma Sullivan's. It was still the blue hour just before the sun rose. Kira was waiting on the front steps.

"Morning, JD. Are you ready for our adventure?"

"Packed and ready. I hope I didn't forget anything."

"We'll be fine if you forgot something. I'm super excited. I hope Uncle Joe shows up soon."

Right on cue, Uncle Joe pulled into the driveway. He was driving his station wagon. It was built for rugged terrain. Uncle Joe used it for work. He got out and walked over to JD and Kira.

"You two ready to head out?"

"Let's rattle our dags," Kira said.

"What?" Uncle Joe said.

Kira stood up and saluted, "Sorry, I meant, we're ready to move out, Sir."

Uncle Joe laughed, "Listen up, privates. I got a surprise for you two. Come check out the gear I have for you."

Kira and JD walked with Uncle Joe to the back of his station wagon and saw something they had forgotten. "We forgot the inner tubes!"

"Yeah, you did. No worries, I fixed up two small tire inner tubes with some nets and hooks. You can put your backpack on one inner tube and anything else on the other."

"Brilliant!" Kira said. "Thank you so much, Uncle Joe. These are perfect."

"It's been a while, but this is not my first time," Uncle Joe said. "JD, toss your backpack in the back and let's rattle our dags!"

Kira laughed. "Aye, captain!"

The drive to the low-water bridge took about forty minutes. It would have been much longer on bikes. The back ranch road was barely a road. It was a rough dirt road that washed out at times. JD was glad that Uncle Joe was taking them in his vehicle. Biking over a long, bumpy dirt road would have worn them out before getting to the island.

Uncle Joe parked his vehicle on the side of the rocky dirt road just before the low water crossing. A series of round, smooth rock slabs formed the crossing. JD's granddad had brought the tractor and dragged rocks and logs across a shallow part of the river to create a small dam and a crossing. Nature moved all of that debris away. Just the smooth slabs remained. A sliver of water flowed over the slabs most days except during a storm. Even an hour of rain could raise the water level well over the low water crossing, making it difficult, if not impossible, to cross even in Uncle Joe's station wagon.

The sun was peeking over the horizon. Gray darkness muted the colors of dawn. Mourning doves cooed, hoping for a reply. A cool north breeze, cooler than it should be for summer, chilled the air. The rhythmic splash of water hitting the rocks provided percussion support for the mourning doves singing their love song. It was summer, but it felt like fall. Uncle Joe pulled the inner tubes from the back of the vehicle.

"Private JD and Private Kira, listen up. This is your mission brief. Your mission is simple. Travel upriver to the island, find a safe route down into the canyon, and don't get hurt! I'll be back after I run an errand for work."

"Thank you, Uncle Joe. We will plant our flag when we make it to the end of the island closest to the low-water crossing," JD said.

"Okay, when I return, I will look for your flag. Will you be okay until then? Your mothers would never forgive me if something happened to you."

"We will be extra careful, I promise. Thanks for bringing us, Uncle Joe."

"You're welcome, Sport."

"Yes, thank you, Uncle Joe," Kira said.

"Alright, I'm off. You two have fun."

"Bye, Uncle Joe," Kira and JD said simultaneously.

The two privates exclaimed. "Jinx!"

Uncle Joe drove off, leaving Kira and JD standing by the side of the road. Water lapped over the shallow bank just to the right of the crossing.

"We should put our tennis shoes in the backpack, or they will be soaked. And heads up, the water is going to be cold,"

Kira and JD secured the backpack to one of the inner tubes. JD pulled both to the water's edge.

"Barefoot it is," Kira said. "No worries on the cold water."

JD started to say he would help Kira into the water, but she was in before he was.

"Whatcha waiting for? The water's fine. Let's go slow poke."

JD carefully pulled his inner tube as he waded into the water. Icy fingers crawled up his legs, and the shivers began as JD slid into the river. The water was chilly for an early summer morning, but he had to soldier on with Kira watching him. Once in the water, it wasn't so bad.

Rapid shallow currents carried the river over the middle of the crossing, but the water was deeper and ran still along the banks.

"We'll be wading upriver against the current, but it shouldn't be a problem if we stick to the sides. Let's wade to the other side."

"Roger that," Kira said. "This is great! A cool, clear morning, wading in a clear river on an adventure to an invisible island. It doesn't get much better than this."

"Be careful where you step. There could be holes and whirlpools,"

"Say what? Holes and whirlpools? Any other dangers I should worry about?"

"Not really. A water moccasin snake might swim by, but they won't bother you. Just don't panic."

"Snakes in the water? I don't like snakes in or out of the water."

Kira already had one encounter with a Texas snake. It was not a joyful experience.

"Don't they have snakes in New Zealand?"

"Not in any rivers. I read about sea snakes, but New Zealand doesn't have any river snakes."

"We're getting into the deeper part. The current is going to pick up. Let's move closer to the shore, but not too close."

Kira screamed. "What the bloody hell is that?"

Fish with long, toothy snouts hung out under a spreading oak tree in the deeper water at the river's edge. The still clear water provided a window into this gathering.

"Oh, yeah, we want to avoid the banks. Those are alligator gars."

"Alligators! And you are just now sharing that?"

"Don't worry, they aren't alligators and don't usually attack humans. Just give them some space."

"They have a long snout and teeth!"

122

"Yeah, but they just use the teeth to hold their prey before swallowing it. They mostly eat other fish and a small mammal or two."

"Texas is more like Australia than New Zealand. We don't have any predators in New Zealand unless they were brought there."

"Texas has its share, but I don't worry about it."

"If you aren't worried, then neither am I! We're the Two Amigos!"

"Come on, amigo, we are almost there."

"Despite the snakes and fish with teeth, I love this. Say, are those dragonflies on the water?"

"Probably or damselflies, I'm not a bug expert."

"I am kind of an expert on bugs in New Zealand. I love studying them. In New Zealand, there are Weta bugs. They are like giant crickets, but they can't fly. They can bite with their mandibles."

"I'd love to see one of those!"

"New Zealand has over 20,000 species of insects, but no snakes.

"Wow, you are a nerd!" JD laughed.

"Hahaha, touché"

Just ahead, the sound of water rushing over rocks grew louder. Rapid currents spread across one side of the river. The swift-moving current found a hole and swirled down it, creating a small whirlpool. The water gushed up from another hole, creating a small fountain.

"Look ahead where the river splits and comes back together. The river splits around a chunk of that higher ground. So, land with water on all sides is technically…"

"An island!" Kira exclaimed. "Awesome! I can't wait to be back on dry land. I think something has been nibbling on my feet and legs this whole time."

"Probably bass or minnows. We need to move back out from the bank and towards the middle. Stay away from the whirlpool. We will work our way around to the side of the island."

"Roger that, lead on. I'm right behind ya."

"It's going to be deep for a while. You probably won't be able to touch the bottom, so hang onto your inner tube and paddle with your feet."

"Hang on and paddle. Got it!"

Kira and JD paddled their way around the long side of the invisible island to the shallow area next to a grassy bank that sloped into the water. As they navigated around rocks sprayed by the rushing river, water splashed over their bobbing inner tubes, soaking every part of their bodies.

JD and Kira pulled their inner tubes up onto the embankment. JD had brought a small towel. He pulled it from his backpack and gave it to Kira, "Here, this might help you dry your feet before you put your tennis shoes on. We'll leave the inner tubes here."

"Thanks, my hair is all wet too," Kira said. "I'm all wet, but I love it. That was so much fun. Where to now?"

"I don't know. This is my first time. I will look for something we can use for the flagpole."

The sun was now well above the horizon, and the air temperature was rising. The morning sun would dry their wet shorts and T-shirts. They both used the towel to dry their feet before they put on their tennis shoes. JD looked around and found just what they needed—two Sotol plants with tall, sturdy stalks. He snapped off the dry stalks and used his knife to smooth one end.

"Here, we can use these as hiking sticks," JD said. "And if we have to walk through tall grass, beat the grass with the stick. It will help alert the snakes, allowing them time to move out of the way. Just don't go poking any holes with it. You might get an unwelcome surprise."

"Got it! Beat the tall grass, but no poking! What next?"

"Look around for another one of these or something we can use for the pole."

A long metal pole lay in the grass with one end exposed. A pile of rocks hid the other end of the pole. Kira pointed at the pole. "What about this?"

Kira and JD stared at each other. "The Four Amigos!"

JD pulled the pole upright. "We need to put this at the island's far end where Uncle Joe can see it. The brush is too thick in the middle, but we can hike around the island's edge. I'll bring the backpack if you can drag the pole."

"Roger that, but I'm a bit peckish. That means I'm hungry. My brekkie was very early this morning."

"I brought just the thing to help with that," JD said as he pulled out two sticky buns and a thermos of hot chocolate.

"Brilliant! You're my hero!"

JD smiled. "A boy has a good mother."

Kira smiled back. "A boy has a good heart."

Kira and JD sat on the sloping bank, enjoying their snack, watching the currents pound the rocks that dared poke above the water. A cool breeze was still coming from the north, but it was countered by the growing warmth of the sun now well above the horizon.

"I love how the sun shines through the trees, making light dance across the water," JD said.

"JD, that was beautiful. Are you a poet too?"

"I don't know. I like to write but I love science, nature, and baseball. I don't like doing chores much, but taking care of the garden with Dolly was one of the best times. The best summer mornings were going out to find what had sprouted and what was ripe enough to pick. Dolly would dig in the soil after I pulled up a carrot or onion. She was always looking for a grub to eat."

"In New Zealand, we have the huhu beetle. The Māori call huhu beetle grubs 'tunga haere' or just huhu grub. The grubs can be eaten if you know when to pick them from the trees."

"People eat them? Have you eaten one? What do they taste like?"

"I have eaten a few. They taste a little like peanut butter and chicken."

"Wow, I'm calling you Bug Girl!"

"And I will give you a knuckle sandwich if you do!" Kira laughed. "Come on, amigo, we've got exploring to do."

"Aye, aye, Bug Girl!"

Kira turned and raised her fist. "Watch it!"

"Hey, you call me Nerd Boy. Why can't I call you Bug Girl? I mean it with respect.

Kira stood silent for a moment, pondering. "Alright, Nerd Boy, but only between us. No one else can know."

"Agreed."

JD had picked a grassy clearing next to the river for their landing and snack, but thick vegetation covered most of the island, blocking the path to the other side.

"How will we hike to the island's far end?" Kira said. "I don't think there's a way through the bushes or these other plants. They even go to the edge of the water."

JD pulled out a long, wide knife. "I brought this."

JD had brought his granddad's old machete to help clear a path. He snuck it into his backpack without his mom's knowledge. His mom would not have let him bring it or his twenty-two rifle, which was too long to stuff in the backpack.

"What is that?"

"It's a machete. It was my granddad's. We can use it to clear a path along the side of the island."

"What about just using that trail?"

"What trail?" JD said, looking around.

"The one behind that tree."

JD realized their snack area was probably where deer bedded down at night. The deer seeking water created the trail.

JD put the machete back into his backpack. "That works for me."

Even with the trail, the thick vegetation and tree limbs bending to the ground made for a rough hike to the island's far end. JD had to pull out his machete several times. The two took turns pulling back the tree limbs to let the other slip past. JD started to wonder if something else created the trail. Then he saw it rooting in the ground just ahead.

Kira pointed to a critter with armor plating, a long tail, a snout, and two tiny ears. "What is that?"

"Armadillo. They usually only come out in the evenings. I guess this one is late getting home. I thought deer made this trail, but it might be a rodent trail, so we'd best look out for snakes looking for their next meal."

"I did mention I'm not a fan of snakes."

"Me neither. Look, there's a clearing. We might be close to the far end of the island."

The thick vegetation gave way to a small clearing near the end of the island. To one side, a tall rock rose from the ground. Bushes and nearby trees covered a dark, foreboding hole in the side of the rock.

"Look over there. That might be the armadillo's home."

"I don't think so," JD said. "They prefer to dig homes in the ground. That looks more like a cave. I didn't expect to find a cave on the island. I wonder where it goes."

"Sweet as! Let's find out."

JD pointed to some yellow flowers. "Careful, don't get too close to that plant. It's a prickly pear cactus. Land on it and you will spend days pulling thorns out."

"Pretty yellow and orange flowers. The thorns look easy enough to avoid."

"It's not the long spines, but the tiny ones with barbs. After the flowers bloom, a reddish fruit develops."

"Can it be eaten?"

"Yes, my mom has made jelly from the fruit. My grand-dad even made wine from it. I don't like harvesting its fruit much. The plant makes it a thorny task."

"Hahaha. New Zealand doesn't have any native cactus plants. Wait, stop, look, a bee is landing on one of the flowers. I love finding critters on flowers."

"You came to the right state, then. Texas has over five thousand species of flowering plants and lots of bees and butterflies. I know where we can see monarch butterflies in the fall."

"Fantastic, I love monarch butterflies. We have them in New Zealand, and they are native too."

"Wow, that's something I did not know. Think about that. Monarch butterflies somehow found a way to migrate to New Zealand."

"Maybe Nerd Boy will find his way to New Zealand sometime. Right now, let's check out this cave."

JD and Kira walked over to the opening in the side of the rock. The rock stood over ten feet tall. Something had carved out an opening on one side. The large rock was tilted or slanted to one side, like it had been pushed up. The half-moon-shaped opening was dark and covered with bushes and tree limbs.

JD used his machete to carve out an opening through the brush. JD pulled back the branches as Kira pushed through the bushes. The two stood before the dark, ominous opening in the rock.

"Come on, let's peek inside," Kira said, hoping JD would discourage that idea.

JD pulled out his flashlight and stepped forward past the entrance. Kira followed with her hand on JD's shoulder. The two could vaguely make out a shimmering on the side of the wall before them. JD shined his flashlight at the shimmering, revealing hundreds of critters with long legs clinging to the wall. "That's a lot of daddy longlegs."

Kira walked up to the shimmering. "Crikey, it is. Wait, let me see the torch."

"Torch?"

"Your flashlight. I want to get a closer look."

Kira walked to the wall for a closer look at the hundreds of critters hanging from the ceiling of the cave to the floor. "Yep, that's what I thought. These are harvestmen. They are not what most people call daddy longlegs, but there's another species properly called that. No worries, they are not venomous and can't bite you."

"How do you know that?"

129

"Remember, I'm Bug Girl. You might be good at science nerdy stuff like radios and stuff, but I am nerdy about bugs. These are wonderful bugs. There are a few species only found in New Zealand."

"Well, Bug Girl, no matter what they are this is more than I am comfortable with. This cave doesn't go anywhere, let's back out and keep going."

"I would love to study them. It's weird how they are all hanging on the wall, dancing, but I agree it's also creepy-looking."

The two backed away from the opening of the cave and as they did Kira tripped on a rock poking up from the ground. The rock had been broken on one side. The exposed side was dark in the center with a creamy white coating on the outside.

"Whoa, are you okay?" JD said.

Kira bent down to pull the rock out of the ground. "Yeah, I tripped on this rock."

"Hey, I think that's flint!"

"You mean the stuff arrowheads are made of?"

"Look around and see if you can find more of it."

JD and Kira walked around the cave's opening, looking for more flint rocks. Then, JD headed back into the cave.

"Where're you going?" Kira said.

"I have a hunch, and I am going to check if I am right."

"Right, I'm coming too, then. I'm not going to be the scaredy-cat during this trek."

JD shined his flashlight back into the cave entrance and slipped past the shimmering on the far wall. He kneeled on the damp ground with his back to the hundreds of harvestmen. In his mind, he felt like they would surround him at any moment.

Kira said they were not venomous and couldn't bite him, but his growing creepy feeling suppressed that knowledge.

Both of them could both comfortably fit inside the shallow opening, but the entire depth of the cave was no more than six to ten feet, making it more like a grotto than an actual cave. JD used his machete to poke around on the ground.

Kira kneeled beside him. "What are you looking for? It's dark and creepy in here."

JD poked around until he found something. "I think I found it. Look at this."

"What is it?"

"I'm not positive," JD said. "It's a piece of flint. It looks like someone chipped it off a larger flint rock. Uncle Joe will know for sure. I am putting this in my backpack. Come on, let's get out of this creepy place."

"You think it might be an arrowhead? Do you think early humans made it? Like American Indians?"

"Maybe. I'm not an expert, so I will wait until Uncle Joe has looked at it. I know it's flint or cert, and that fracture usually doesn't occur naturally. Let's talk about this later. These harvestmen are creeping me out."

"Don't worry, I'm Bug Girl! They won't attack unless I command them to."

"Hahaha, so I can call you Bug Girl then?"

"Yes, you can call me Bug Girl, but remember only in private, never in public, 'cause you would give away my secret identity!"

"Okay, mild-mannered Kira, we're out of here!"

"Roger that. Where to next?"

"We can't be too far from the end of the island. We need to plant the flag before Uncle Joe returns."

JD and Kira pressed on around the rock grotto. The river formed the island from higher ground that originally stuck out from the shore. Flash floods opened a path through the protrusion, isolating the island from the shore. The stream between the island and the shore was narrow and shallow. Sand deposits from flash floods left behind sandbars that animals, including deer, used to cross over to the island.

JD and Kira found a rocky edge at the island's far end, closest to the low-water crossing. Kira attached the green scarf to the pole, lifted it upright, and pressed it into the ground as far as possible. JD gathered some rocks and placed them at the base of the pole.

"I claim this island in the name of the Two Amigos, Queen Kira and King JD," JD said. "Henceforth it will be called Invisible Island."

"Hear, hear! Would Your Majesty agree to a short break before we press on? The queen is a bit thirsty."

"Yes, my queen," JD said. "I believe I have one more sticky bun. Would the Queen like half?"

"Yes, please!"

JD found a dry spot and placed the towel on the ground.

"My lady," JD said as he gestured for Kira to sit down.

"Thank you, kind sir."

Kira sat down, and JD sat down next to her. JD pulled out the thermos and handed Kira the sticky bun. Kira pulled it apart and gave JD half.

The two amigos sat having a snack, looking down the river toward the low-water bridge. River water flowed around both sides of the island, heading to the bridge. The water rushed around the left side of the island while the right side gently flowed into the shallows near the riverbank.

With no shade and the sun warming the sand, it felt like they were on a beach somewhere—butterflies passed by looking for their energy snack on a flower. Fish leaped out at anything that stopped too long on the surface of the clear. The river ran still and deep closer to the riverbank. A cloudless sky provided no shade. A light wind swirled, warming air around, mixing it with the cooler north breeze.

"I love this so much. I wish every day were like this. I want to sit here feeling the sun on my face and listen to the water rushing by. Tell me, my king, what do you want to do when you grow up?"

"I haven't decided. I know I want to do something in science, but I love to explore too. I think my mother wants me to take over the farm. I know that was my granddad's dream. Farming is okay, but I want more. Uncle Joe gets to go around and investigate stuff since he is a geologist, but he's stuck in this county unless he moves. One of my aunts got me a subscription to National Geographic. I want to travel the world and visit the places I read about. What do you want to do?"

"I want to explore too, but I don't know what else. I love being out in nature, so maybe a biologist? I missed the time exploring with Nana when she came to visit last year. She wants to return to New Zealand but loves the ranch so much."

"I wish you lived here," JD said. "You're not like all the other girls around."

"You're not like any of the boys, I know. We have time to explore. I'll be here the entire summer and longer if my mum decides to stay to help Nana."

JD and Kira saw the dust trail of Uncle Joe's station wagon coming down the dirt ranch road to the low water crossing. The station wagon stopped before the crossing. Uncle Joe got out and stood by the riverbank. He saw the green flag waving in the breeze.

"There's Uncle Joe!" JD said. "Come on, let's wave."

JD and Kira stood up and waved. Uncle Joe waved back, holding up a sign. JD pulled out his binoculars.

"What's the sign say?" Kira said.

"I'll be back later."

JD used hand signals to tell Uncle Joe they received the message. JD packed the towel and thermos in his backpack.

"Well, we'd better go," JD said.

"Do we go back the way we came?" Kira said.

"I think the best way is to follow the island's edge until we come to the mouth of the canyon. The water is shallow, so we shouldn't have a problem crossing."

"Okay, lead on. I'm so excited. I can't wait to explore. I hope we can find a way into the canyon."

TREK TO THE TOP OF THE WATERFALL

JD and Kira walked along the edge of the island near-est to the riverbank. The river, not much more than a few feet wide, rushed through narrow paths in the sand on that side of the elongated island. Scrub bushes lined the riverbank across the narrows. Movement and a rustling sound alerted JD and Kira. They both stopped and peered toward the rus-tling. Out came a doe and her yearling, walking to the edge for a drink. JD saw the doe first. He crouched down, pulling Kira down with him.

JD whispered. "Look over there."

"Wow, would you look at that? White-tailed deer!"

The deer heard the two whispering and stared right at them, assessing whether they were a threat. JD and Kira crouched motionless and quietly until the two deer left the area.

"That was so cool!"

"How do you know about white-tailed deer?"

"We have them and others in New Zealand. They were introduced to New Zealand. I've read about them."

"I'm thinking Nature Girl is a better nickname for you."

"I like that, Nerd Boy! But Bug Girl is more me. I love bugs, especially creepy crawly ones."

JD laughed. "Bug Girl, it is!"

"I hope we find even more wildlife, except snakes."

JD and Kira continued their hike around the island to the mouth of the canyon. Kira pointed to a bird swooping down. "That looks like a bush hawk."

"It's some hawk, but I'm not a bird expert. We might come across some Texas vultures, but they like the roads more these days. I call them the county road sanitation crews. They come and clean up the roadkill."

"Yuck, I guess they serve a purpose."

"Snakes do, too, but I'm not a fan of them either."

The vegetation thickened and crowded the island's edge, making it impossible to continue on dry land. JD pointed to the shallow part. "We'll have to walk along the sandbars and wade through the shallows."

"Then I'm taking my shoes off. I want to feel the water and sand in my toes."

"Me too. Hand them to me, Bug Girl, and I will tie them to the backpack."

Kira stopped and let the water trickle through her toes. "This is the greatest adventure of my life. I am so happy right now. I never imagined I would have this much fun in Texas on an adventure with a nerd boy."

"I'm happy to be sharing this with you. I do have a confession."

"Yeah, what's that?"

"My mother said I had to show you around this summer. I was not happy. I didn't want to spend the summer with a girl tagging along. But now I am happy you are here. You aren't like all of the girly girls, I know."

Kira stopped, turned, and faced JD. "I am a girl. I love being free to do what I feel like doing. I can be girly, too, when I want to be."

"Yeah, I know, and that's the weird thing. I loved seeing you all dressed up girly-like. But I love seeing you like this in shorts and barefoot, walking through the water and the sand."

"I like that you like me both ways," Kira said with a smile.

"Okay, glad we got that all straightened out. You're Girly Kira, whose secret identity is Bug Girl!" JD teased.

Kira bent down, scooped up two hands full of water, and splashed JD, "Watch it, Nerd Boy!"

The two laughed and had a short water fight in the middle of the shallows of the river.

"Alright, uncle, uncle! I give! Let's keep going."

"Ok, truce!" Kira said. "Lead on, amigo."

JD and Kira continued up the narrows, walking across the shallow streams that cut their way through the sandbars. The sound of birds filled the air as they made their way to the mouth of the canyon.

"That's a lot of different bird sounds."

"It's probably a mockingbird," JD said. "They can mimic many different birds. I think I hear something else?"

"Yeah, me too. It sounds like a giant shower."

"We must be close to the mouth of the canyon. Come on!"

JD and Kira tried to run toward the sound, but the sand and streams slowed their pace. The top of the shoreline across the shallows rose as they went until it was taller than JD's house. Soon, they came to a slab of rock leaning against the opposite shore from the island. The top of the rock was higher than the shore, now a hillside. Just around the rock, they saw water rushing out over other large rocks that had fallen like dominoes.

"Is this the waterfall?" Kira said.

"I don't think so. This must be where the cave-in happened. Look, on the right side, there's a small opening with only a stream of water flowing through it. That's where..."

Kira finished JD's assessment. "The Four Amigos used that to enter the canyon before the cave-in."

"Right, but it is not wide enough to squeeze through. We will have to find another way."

Kira pointed to the side of the mouth of the canyon. "How about that trail going up the side?"

JD looked over at the trail. "Yeah, it's either a deer trail or a wash where rain came down."

Water rushed over and through the rocks, blocking the entrance to the canyon. The water settled below the rocks, creating a clear pond. Thick vegetation along the far bank blocked the route around the pond, so the only access to the trail was across the water.

JD pointed to the pool. "We need to cross this water first. It looks shallow enough."

Kira stepped into the pond. The water level reached her knees, but her feet sank deeper into the sand, making walking difficult. The water rushing from the canyon mixed with the sand, making it like quicksand.

"Stick to the edge of the pond. As I walk to the middle, my feet sink into the sand."

"Like quicksand? We should keep the hiking sticks ready. Let me go first and make sure it's safe."

"I'm in the lead. I'll go first."

JD started to say that guys should go first, but he realized that would not go well with Kira. He wanted a girl who wasn't like all the other girly girls, and he got his wish. Now, he had to make sure not to upset her by treating her like a girly girl.

"Roger that!" JD said.

Just beyond the right side of the pond, a small, narrow opening in the bushes led to the trail up to the top of the canyon. As JD and Kira made it to the opening, a five-foot-long snake crawled out in front of them.

Kira pointed and yelled. "Snake! Snake!"

"No worries, it's a rat snake. It's probably coming down for a drink or something to eat. We are not on the menu. Snakes, even rattlesnakes, don't hunt large prey like humans. It's best to let it be and keep your distance. Look, it is slithering away."

"Texas has too many snakes!"

"Come on, it's gone. We need to check out the trail up to the top before lunch."

"Okay, but you take the lead,"

"So, I'm the snake bait?"

"Roger that and bait for anything else hiding in the bushes. It's your home. I'd be the exciting new dish on the menu! Besides, you are my king and knight. Be my champion, and I will let you wear my colors."

"I am happy to be your knight. Okay, here's the start of the path up. It's steep going up. We'll still need the hiking sticks and shoes back on."

"Aye, Sir Knight! Sticks and shoes."

Rainwater had cut a rocky V-shaped groove down the side of the canyon from the top down to the pond's edge. Thick bushes lined the path opposite the canyon wall. Shade from the trees covered most of the path up. The uneven, rocky path created a slow trek up. At the top, JD and Kira stopped to catch their breath.

Kira surveyed the landscape below. She saw the river winding around to the northwest and Granddad's crossing to the east. Grassland dotted with oak trees spread out beyond to the north and east. "Wow, what a view! That was a rough trek up, but well worth it. I have goosebumps just standing here looking out. If I were a millionaire, my house would be right here with my porch looking out across the river."

"I have the land, so all you need is the money to build that house," JD said with a wink. "According to Uncle Joe's map, the waterfall is about five hundred feet in that direction. Let's try to stay closer to the rocks along the edge, but a little tapping the ground might be good."

"I'm right behind you, snake bait!"

The canyon stretched mostly west from the river. To the right of the canyon, prairie grass dotted with oak trees covered the ground. A narrow path along the canyon's rim allowed the two to avoid the grass and the rocky edge. Halfway to the waterfall, JD and Kira heard the faint sound of water crashing on the rocks.

"Do you hear that?" JD said.

"Yeah, sounds like the waterfall. I can't wait. Do you think we can see it from up here?"

"I don't know, we might be able to get a sneak preview. I'm just hoping we find an easy, safe way down so we can return and enter the canyon."

"Right, our focus must be on finding the way down."

The sun was now high in the sky. Beads of sweat formed on Kira's neck, rolling down her back. A buzzing sound near her neck brought an immediate slap from her right hand. "I think I need my hat and some insect repellent!"

"Can you hang on a bit? We're only about a minute or two from the springs. We can take a break in a bit and have some lunch."

"Okay, but if Bug Girl turns into a giant mosquito and eats you, it will be your fault for not stopping."

"Hahaha. Look, see that oak tree. We can take a break under it."

Kira wiped the sweat from her eyes and neck. "Just in time before I melt. I can feel a cool breeze, but that sun. This kiwi is not used to it being so bloody hot."

"How hot is it during your summers?"

"Where I live in Auckland, it usually is around 24 for high."

"Only twenty-four? Wow!" JD said.

"Well, that's 24 degrees Celsius, I don't know what that is in Fahrenheit."

"I can't do that math in my head, but I remember that thirty Celsius is about 80 to 90. I guess twenty-four is about seventy-five?"

"The sun can get hot in Auckland, but on the forest trail, it's not like this," Kira said. "What did ya bring for lunch? I have a bottle of pink lemonade. My mum froze it, so it should be nice and cool."

"Pink lemonade! That's my favorite!"

"Yeah, I know," Kira smiled. "You're not the only one who does their homework."

"I brought hiker food, peanut butter, and jelly sandwiches."

"I like peanut butter, so I am in."

141

"My mom used some of her strawberry preserves. I grew and picked the strawberries."

"Sweet as! I love strawberries! Pass me one of those sandwiches."

"Coming right up, and a bag of chips. I slipped in the chips."

"We call those crisps in New Zealand. What you call French fries, we call chips. Do you like gardening? I picture you more with your nose in a science magazine than in the dirt."

"I loved working in the garden with Dolly. I don't know, I guess I have lots of interests. To me, science is all about exploration and discovery, trying new things, and figuring out how stuff works."

"Exploring is my favorite thing to do. I think that is one reason I joined the bike gang. I preferred going with Nana when she came 'cause she taught me about stuff on our hikes. I think that is one reason I like you."

"I like you too. I'm glad you came to visit."

Kira smiled and touched JD's arm. "Yeah, me too. I am glad I came to meet Nerd Boy."

Beyond the oak tree's shade, a meandering creek flowed into a grassy pond above the waterfall below. The soft sounds of water gurgling and the raspy noise from cicadas provided the background music for lunchtime.

Peanut butter and jelly oozed out of Kira's sandwich. "Did you bring anything like napkins?"

JD searched through his backpack, pulled out one of the napkins his mother had thoughtfully packed, and handed it to Kira. "See that pond over there? I bet that feeds into the waterfall. This creek fills up the pond, and the water overflows below."

"I wonder where the creek comes from. I want to explore that too."

"Based on Uncle Joe's map, there's a spring somewhere higher but farther up from here. Let's look for a way down. How about on the left side of the pond?"

"Agreed. Give me a minute to finish this sandwich and take another sip of lemonade."

After their lunch break, they walked between two boulders to the left of the pond and the oak tree. As they got closer to the canyon's edge, the sound of water pounding rocks below grew louder. Smaller rocks covered part of the ground between the two boulders. Rainwater runoff cut a path down the side of the canyon to the canyon floor.

"Look at that!" JD said. "That looks like a natural trail down."

"Let's check it out partway. We will keep to the agreement and not go all the way down, but we were told to find a safe way down, so we must at least check it out."

JD agreed. "We'll go partway down to ensure it goes all the way. We might get a side view of the waterfall!"

"Agreed, lead on, amigo! I'm excited to see that waterfall."

Rocks dotted the path down. Rainfall from storms over the years had cut ruts or grooves in the path, making walking down difficult without checking your steps. Halfway down, it was clear to JD and Kira that the path went all the way down, and they could make it with some care. The sound from the waterfall was now loud. The two turned and saw the spray coming off the side where the water spread along the canyon's edge, falling like a shower. Beyond the spray, the water rushed over and between rocks, falling straight down until it slammed into the ground below.

JD and Kira stood staring with amazement and growing excitement. They both wanted to keep going.

Kira leaned on her hiking stick. A faint mist from the waterfall fell on her face. "Wow, just wow! I have read about waterfalls in New Zealand but have never seen one. JD! I'm...I...I..."

"I know; I want so bad to go down right now."

"Me, too, but we promised."

"Yeah, you're right," JD agreed. "So close. But we found a safe way down. We'll return. Let's head back up."

The wind changed, sending a cool breeze down the trail.

JD stopped. "Did you feel that?"

"Feel what?"

"The wind suddenly changed direction. I felt a strong, cold breeze going down the trail. At this time of day, the air should be warm and rising. We need to hurry back up. I don't like this."

A STORM IS COMING

At the top of the trail, JD glanced up at the sky and noticed something disturbing. Thick clouds were beginning to stream across the sky from the west. He understood from the sky what that meant.

"We need to go back down now!"

"Why? This is so beautiful. Can't we stay a little longer? Uncle Joe is probably not back yet."

"No! We have to go now! Look at the clouds."

"Yeah, so? The sky's beautiful. What's so special about the clouds?"

"A storm is coming. Trust me, we need to go now."

"Roger that, let's go!"

Kira and JD quickly returned to the oak tree and grabbed their gear. The wind changed directions, coming out of the southwest instead of the north. JD sensed something was wrong. As a science nerd, he delved into anything and everything. Summer storms in Texas brought more than rain.

A Storm is Coming

"Do you feel that and smell that?" JD said as he grabbed his backpack. "We have to get down as soon as we can. Can you keep up with a quick pace?"

"I can match whatever pace you set. Let's go!"

"Watch your step as you go and use the hiking stick."

Shadows from tree limbs flickered on the rock face as Kira and JD inched their way down the trail from the top of the canyon. Tree limbs swayed back and forth, slashing out at the two.

The sun hid behind dark and foreboding clouds. Rain began to fall as JD and Kira returned to where they had left the inner tubes. The wind turned the rain into a shower, spraying water everywhere. JD struggled to find some rope in his backpack. He tied the two inner tubes together with a stretch of rope.

JD pulled the inner tubes into the water. "Paddle or wade, whatever is faster. If you drop something, leave it."

Kira sensed the growing apprehension in JD's voice, and it spread to her. "We're not going to make it! We're already soaked."

"Yes, we will. I'm not worried about the rain. I'm worried about what could be happening upriver."

"What could that be?"

"A wall of water!"

Kira paddled faster. "A flash flood!"

"Yes!"

The wind blew hard across the water, drowning out softly spoken words. The water level began to rise, and the current sped up, helping to speed the two towards the low-water crossing. Water rushed over the crossing ahead, hiding the top of the road from view.

Waves rose up, sloshing river water into Kira and JD. Kira lost her grip on the inner tube and slipped beneath the surface. She bobbed back up and yelled. "Help!"

JD turned and grabbed Kira before she went under again. "Gotcha!"

"Don't let go!"

The windblown waves picked up the inner tubes, trying to rip them from Kira and JD's hands. The constant wind and wave action made pressing forward to the crossing difficult. The wind whipped around from the front, back, and sides. JD and Kira bobbed around trying to find footing to inch their way to the crossing.

"I can touch the bottom," JD yelled. "Use your feet!"

"My feet keep slipping. I don't think I can go much further."

JD reached out his arm to Kira. "Yes, you can. You have to. Just a few more feet to go. Grab my arm, we're almost there."

Dark storm clouds turned day into night. JD squinted to see the crossing. Through the blowing rain and the frenzied waves, he saw the station wagon. "We're here. I see Uncle Joe."

Soaked and exhausted, the two crawled up the embankment at the crossing. Uncle Joe was sitting down by the car. "Thank God, you saw the signs in the sky. We have to go now! But I have a problem."

JD tossed his backpack and the inner tubes into the back of the station wagon.

"What problem?" JD said.

"I started to go after you to warn you about the storm. As I walked down the bank, I slipped and fell. I twisted my right ankle and aggravated an old knee injury. I won't be able to drive. You're going to have to drive."

"What? Uncle Joe, I can't. Sure, you have shown me how to, and I have driven the station wagon – but only on clear, dry days. I can't drive in pouring rain!"

"We don't have any time to argue about this. Unless Kira can drive, you're it. We have to get out of this valley."

"I don't know how to drive!" Kira said. "JD, you can do this. You have to do this!"

"Help me into the passenger side," Uncle Joe said. "I will help as much as I can. Kira, jump into the back seat."

The Storm

Rain pounded JD and Kira as they helped Uncle Joe into the station wagon. Dark rolling clouds shut off the light of day, and only the lightning in the sky brought it back for a split second. JD got into the driver's side of the station wagon, and Kira got into the back seat from the passenger side.

"Okay, Sport, start her up. I'll help with the steering if we start to fishtail. Remember to take your foot off the gas if you feel it lose traction."

"Fishtail, foot off," JD repeated over and over.

"Breathe and go slow. You'll be fine."

JD tried to find the road ahead. All he could see were sheets of rain falling and pounding the hood of the station wagon. "I can't see the road! I can't do this!"

"Calm down, all you have to do is dim the lights and follow the road's edge. Mostly bushes or tall grass are along the edge, so use that to help. We need to get out of this low-lying area. You know that and you know why."

Kira closed her eyes, placed her hand on JD's shoulder, and whispered something. Voices whispered in her ear. "If you help, we gain the advantage. You are putting yourself at risk. You know the law." Kira ignored the voices and continued to utter a mantra while touching JD's shoulder.

JD put the station wagon in neutral, pressed the clutch to the floorboard, and turned the ignition. He pressed down hard on the gas pedal, and the engine roared.

"Back off the gas and put it in gear."

JD selected first gear and pressed down on the gas pedal again. The station wagon lunged forward, and the engine stalled.

"It's fine," Uncle Joe said. "Remember, apply the gas slowly. Start again."

JD breathed deeply, started the process over, and the station wagon moved forward slowly. He turned the lights on the low beam and followed the edge of the road, glancing back at the center of the road at times. The station wagon rocked back and forth as the wind and rain smashed into it. Then the hail came. Hailstones pelted the roof and sides of the station wagon in rapid succession like a machine gun.

"Keep it under twenty-five miles per hour. We don't have too far before we are out of the valley."

"Roger that," JD said, feeling more confident.

"You're doing great," Kira said as she squeezed JD's shoulder.

JD turned on the radio and tuned it to a lower AM band, and he heard what he didn't want to hear: "Uncle Joe, does your station wagon have the..."

"NOAA Weather Alert channel? Yes, it does! It's still in the experimental stages, but I got our office in the test program. I don't think we will get much of a signal this far out. I will try it."

Uncle Joe switched to the VHF band and tuned the radio to the NOAA Weather Alert channel. JD and Uncle Joe heard a tone and words, but static blocked the message from coming through clearly. JD heard the word "severe," and that was enough. They were in a severe thunderstorm. Heavy rain and hail hammered the road ahead, creating holes and exposing rocks. The inner tubes, hiking sticks, the backpack, and anything not tied down bounced around as the station wagon rocked back and forth.

"Slow down, we're almost to the highway crossing. Roll down your window. Check for lights and the sound of an engine or loud horns. JD brought the vehicle to a slow stop at the crossing. Rain sprayed JD's face as he squinted to check for traffic on his side of the car. Since the highway was the state's north-south route, trucks used this route. Accidents happened all the time along this stretch of the highway. JD had to get everyone across safely in the pouring, blinding rain. As rainwater slid down his soaked hair, face, and eyes, JD squinted and looked both ways. He slowly applied the gas and eased the station wagon onto the highway.

Kira looked at the highway and saw a vision of the events about to unfold. A truck would come out of the rain and hit the station wagon sending it spinning and flipping over.

Kira grabbed JD's shoulder. "STOP! Truck! Stop!"

JD slammed on the clutch and brake pedal with both feet. Out of the darkness, a truck with no lights appeared from the left, as if coming from another dimension. The truck blared its horn as it zoomed past, just missing the front end of the station wagon.

As soon as the truck zoomed past, Uncle Joe checked the far side of the road and shouted, "Gun it!"

151

JD pressed the gas pedal to the floor, and the station wagon surged forward, nearly flying across the intersection.

"Let off the gas and don't use the brake!" Uncle Joe yelled as they made it to the other side of the highway.

The station wagon rattled and swayed side to side as it sped down the rocky dirt road, not slowing down much. The tangled jumble of gear in the station wagon's rear tossed up and down like salad. Up ahead, JD saw the sharp turn to the left to JD's house. He tapped the brakes and tried to steer the station wagon into the turn, but the rear end swung to the right. Uncle Joe grabbed the wheel and steered the station wagon to the right. The station wagon slid across the road, coming to a full stop on the side of the road in some bushes. It just missed a tree.

JD's eyes were wide open. His hands shook, gripping the wheel. Shivering from the cold rain, he turned and stared at Uncle Joe. "I can't do this! We're not going to make it home with me driving!"

"We're okay. It's okay, you're doing fine. Hang in there. We're almost home."

The wind drove the rain sideways and returned from a new direction. A wall of heavy rain and hail faced JD as he drove slowly down the rocky, muddy road home. The NOAA Weather Alert channel now came in clearer through the static. JD and Uncle Joe heard the message: Tornado Warning, Take Cover Now!

JD glanced at Uncle Joe. Uncle Joe nodded yes.

A calm spirit flowed through JD. "I can do this," JD thought.

"Kira, we are going to your house and pick up your mother and Grandma Sullivan."

"Okay, but why?"

"The storm is getting worse. We have a shelter at my house."

"Oh, wow, okay. Can you help me get Nana into the station wagon?"

"Sure, of course."

JD and Kira dashed through the rain to the door at Grandma Sullivan's house. JD banged on the door and pushed the doorbell button over and over. Kira's mom opened the door and saw two soaking wet kids shouting. "We have to go now!"

"Yes, I know," Kira's mom said. "Nana is right here. Where's Joe? We need his help getting Nana into the car."

"Ankle hurt, bad knee, he can't help," JD blurted out. "We have to do it. Hurry, let's go!"

Grandma Sullivan bent over with a raincoat draped over her. She walked, steadying herself with her cane, checking each footstep.

"I'm fine," Grandma Sullivan said. "I don't need any help!"

JD and Kira ignored that statement, grabbed an arm on each side of Grandma Sullivan, and escorted her to the station wagon. Together, they helped her into the back seat of the wagon. JD got back into the driver's seat and headed for his house.

"Well, isn't this cozy?" Grandma Sullivan said. "Joe, are you okay? I heard something about the ankle and the knee."

"Yes, ma'am, I'll manage. There's nothing to worry about."

"Well, my, my, my, and JD is driving," Grandma Sullivan said.

"Yes, he is," Uncle Joe said. "He's doing a great job."

The Storm

"I didn't know JD could drive," Grandma Sullivan said with a wink. Grandma Sullivan certainly did know JD could drive. Grandma Sullivan knew everything that went on in the area.

Darkness now covered everything. The headlights only reveal sheets of rain. JD barely saw a sliver of the road ahead. The trip to JD's house was slow going. When they arrived, JD's mother was waiting on the front porch. She rushed over to where Grandma Sullivan was seated. With Sheila's help, the two women got Grandma Sullivan out and to the shelter's door. JD grabbed his backpack and helped Kira get Uncle Joe to the shelter.

JD's mother used the shelter to store her preserves and other canned goods. JD's dad and granddad built it before JD was born. They made it big enough for a bed, a small table, and one single chair. His granddad would sneak into the shelter and sit in the chair listening to baseball games on the radio. He sat there with a cigar in his left hand and a glass of whiskey in his right. After the game, granddad took a nap on the bed.

A creaky hinge on the door and the stairs gave enough warning to Granddad to hide the cigar and the whiskey. No one ever entered the shelter while granddad was down there, not even JD's mom. Being a devout Baptist, JD's mom did not approve of the smoking and drinking, but she did not interfere. She figured Granddad Jayson had lived through enough and lived long enough that he could do whatever he wanted to do.

JD's dad and granddad were neither Baptists nor religious. His dad attended church with JD's mom. Like granddad, he was more of a realist than a Baptist. He did take "love your neighbor" to heart. He and JD's mom spent many weekends in the Black community providing free medical help. This was during a time when no white person would even drive through the Black community unless they were up to no good. The attitude and actions of JD's dad help moderate the views of JD's mom. She was still strict. Yet, she often chose to ignore something or not judge.

JD opened the door to the shelter. He switched on the one light hanging from the ceiling by the door. The group slowly made it down the stairs. Dim shadows of the group crawled across the wall. He sneezed, and Grandma Sullivan replied. "Bless you."

The smell of damp earth and mold filled the air. This was not a home. Hopefully, it was a safe haven. The wind howled and beat against the door like a giant demanding entrance to a castle. The door flew open. The wind roared and slammed it shut and then yanked it open again. JD rushed back up the stairs and struggled against the wind to pull on the door. He latched the door shut and said, "Crikey, that was full on." Kira burst out laughing. Everyone joined in. Laughter was better than fearing what might be happening outside that door.

The root cellar would probably not pass a "storm shelter" certification. It had a steel roof and concrete rock walls. Granddad used steel beams for the shell. Dirt covered the steel and concrete frame to the roof. It was strong enough, but it could have been better. The storm outside created a deafening noise. The wind kept struggling to rip the door off, making its presence known to the six people stuffed inside.

Kira and JD helped Grandma Sullivan to the bed, where she sat on the edge. JD and Kira sat together next to Grandma Sullivan.

"You kids look like drowned rats," Grandma Sullivan said. "Here, put this blanket over you, before you catch your death of cold."

"I'm fine," JD said as he pulled the blanket over Kira.

Kira wrapped one end of the blanket around JD and both of them. Under the blanket, she reached over and squeezed JD's hand. He turned and smiled.

"Thank you for getting all of us home," Kira said, looking at JD.

"Yes, thank you, JD, for getting us here safe," Grandma Sullivan said.

"Yeah, you did well, Sport," Uncle Joe said.

JD's mom glanced at Grandma Sullivan and then at Uncle Joe. She started to piece the facts together, but she did not like the conclusion.

"Joe, how were you able to drive with your bad knee and ankle?"

"Uh, well, uh," Uncle Joe stammered.

"JD drove," Grandma Sullivan said. "He drove from the crossing to my house and your house."

"What? Is this true, JD? You drove Uncle Joe's station wagon through the storm with the rain and wind along that dangerous dirt road?"

JD thought. "This was a set-up." He wanted to answer proudly, but his mother was somewhere between upset and horrified. Her one and only little boy had driven a vehicle along a dangerous road, across a busy highway, and through a severe thunderstorm.

"Yes, ma'am," JD said sheepishly with his head down.

"Well!" JD's mother said with her arms crossed and her best concerned mother look.

"Here it comes," JD thought.

JD's mother paused, stood up, reached out her arms, and said, "Come here."

JD was convinced his mother would scold him right in front of everyone, including Kira, in the damp, dimly lit, crowded storm shelter. Only the collapse of the shelter roof could have been worse. He stood up and walked to his mother. His mom hugged him and held him at arm's length.

"Just to be clear, you still have to have your learner's permit before you can drive with or without me," JD's mom said. "But I am proud of you for getting everyone here safely. How were you able to do that?"

"I've just been reading a lot about it. Uncle Joe has been showing me stuff like how to start the engine and put it into gear. You know, just general stuff."

JD technically did not lie, but he strategically left out the part about Uncle Joe actually letting him practice driving the station wagon.

"Well, that should make Driver's Education much easier for you," JD's mom said.

JD turned and walked back to the bed. He glanced at Uncle Joe, who winked, indicating his secret was safe.

Just as JD sat back on the bed, the wind increased in intensity. The shelter door vibrated and shook. Everyone turned and stared up at the door. They expected the door to be ripped off its hinges at any moment. Instead, they heard a loud cracking noise followed by something crashing against the door. The door stopped vibrating.

"There went the old oak tree," JD's mom said. "Generations just died."

The old oak tree stood in the backyard. A swing hung from one of its branches. JD's great-grandfather built the house near that old oak tree over a hundred years ago. JD often took a break under that tree after working in the garden. JD's dog, Dolly, would sit next to him, panting, hoping JD had brought some treats.

The tree rested on a small rise in the backyard. From under the tree, JD could survey the nearby garden. Some of the branches nearly touched the roof of the back porch. A squirrel often taunted Dolly from the roof. Dolly would race up to the back porch, shouting her disapproval of the squirrel trespassing into her domain. The squirrel raced back and forth along the roof with Dolly below on the ground. JD would try to convince Dolly the squirrel was taunting her. Dolly refused to accept that conclusion and would continue to chase the out-of-reach squirrel back and forth. Eventually, the squirrel tired of the game and leaped back onto the branch, retreating to the tree. JD wondered if the squirrel had survived the storm.

The wind kept pushing on whatever was now pressed against the door. It made a scratching noise, like a giant cat scratching on the door, wanting to come in. The scratching noise replaced the vibrations.

The shelter's light flickered several times and went out. JD pulled out his flashlight from his backpack, and JD's mom lit the candle on the small table. The scratching sound stopped. It was all quiet in the dimly lit, damp shelter. Everyone sat silently for a minute or two.

"Is it over?" Kira said.

"Might be," Uncle Joe said. "Let's give it a few more minutes."

JD's mom started singing "Amazing Grace." Kira joined in. JD was surprised and stared at Kira. Soon, everyone but JD was singing. Reluctantly, JD joined in too. After the song, it was still quiet. Only the candle provided light.

JD turned his flashlight on and said, "I'm going to check outside."

"Listen at the door first," Uncle Joe said. "We might be in the eye or between storm cells."

JD listened at the door but didn't hear anything. He unlatched the door and pushed on it, but it did not budge. "I can't open it." Kira got up and walked up the stairs. "Coming, maybe the two of us can nudge it open."

AFTER THE STORM

JD and Kira both pushed on the door. It gave way a bit with more scratching noise. They squeezed through the opening. The branch that had once nearly touched the back porch had been torn from the tree and thrown against the shelter door. Its limbs and leaves created the scratching noise on the door.

JD stared down at the fallen limb, thinking about Dolly. The link to a memory was gone in the storm. The house still stood, but some galvanized roofing sheets were torn off or pulled back. Then they saw the garden. Water from the creek had come up and flooded the garden. That much water certainly drowned the vegetables.

The storm had passed to the east. The sun tried to shine through the receding clouds. JD and Kira went inside the house from the back porch to check on the power and water. Water came from a well on the property, but power from the city ran the pump. With no power, water could not be pumped to the house. The pump filled a tank in the pump house. Water could still be drawn from a faucet on the tank. They had enough water for a few days if needed. The two pulled the branches away from the door and returned to help everyone out.

"Well?" JD's mom said.

"Power and water are out. I saw a few windows broken, and some roofing sheets are gone or bent back."

"What was jamming the door shut?" Uncle Joe asked.

"A branch from the oak tree broke. The wind pushed it against the door. Kira and I have cleared it away enough to open the door."

"Well, let's get out of this hole," Grandma Sullivan said. "I feel like I am in an early grave, and I am not ready to go just yet."

Kira and JD helped Uncle Joe up the stairs. The two moms followed with Grandma Sullivan. JD's mom stood by the open door, staring at the tree and the garden. Tears welled up in her eyes. "Damn it."

JD had seen his mother cry, but he had never heard her utter one single curse word. The garden was her unique pleasure in life. JD got the garden ready and planted, but his mother cared for it. After breakfast, you could find her in it, visiting each area, stopping to remove any critter wanting to attack and devour a plant. In the afternoon, she pulled out the unwanted, broke up the topsoil with a small gardening fork, and carefully watered each area according to its needs. When JD came home from school, he would find his mom singing a hymn while tending the garden.

In the evenings, JD came and sat with his mom on the back porch swing. She sipped on tea, looking at the garden. It represented more than just the vegetables in it. Memories floated like a cloud of fireflies above the garden. He could picture his dad with the wheelbarrow hauling away the un-wanted to the compost pile. The best joy for his mom came when she harvested the fruits of her labor. Now the garden was covered with dirty, muddy water from the creek. To her, it was gone along with all the memories and happy times she spent caring for it.

JD's mom turned to everyone. "Let's all go inside. If the creek flooded, then the river did, too. I need to call the pastor of the African American church and ask if they need medical help. Joe, when we're inside, I want to check out your knee and ankle. And no arguments."

"It's all feeling much better, but you're the nurse."

JD's dad was a doctor, and JD's mom was a nurse. Be-fore his dad went to join a MASH unit at the start of the Korean War, the two would go to the African American church on the west side of town to provide routine medical care. The locals called that area of town "Shanty Town."

In the 1960s, a person of color could not always walk into a clinic, hospital, or store. Some stores did have a back entrance marked "Coloreds Only" or something similar. JD's dad and mother provided free medical help to those who lived in Shanty Town.

A mortar attack hit his dad's MASH unit shortly after it was deployed to the front lines. His dad had only been with the unit for nine months. His dad died the day JD was born. Uncle Joe intercepted the War Office telegram before it was delivered to the hospital. He did not give it to JD's mom until she came home. She was devastated by the news but continued doing her best to be a single mom, managing the farm. She continued to provide medical help for the African American community. She did it because they needed the help, but deep down, she did it to remain close to the one she lost.

Women in the 1940s had to break through thick walls and high ceilings to become doctors. Those walls and high ceilings kept JD's mother from earning her doctorate degree and the M.D. designation, but that did not stop JD's dad from teaching his mom everything she needed to know.

His dad was a resident doctor at the clinic and an adjunct professor at the university. JD's mom was his at-home student. She was the first to receive the lessons and benefit from them. She would often wait in the library reading medical journals while his dad taught a class. After class, they went to the drugstore across the street and talked about what she had read that day.

JD's mom did not have the M.D. designation, but she had the preparation. She could treat anyone for anything a male doctor could. Still, she was limited in what she could do legally. In some cases, patients had to be referred to a doctor. The clinic had an attending physician who would see African Americans after hours. Those patients were ushered through the garage access below the clinic.

"I just spoke with the pastor at the church," JD's mom reported. "The entire westside of town is flooded. Many of the roads are under several feet of water. There's no access except to the church from the town square. Most of the folks are safe in the church for now. Luckily, the church was built on higher ground, figuratively and literally. Joe let's get you into the kitchen. Time for your examination."

"Okay, but be gentle."

Sheila and JD's mom helped Uncle Joe into the kitchen.

"Alright, drop the pants," JD's mom said.

"What?" Uncle Joe replied in shock. "There's no way I am doing that in front of present company."

"Poppycock," Grandma Sullivan said. "I used to babysit you when you were a wee thing. I changed your diapers. I have seen it all! I'm sitting right here. Tomorrow, I'm going to make some calls. Joe and the disaster team are going to need supplies. I know a few people in high places."

"Mom, He doesn't mean you. He means me," Sheila said. "I'll check on what JD and Kira are doing and keep them out."

After Sheila left the kitchen, Uncle Joe took off his pants.

"Alright, let's take a look. Hmm, your knee is a bit red and bruised. Your ankle is swollen. Can you move your toes and the ankle?"

"Yeah, a little, but it hurts."

"It would have to be that leg. How did this happen?"

"I saw the storm coming and was going to help JD and Kira. As I was trying to get into the river, I slipped and down I went."

"I'm going to wrap the knee and ankle," JD's mom said. "I'll give you something for the pain. I want you to keep that leg elevated as much as possible. We'll need to go to the clinic and have some X-rays done. We can do it tomorrow before I head to the church. In the meantime, you can use granddad's old cane. I think it suits you. Next time, look before you leap."

"Thanks, doc, you're all heart."

"Brains you have, common sense has always been your shortcoming. You were supposed to keep the kids safe. Yet you are the one who is hurt. I'm just thankful it wasn't worse. I nearly lost a brother as a young girl. I am not ready to lose you now."

"Sorry, sis, I'm not ready to go either."

JD's mom gave Uncle Joe a quick neck hug and kiss on the head. "Please stop going around my parenting. I can't bear the thought of losing JD. I am glad JD got everyone home okay, but he's not ready to be driving."

"Sis, the boy doesn't have a father and has lost his granddad. He needs someone to help fill those voids. You won't be able to keep him in the nest forever. He is going to leave one day. You know that. I know that. I want him to be able to fly when he does and not fall flat on the ground."

JD's mom wiped tears from her eyes. "I know; I know. It's just so hard. I am truly thankful I have you to help. All done, you can put your pants back on now, bashful. Anyway, let's focus on getting everyone situated. I think we should all stay put until tomorrow."

JD's mother was a born leader, but being a single mom turned her into a tough CEO. If she weren't such a devout Baptist, she would have had a cigar in one hand and a shot of whiskey in the other. Despite the toughness that life required, she was still a tender, loving mom.

"I'm sitting at the kitchen table," Grandma Sullivan said. "I am not up to moving."

"That's fine," JD's mom said. "You and Joe stay put."

Sheila walked back into the kitchen. "Is it safe to come back in?"

"Yes, it is. Bashful Joe has his pants back on. Where's JD and Kira?" JD's mom said.

"They went up to JD's room to change clothes," Sheila said.

"Hmm, I don't much like that."

"They'll be just fine," Grandma Sullivan said. "Those are two smart and dependable kids. I, for one, am thankful for both of them."

"You're right, of course. They are like two peas in a pod."

JD's mom looked at Sheila and her brother. "They remind me of two other kids I used to know. That's what has me concerned."

"Life has a way of snapping two peas apart," Sheila said, looking over at Uncle Joe.

JD and Kira stood at the door of his room. The storm had blown in the window. Shattered glass covered the floor below the window. Everything not secured on something was now on the floor. The wind had sent rain through the broken window, soaking memories and scattering them around the room. JD walked in, dropped his backpack, bent down, and picked up the rain-soaked photo of Dolly. He sat on the bed motionless, staring at the photo of Dolly. Kira sat next to him and put her hand on JD's shoulder.

"No worries, we'll clean it all up and sort it out."

JD stared at the photo of Dolly. "Right, it's just stuff."

His mother came up the stairs, stood at the door, and saw the chaos in the room. "What a mess. I'm so sorry."

"It's fine. I'll clean it all up, Mom."

"I'll help," Kira said.

"Could you two help gather some candles right now? It will be dark soon, and we don't know when the power will be back on."

"Sure, Mom, we'll be down in a minute."

JD stood up and laid the rain-soaked photo of Dolly on his desk. "Come on, let's go downstairs. We can worry about this mess later."

Kira stood up and hugged JD. "You did good today. Thanks for getting everyone here safely."

"You helped. We'd all be dead if you hadn't seen that truck. How did you do that?"

"I don't know. I had a feeling, I guess."

"Whatever it was, it saved the day."

Kira squeezed JD's hand. "We're a team. Right now, I'm soaked to the bone. Do you have any dry clothes I can borrow?"

"Oh, sure. I guess. They might not fit."

JD rummaged through his dresser and found a T-shirt and shorts. Although he and Kira were the same age, JD was taller, and Kira was thinner.

"How about these?"

"Perfect. And hand me that small bag I stuffed in your backpack."

"What? What's in the bag?"

Kira took the small bag from JD. "Never you mind. Turn around. I don't want you looking while I change clothes!"

"Oh, yeah, sure. You can use my bathroom if you want."

"Super, I can wash some of this mud off me."

"There are clean towels in the cabinet. I'm going to change clothes too."

After a few minutes, Kira shouted from the bathroom. "You done out there?"

"Yep, I'm all changed. When you are done, I want to wash my hands and face. I smell like fish.

Kira emerged from the bathroom wearing JD's t-shirt and shorts. "I'm done."

She stood in the doorway. The light from the bathroom window silhouetted her figure through the t-shirt. Her long, golden red hair flowed down in front of her shoulders.

JD had not forgotten Kira was a girl. The anxiety he felt around her had disappeared. JD stood there, staring at Kira standing in the doorway. A new feeling about her replaced the old anxiety.

"I told you I was all girl. Now close your mouth. Let's find those candles in the closet."

"Yeah, you're right. Sorry for staring."

"Stare all you want. Just remember. I might be a girl, but I am just as tough as any boy. Got it? Now go wash up."

JD smiled. "Yes, ma'am!"

JD came back into the room after washing his hands and face. "Alright, to the closet."

Kira walked ahead of JD with a sassy sway in her hips. A new chapter in Kira and JD's relationship had begun.

ONE SUMMER NIGHT

JD stood there, watching as Kira walked to the door. Kira glanced back over her shoulder. "You going to show me where those candles are, or are we going to stand here all night in the dark?"

"Yeah, right, they're in the hall closet downstairs. Follow me."

JD opened the hall closet door and saw the family photo albums covered with a muddy film of water. The roof above the closet had leaked. "Crap, mom's not going to like this,"

Those albums contained JD's family's lives and memories, including photos from the 1800s to when his dad left for Korea. JD's mom put them away in the closet, hoping the ghosts from the past would stay there. A photo album of JD's photos sat on the living room coffee table.

Kira picked up one of the albums, opened it, and flipped through a few pages. "The pages are mostly okay. Just the covers were damaged. Hey, are any of your baby photos in these?"

"No, mine are in the album in the living room," JD said, immediately regretting he uttered that confession.

"I'm going to need to look through that album."

"Fine, but it's boring."

"Oh, I doubt that!"

"Here are the candles. Let's put some in the living room and take some to the kitchen."

JD set the candles on the coffee table, and Kira picked up the photo album. JD felt uneasy. Although the album did not contain anything incriminating or embarrassing, he was nervous Kira would find something that would change how she felt about him.

"I can't wait to flip through this."

JD rolled his eyes.

His mother entered the living room, saving him from shame and humiliation. "You found the candles, thank you. Kira, you, and your family are going to spend the night. It's late, and we all agreed it would be best to stay put. I will try to fix something for us all to eat."

"Oh, goodie, a sleepover! Aunt Susan, I would be happy to help in the kitchen. My mum usually works late, so I always cook at home."

"Yes, thank you, that would be helpful."

"Can JD and I camp out here in the living room?"

"Sure, you'll have to share it with Uncle Joe. I am going to put your mother and Grandmother in the guest room. I figure Uncle Joe can sleep on the sofa. Will you two be okay sleeping on the floor?"

Kira side-looked at JD. "That would be super! JD, we can play some games or look at some photos."

"Yeah, sure, whatever."

"Finish here and join me in the kitchen."

Kira held the treasure trove of memories in her hand. She grinned with eager anticipation. "I hope you have extra batteries for your flashlight. I am going to be up late."

"Whatever," JD said.

"Don't be so gloomy, JD. I won't eat you in the middle of the night."

"Not worried about that. I don't want you to look at me as a baby. I was a dorky baby."

The months Kira spent with the bike gang, standing up to the boys, rose to the surface. She walked up to JD, nose to nose. "You're being a baby about it now. You're not the baby in those photos, but that baby turned into the boy I like. I want to know everything about that person. Got it?"

"Okay, okay," JD said without flinching.

Kira kissed JD on the cheek, walked to the kitchen, paused, and turned back. "Come on, dorky baby. We are wanted in the kitchen. I got cooking to do."

JD smiled. "I hope we survive your cooking. I plan to beat you at several games tonight."

"You wish," Kira laughed.

Back in the kitchen, Kira's mom looked through the refrigerator for something to fix for dinner. "Susan, the only things I can find in the fridge to fix without cooking are milk and salad fixings."

"Our stove is hooked to propane," JD's mom said. "We just need a match to light it."

"Mom, you go keep Uncle Joe company," Kira said. "I'll help Aunt Susan with dinner."

"That's probably safer for everyone," Kira's mom said.

172

"It's already getting a bit dim in here. JD, please grab the matches from the cabinet. Light the stove and the candle on the kitchen table. It'll be tight, but we can all squeeze in."

"I'm on it. If you want, Kira and I can eat in the living room. We don't need to eat at the table."

"I don't much like having food in the living room. But it would help. Just this time."

Grandma Sullivan waved disapprovingly. "We can all fit. We weathered the storm together. We damn well can find room to eat together."

Kira's mom sat down next to Uncle Joe at the kitchen table. She glanced at Joe, then nervously stared at the candle. Uncle Joe glanced back at her and then at the candle.

She stared at the flickering flame. "So, Joe, how's the knee and ankle?"

"Better, much better. Thanks for asking."

"Good, good."

A minute passed with the two staring at the candle in the middle of the kitchen table.

"Look, I, uhm, you know, I had to get Nana and Kira sorted out. I'm sorry I didn't call you. I meant to but just got so busy. Sorry."

"You don't have to explain. I understand. I've been super busy too. We'll catch up later. Let's have lunch sometime."

Kira's mom touched Uncle Joe's arm. "Yes, lunch. That will be fine. I'd like that."

Uncle Joe smiled back. "Me too."

JD's mom announced. "Okay, everyone, the Jayson Café is open. Our selection is more like breakfast than dinner. I apologize. I was on the way to the store when, well, you know. We have scrambled eggs, toast, and bacon. And I have some of my strawberry preserves. Kira did the cooking, and she added some New Zealand dishes. I'll let her explain."

Kira stood by the stove holding a spatula. "I cooked fritters, bangers, and pikelets."

"What?" JD said.

"Potato fritters, sausage, and tiny pancakes," Kira's mom translated.

"All that sounds like hardy food to me," Granda Sullivan said. "I'll set the table."

"Grandma Sullivan, you just sit," JD's mom said. "JD will set the table."

"Nonsense, I've been sitting on my ass way too long today. Just help me up and point me in the right direction."

JD's mom motioned to JD to help Grandma Sullivan.

"Here, let me help you."

"Thank you, JD."

Grandma Sullivan reached up and put her hand on JD's shoulder. She whispered something to herself in Māori. "You're a steady young man. You did well through this storm. Stay strong and always be ready to help when needed."

"Yes, ma'am, I will. I'll do my best."

"Now let's get this table ready. I'm peckish."

Kira looked over at JD helping Grandma Sullivan. She smiled and whispered something to herself in Māori.

JD said grace at the table without even being asked to do so. Kira sat next to him and bumped his knee with hers. They had all weathered the storm, and, for now, everyone was safe. After the breakfast-style dinner, JD and Kira went to get the living room ready for their sleepover. The rest of the survivors had coffee and some cookies from the never-ending cookie jar. JD's mom went to check on JD and Kira.

"Here are some cookies and lemonade for you two," JD's mom said. "JD, grab the extra pillows and linen from the closet in the guest bedroom. Get some for your uncle to use too. That floor is going to be like sleeping on a board. I don't know what to do about that."

"We'll be fine, Mom. I'll fold some blankets, and we can sleep on them. We'll figure it out."

"I guess that will do. It will have to, I suppose."

"I've been tramping a few times. I mean camping. I slept on the ground in just a sleeping bag," Kira said.

"Sleeping bags!" JD said. "I forgot. We have sleeping bags."

"Brilliant, we'll use those!"

"Well, it sounds like you two have it all figured out. I am going to fix up the guest bedroom."

"JD and I are going to play a board game."

"Did I hear board game?" Uncle Joe said as he walked into the living room using Granddad's old cane.

"Right you are," Kira said. "Do you want to play?"

"Sure, I'm always up for a board game."

When JD's granddad was alive, Uncle Joe would come over Saturday nights for dinner and a fun evening playing board games. Lively disputes broke out, but fun and laughter filled the living room every Saturday night.

Kira, JD, and Uncle Joe played for a few hours with the same cries of unfair play and fun-filled laughter. Darkness had come, and the coffee table candle sank into a melted wax pool.

JD saw the candle melting and replaced it with a fresh one.

"Kiddos, I am calling it quits," Uncle Joe said.

"Do you mind if JD and I stay up a bit longer? I want to check out the photo album. We'll be quiet."

Uncle Joe stood up to spread the sheets on the sofa and position the pillow. "Fine with me. I think the painkiller is kicking in. Anyway, noise doesn't keep me from falling asleep. Just don't expect my sleep to be without noise. I do snore."

Kira walked over and took the sheets and pillow from Uncle Joe. "Please, let me help you with that."

"Thank you, Kira," Uncle Joe said. "The last thing I need right now is to fall trying to make my bed."

JD saw Kira helping his uncle and whispered to himself, thanking God.

JD got the sleeping bags and laid them out on the floor side-by-side. Kira grabbed the photo album from the coffee table. She pulled her sleeping bag right next to JD's. "Where's that flashlight? We got some viewing to do."

"Yeah, okay, it's right here," JD said reluctantly.

The two lay side-by-side, flipping through pages of memories, returning to a time before JD was born. He had forgotten the album had photos of his dad and granddad. He relayed stories that his granddad had told him. Laughter often accompanied a story that popped up from the page. Some photos brought a few reflective, sad moments, but laughter soon broke through as JD remembered some funny anecdotes, especially about Dolly's antics.

In the morning, JD's mom found the two on the floor with the photo album between them like a bridge of memories between two different shores. She looked down at the two peacefully sleeping beside each other and smiled. It was a moment she did not want to let go of. JD's mom bent down and gently shook JD, trying not to wake Kira.

"Mom? What time is it?"

"It's early. I just wanted to let you know I am taking Uncle Joe to the clinic for an X-ray on his knee and ankle. I'll take him home and then go to the church to help there."

"I want to come and help."

Kira rolled over, rubbing her eyes. "I'm coming too."

"I need you two to stay here and help with Nana."

"Aunt Susan, my mum can do that. She does it at home."

"That's true. I could use the help with Uncle Joe. Alright, you can both come and help. But right now, how about breakfast?"

THE FLOOD

After breakfast, Kira and JD helped Uncle Joe into the car to go to town. JD's mom figured the back road through the park would be flooded, so she took the highway across the new bridge. As she crossed the bridge, she slowed the car to look down the river. The water level had risen almost to the bottom of the bridge. Water covered most of the park. The crossing near the springs could not be seen, nor could the springs. It was worse than JD's mom had feared.

"Wow, I have never seen anything like this before," Uncle Joe said. "We're going to be busy at the office."

"You're not planning to go into the office, are you?" JD's mom said. "How're you going to get there?"

"Someone will come pick me up. I'm the chief of the disaster response team. I won't sit at home while I'm needed at the office. Would you?"

"I guess not. But if the X-ray shows even a fracture, you will be in a cast or wrapped up tight. You'll probably need physical therapy either way."

"People are going to need food, water, and medical supplies. I can help coordinate that from my office. I can't do that well from home. And remind me where you are going after you take me for the X-rays?"

"You're right. I know. We did have the same father, and he would have done the same. No need to call anyone, I'll drop you by the office on my way to the church. But Kira and JD are going to help you up those stairs. That's not negotiable."

"Agreed."

Kira and JD sat in the waiting room while Uncle Joe completed his X-ray. The clinic in town and the attached small hospital served the entire county. Thanks to the efforts of JD's dad and mom, the latter had the latest medical equipment.

Uncle Joe's near-death experience during the cave-in at the canyon was one reason JD's mother decided to become a nurse. The real heroes that day at the canyon were Kira's mom and JD's father. Two rocks from the ceiling splintered and slid down like cards. Uncle Joe's right foot was pinned. Right above were two more rocks, ready to slide down and cut off Uncle Joe's leg like a guillotine.

JD's dad used two hiking sticks tied together to lift the rocks enough for JD's mom to help Uncle Joe free his leg just before the other two rocks slid down. The first rock had cut deep into Uncle Joe's big toe. The second slab sliced a gash in his ankle. Kira's mom and JD's mom had first aid training. They helped stop the bleeding. The top part of the toe was lost, but Uncle Joe's life was saved.

JD's mom had already considered becoming a nurse, and that incident convinced her. Her decision led to JD's dad deciding to become a doctor.

JD's mother came out to the waiting room. Uncle Joe walked behind her using the cane. JD had found a National Geographic magazine to read. Kira was pacing around the room.

"There's no fracture, but the knee and ankle are still swollen. Your uncle insists on going to the office. Could you two help him up the front steps and the stairs? With the power out, I don't think the elevator is working."

"Yes, ma'am," Kira quickly said. "We'll take good care of him."

"Thank you; that would be helpful. After that, I can take you two back home and then go to the church."

"Mom, we're coming with you to help. Aunt Sheila and Grandma Sullivan will be fine. Please let us help."

"I agree. Let the kids help. It will be a valuable experience for them."

"It could be dangerous. You saw the water level at the bridge. More water could be coming. I would prefer they went home."

"Just so you two know, my sister can be stubborn. Susan, remember what we talked about."

"Yes, fine, but I have a bad feeling about this."

At the county courthouse, Kira and JD safely got Uncle Joe up to his office. The three heard the sound of chaos down the hall. People crowded into the small space, demanding requests and updates about the flooding. JD saw deputies from the Sheriff's office and officials from the fire department. Everyone was talking over each other. No one was taking charge. Uncle Joe beat his cane against the side of the door like a judge slamming the gavel to bring order to the court.

"Quiet! Quiet!" Uncle Joe yelled. "Will everyone please shut up! What the hell is going on here! We have a disaster plan. Stick to it. I'm the appointed disaster response chief. I want all of the disaster response team leaders in my office now. The rest of you get the hell out!"

One of the men came up to Uncle Joe. "Here's the latest report from the weather office. More storms have formed upriver. Heavy rain is accompanying these storms."

"That means more flooding is coming," Uncle Joe said.

Uncle Joe turned to Kira and JD. "You two go on. I've got my hands full here. I appreciate your help."

"Are you sure you're going to be okay?" JD said.

"I'll be fine, Sport. Your mother needs you more right now. Please make sure she doesn't overdo it. Tell her that more storms and more flooding are coming from upriver. They need to get everyone to the church as soon as possible."

"Yes, sir, will do."

"We'll take good care of Aunt Susan," Kira said.

"Thank you, now off you go."

JD and Kira walked back outside and stood at the courthouse steps. They saw that water had come up and covered the street leading to the west side of town. They returned to the car and told JD's mother they had safely taken Uncle Joe to his office. They did not tell her about the chaos in Uncle Joe's office.

"Thank you both for doing that. "When we arrive at the church, I will ask the pastor if you two can help do anything."

"Mom, water is covering the street to the westside. We saw it from the courthouse steps. Uncle Joe said to tell you more storms have formed upriver. More flooding is coming."

"I was afraid of that. That means more homes are going to be flooded. We're running out of time. I'll take the back road by the feed store; it is a bit higher and closer to the church. The water shouldn't have reached that far yet."

The town square lay on flat ground. The land rose to the highway bridge to the north of town and sloped down to the west. The west side of town was built around a low-water bridge west of the church. The river bent around the west side of town and passed the low-water bridge.

A deep part of the river on the east side of the bridge was a popular swimming hole. JD and his friend Ben would swim there while JD's mother held a clinic in the church. Ben's dad was the Black pastor at the church.

The old bridge below could be seen from the church, higher on a hill. JD's mom parked the car in front of the church. The sound of water rushing under the bridge was easy to hear. The flood water was close to flowing over the road and the metal railing.

Pastor Martin came out to greet them. "Thank you so much for coming. Some folks have cuts, bruises, and broken bones inside. I see you have brought some extra help. Hello JD, who is the young lady with you?"

"This is Kira. She's Sheila's daughter," JD's mom said.

"Ah, yes, you must be Grandma Sullivan's granddaughter. Please send our regards to your grandmother. Her continued support helps keep so many folks fed and clothed here on the west side."

JD's mom pulled Pastor Martin aside. "Joe said more flooding is coming. You need to get as many people as possible to higher ground as soon as possible."

"God knows, we have been trying. The Community Action Team worked all night knocking on doors."

"Do you have anything to keep these two busy and out of trouble?" JD's mom said.

"Why yes, they can help Ben bundle up supplies. He's over on the side of the church, tying rope together. We have some folks trapped on their roofs. We were hoping we could toss a rope to them to lift some food and water until we can get them down. JD, Ben will be happy you came."

It had been some time since JD had seen Ben. Racial tensions had existed in the town since the Civil War. The town fathers ensured segregation remained intact. The fact that Ben was Black never bothered JD when he was a kid. He just wanted to come and spend the day playing with his friend. He let his friends in school convince him that he shouldn't be pals with a Black kid. Now it was awkward for JD to see Ben. He hadn't seen him in years.

"Well, look who's come to slum with the poor Black folk," Ben said.

"Hey, Ben, how are you?" JD said.

"I've been busy, not that it's any of your concern."

"Look, I'm sorry, okay. We came to help."

"Who's your friend?"

"This is Kira. She's come from New Zealand. She's Grandma Sullivan's granddaughter."

"Any relative of Grandma Sullivan is welcome here. She never forgets a friend."

JD hung his head down. "I'm sorry I ignored you. I was a bad friend. I don't know what else to say. Kira and I are here to help. Please let us help."

Kira reached out her hand. "Howdy Ben, what can we do?"

"You two can sort through the supplies we gathered. We need to put them in bundles that include some water, food, and medical supplies."

A pickup truck pulled up and stopped beside where they were preparing the bundles. JD heard someone shout, "Hey Nerd!"

JD turned and saw Billy and his brother Donald in the pickup truck.

"Hey, I'm talking to you, nerd. Did you come to play with your little Negro friend? Aww, did the mean flood come? This place needed a bath anyway."

Donald and Billy laughed.

JD stared back. "What do you want?"

"From you? Nothing. If we didn't have to deliver these supplies to my grandparents, I'd get out and beat the crap out of you and your friends. That'd be fun."

JD wasn't going to warn Billy and Donald about the flooding coming, but Kira nudged him, whispering. "Say something."

"You can't cross the bridge right now. It's not safe. More water is coming soon."

"Shut up, nerd, we can do whatever we want. Have fun with your little Negro friend. I can't wait to tell everyone at school you're a Negro lover."

Donald drove off with Billy in the passenger seat. The flood waters rushed towards the bridge. The water in the middle flowed over the bridge close to the top of the railing.

JD, Kira, and Ben watched as the pickup truck drove down the hill from the church. Donald eased the truck into the rushing water.

Ben watched as water rose past the wheels of the truck. "Are they crazy?"

A wall of water upriver rolled towards the bridge. JD noticed it first. "They're not going to make it across. Grab some rope."

"Already got it," Ben said. "Let's go."

"Wait," Kira said. "Where're you going? What's happening?"

JD pointed upriver. Kira saw the wall of water coming. "Oh my god! They're going to drown."

JD and Ben ran down the hill, dragging the rope behind them. Kira followed behind.

The wall of water sailed over the road, slammed into the side of the pickup, lifted it on its side, and pinned it against the railing. Donald climbed out of the driver's side, but Billy was trapped. Donald jumped off the truck just as the water surged again, flipping the pickup truck over the railing into the raging waters below. The pickup flipped again, hit the water right side up, twisted around, and came to rest flat against the rock used to dive into the swimming hole.

Donald was pushed against the railing. He grabbed the railing to keep from being swept into the floodwaters below. When Kira, JD, and Ben reached the bridge, they saw Donald pulling himself along the railing to shore. The pickup was slanted to one side and pinned against the rock. Billy climbed out of the pickup truck through the driver's side window. JD wrapped the rope's end around his waist and tied it in a knot.

"What are you doing?" Kira said.

"Getting ready."

"For what? You can't go in there. You'll be swept away!"

"I'm hoping you and Ben will be holding the other end of the rope. Besides, it's shallow by the bridge. I should be able to wade out and still touch the bottom."

"You're crazy. You can't fight the force of that water! I didn't come all the way from New Zealand to visit Nerd Boy to watch him drown!"

The Flood

JD wrapped the rope around his waist, tied a knot, and left a length of rope at the end. "I can't just stand here and do nothing. I'm going in. Are you going to help or not?"

Kira and Ben grabbed the rope, letting it out as JD walked forward.

JD stepped out into the shallow part and walked toward the truck. Soon, the water level was up to JD's waist. Another surge of water came over the bridge, sweeping JD off his feet. The rope went taut, pulling Ben and Kira toward the water's edge.

Donald reached the end of the bridge and stood watching Ben and Kira try to hold on to the rope, which was now slipping through their hands.

"Come help us!" Kira shouted at Donald.

Donald shook from fear and shock. Instead of helping hold on to the rope, he ran toward the church yelling. "I'll get help."

Another wave of water splashed across the bridge. Desperately, Ben and Kira tried to hold on to the rope. Kira saw JD bob back up above the surface. Only his head and shoulders could be seen. He struggled to swim to the capsized truck. A wave shaped like a hand came out of the water and slammed JD back under.

JD was still under the water and being pulled downriver. Ben held onto the rope but slipped and fell. He slid into the water feet first until a large rock blocked his forward momentum. Water washed over Ben's head as he braced his legs against the rock. "I can't hold on much longer!"

Kira seized the momentary slack in the rope. She turned to face the railing and slung the rope over her shoulder for better traction. The rope was slipping through their hands. Kira felt herself slipping backwards. A face appeared in front of her. It looked like the head of Medusa. Snakelike protrusions stuck out where there should be hair. The eyes glowed like fireballs. Yellow pointed teeth filled the mouth.

The face laughed. "We warned you, stupid human. Now you will know our power! Say goodbye to your puny nerd boy, silly girl."

Kira replied. "Be gone! Go back to your hole. You have no power here!"

Kira pointed to the end of the rope and spoke two words. The rope's end rose, flew through the air, and then wrapped and tied itself to the railing. Donald was running to the church and missed seeing the face and the rope magically secure itself to the railing. Ben watched as JD's head bobbed above the rushing water.

A voice in Kira's head whispered, "You and your family are no longer protected. You are now fair game. You know the rules. We warned you."

Kira ignored the voice and kept pulling on the rope.

JD had hit his head on a rock when the mysterious wave slammed him under. He could feel and taste the warm blood flowing down his nose from his forehead past his mouth. He struggled to find a foothold as the water rushed around him. In the distance, he could hear his mother screaming his name as she ran down the hill.

The Flood

JD concentrated on swimming sideways to the truck. Billy struggled to find a foothold on the open window. He pushed up and bent over the open window, trying to hold on to the top of the truck. His feet dangled across the open window. Water rushed in and back out of the window as the truck rocked back and forth.

JD inched his way over to the truck bed, grabbed the edge, and worked his way to Billy. He reached out and grabbed one of Billy's legs.

"Billy, slide down. I got you."

"You're nuts! There's no freaking way I'm doing that. The water will sweep us both downriver. What are you even doing here, nerd?"

"I'm trying to save your life. I'm tied to a rope. Ben and Kira are on the other end. Just slide down and hold on. If the water pushes the truck around the rock, it will sink into the swimming hole. You will drown. Now come on, before we are both washed away."

The truck rocked back and forth as wave after wave pounded against it. It started to slip off and around the huge rock. That was enough to convince Billy.

"Alright, I'm coming, but you better not let me go."

"I left enough rope at the end. Just slide down and hold on while I tie it around you."

JD waved back to Ben and Kira to pull both of them back. Kira, Ben, JD's mom, and several others from the church pulled Billy and JD back to the shore.

JD's mom rushed over to JD. "Are you okay? You're bleeding!"

"I'm fine, Mom. It's just a scrape when I slipped."

"It's not a scrape, it's a gash. Let's get you to the church, and I will treat it. You'll need stitches and will probably have a scar there."

"Cool, a war wound."

"Not cool, you could have drowned out there. What were you thinking?"

"I don't know. I don't think I did much thinking. I just sorta reacted. I had to do something."

Kira tapped JD's mom on her shoulder and pointed at the pickup truck. Waves had rocked it to one side. One final surge of water pushed it around the rock and into the swimming hole. Within a minute, it sank out of sight. "JD saved Billy's life."

"Yeah, dude, you saved my life," Billy said. "You're still a nerd, but I won't forget what you did."

JD pointed to Kira and Ben. "I couldn't have done it without their help."

Billy stood up and held out his hand to Ben. "Thank you, thank you both. I'm sorry about what I said before."

Ben shook Billy's hand. "No worries, happy to help. JD was the one who took the lead. I just followed."

"Billy, let me check you, too," JD's mom said.

"I'm fine, Mrs. Jayson, just a scrape on my knee and a scratch here and there."

"I want to check you and JD again at the church. Afterwards, I can take you and your brother home."

"If it's okay, I want to stay and help. If Ben and the pastor are okay with that. I owe them at least that. You can take my brother home. He can tell our parents where I am. They can come pick me up later."

"From what I can tell, you only need some antiseptic and a small bandage. I'll leave it up to Pastor Martin."

"Billy, you can help us gather supplies for those trapped on their roofs," Ben said.

"We best get going," JD said. "The water is rising fast."

The Flood

The pickup and the top of the bridge had disappeared beneath the water. Only rising flood waters could be seen.

The worst of the flood was still coming. The new storms from upriver kept pumping large volumes of water downriver, and the river could not move that much away. Soon, more houses had water at roof level or higher. The raging flood waters ripped a house from its foundation and floated it down the river past the church.

JD's mom called Uncle Joe for help. Grandma Sullivan had called several of her friends. Billy called his father and told him what had happened. In less than an hour, a disaster response team showed up at the church with boats, ladders, supplies, and more rope. That afternoon and through the night, it didn't matter what your skin color was. That night, the town's soul was moved in a new direction, all because of one boy helping another boy.

The dawn of the next day brought good and bad news. The storms had moved off, and the water level receded. The epic flood had ended. However, it wasn't all good news. Three people died during the flood, but many more were saved. The flood devastated Shanty Town, destroying the homes and livelihoods of hundreds.

With Grandma Sullivan's help, Uncle Joe secured tents and cots for those left homeless. JD, Kira, and Billy continued to help Ben at the church. Billy's dad rounded up several of his friends to come and help repair the damaged houses. The local lumber yard donated supplies and construction workers to rebuild the home that floated away—everyone who could come came and helped everyone who needed help.

The beautiful city park was in ruins. Mud and debris covered the park roads and the community center. The mayor requested and was granted a disaster declaration for the town. That would help financially, but it would take time to rebuild. It was only two weeks from the annual 4th of July celebration. The mayor called for help to get the park ready. Folks from all over the county came to help. In less than two weeks, the fairgrounds and the community center were ready for the 4th of July celebration.

THE 4TH OF JULY

"JD, are you going to ask Kira to the 4th of July celebration?" JD's mom said.

"I guess."

"What's the matter?"

"What if she says no?"

"I doubt that's going to happen. She doesn't know anyone else here, so who else would ask her?"

"It's just so hard. I want to, but..."

"I happen to know that she's expecting you to ask her. A little bird told me."

"Aunt Sheila, I bet. That makes it even worse. What if I don't do it right? What if I end up being a doofus and say the wrong thing?"

"Stop making this into a mountain. Just ask her and try not to make it complicated."

"Okay, I'll call her."

"No, you will go and ask her in person. And take this recipe to Aunt Sheila. She and Kira are going to bake a banana cake for the 4th of July potluck dinner."

"Alright, I'm going."

JD had overcome his previous anxiety about girls, but now it seemed a new anxiety about Kira had emerged. His feelings for Kira grew beyond having her around as a friend and fellow adventurer. A deeper feeling for her emerged. He didn't understand what it was. After the flood, he couldn't stop thinking about Kira. It scared him. He thought this over and over in his head as he rode to Granma Sullivan's.

"Hi, Aunt Sheila, Mom said to give you this."

"Thank you, JD," Kira's mom said. "I'm not much of a cook, and Grandma Sullivan's specialty is not desserts. Kira loves banana cake back home, so I figured it would be a great dessert to bring. Here, I am rambling on, I guess you want to visit Kira."

"Yes, ma'am, is she home?"

"She just got back from taking her weekly test at the university. I think she's in the garage. Are you okay? You're a bit pale."

"Yes, uh, yes ma'am. Thanks, I will check if she's in the garage. Okay, well, I'm going now. Thanks again."

JD found Kira in the garage, working on her bike. The moment had arrived. Words and broken sentences rattled in his brain. Why was this so difficult? He could knock a tin can off a branch with one shot from his 22 but could not find the words to talk to a girl. He thought. "What was happening? Why is this so hard to do?"

"Hi, JD, Whatcha up to?"

"Nothing, I just brought over a recipe for your mom."

"Aw, yes, for banana cake. Haven't seen you since the flood. I missed you. Are you up for some adventure? We still need to work on our plan for the trek back to the canyon and the waterfall."

"I've been busy with stuff. So, I guess you're attending the 4th of July celebration?"

"Right you are. I suppose you are, too."

"Yeah, so, uhm, I was wondering."

"Yes?"

"Hmm...well if you are going and I am going. Well, uhm, you want to ride with me and my mom?"

Kira smiled. "You mean like a date?"

"I guess. Or we can hook up there since we're all going."

"I'd love that, but it has to be a real date."

"Whaddaya mean?"

Kira stood up and walked to JD, standing nose to nose. "I mean, I want the whole works. You know with flowers, and you have to ask me properly."

JD wiped his hands on his jeans and swayed back and forth, "Okay, okay. Would you go to the 4th of July celebration with me?"

"Yes, I would love to."

"That's great, I mean cool, right, so, my mom and I will come by at 7 pm."

"I'll be ready, and don't forget those flowers!"

JD nervously smiled, backed up, tripped on something by the garage door, then nearly ran past his bike to tell his mother he needed some flowers. Back home, he rushed into the kitchen out of breath. "Mom, flowers, I need flowers, where? She said yes. Kira said yes!"

"Sit down, breathe, and tell me everything," JD's mom said.

"I gave Aunt Sheila the recipe and asked Kira. She said yes, but."

"Yes, but what?"

"She wants it to be a formal date. You know, the works with flowers and all."

"Smart girl. I'll call the florist in town and ask if they can do anything. If not, we can put together something from the flower gardens. The flowers near the house were spared. And you're going to need a haircut or a touch-up."

"Okay, I guess if they have the flowers, I can pick them up after the haircut."

The town was still trying to put everything back on track. The flood had affected a substantial portion of the state, not just the town, so supplies came in slowly.

"Sorry, the flower shop said they don't have any fresh flowers in stock," JD's mom reported. "I guess between the flood and the 4th of July demand, they ran out. We can check the flower gardens in front of the house."

"I have an idea. Hopefully, there's still some there."

"Where're you going? You're not going where I think you are going. That meadow was probably flooded. I doubt you will find anything there."

"I have to try. I'll be careful, I promise."

"Alright, wrap them in this newspaper and take the scissors. Cut the stems on an angle."

JD hugged his mother and kissed her on the cheek. "Thanks, Mom; you're the best."

"Amazing what puppy love will make you do," JD's mom whispered to herself.

JD was on a mission. He got his haircut, gathered a few blooms from the meadow that still looked fresh, and made it back home in time for lunch.

"Well, these are okay, but they will be better with a few smaller flowers mixed in with them. I'll take care of that. You put these in some water."

"Thanks, Mom."

"After lunch, you still have some chores to finish, and I have some baking to do myself."

"Yes, ma'am, I'll get right to it."

Even with the chores, the afternoon dragged on and on. JD kept checking his watch. He wanted to have plenty of time to take a shower and be ready for his first-ever date. Negative thoughts beat a drum in the back of his head. He ignored the drumbeat. He was excited to be with a girl, not just a girl who acted like a boy, but a real girly girl. More than all of that, it was Kira. Kira was becoming more than just another girl. She was smart, brave, and funny. Something about her pulled at JD's heart. He felt deep inside like he had known her all his life, not just a few weeks this summer.

Finally, the time had come. JD took a carefully crafted shower. It wasn't his usual in-and-out before the water hit the bottom of the tub shower. He meticulously cleaned every nook and cranny of his body. He even clipped his nails and expertly combed his freshly cut hair. He only used a small dab of hair cream to achieve a wild but under-control look. After a quick check in the mirror, he took the towel, dried his hair, and combed it again. It had to be perfect.

The short drive to Grandma Sullivan's seemed to take forever. JD stood at Grandma Sullivan's door, trying to remember what to do next. The door opened as he started to knock. Kira stood in the doorway with the hall light creating a halo around her head. The setting sun beamed into the doorway with a soft glow.

JD stood admiring this girl with the long, flowing, golden red hair. She wore her hair in a ponytail with bangs in front. She had put on some makeup. Her steel-blue eyes glistened above her red lips. She wore a pinkish-red skirt with a baby blue top. The pleated skirt went down just below her knees. A thin black belt went around her waist. This was not something a teenage girl would wear to church, at least not more than once.

"Well, what do you think?"

"Wow, you look amazing!"

"Thanks to Grandma Sullivan and my mom. It's more girly frilly than I like. You cleaned up nicely, too. Did you get a haircut?"

"Yeah, I did," JD said, staring at Kira.

"So, where are my flowers?"

"Oh yeah, one minute," JD said as he turned to go back to the car.

JD's mother was standing behind JD, holding the flowers. "Did you forget something?"

"Yeah, thanks, Mom."

JD handed the flowers to Kira. Kira stepped out onto the porch and looked down at them. A tear found its way down her cheek as she held them in her hands.

"Sunflowers! You remembered!"

"I figured you might like them."

"I love them!"

Kira took the sunflowers and went back to the door. Her mother was standing in the doorway, watching. More tears dripped from Kira's eyes down her cheek. "Mum, look! Sunflowers, he remembered!"

"I see that. Well done, JD. Kira, we need to freshen up your makeup. JD, give us a minute, we'll be right back."

JD turned to his mom. "Is she crying? Did I do something wrong?"

"No, JD, you did everything just fine."

Grandma Sullivan walked out the door using her cane. "Making girls cry already, are we JD?"

"What?" JD said. "I didn't mean to. I just wanted to give her something that would make her happy. Something she said she liked. I didn't think it would make her cry."

"I'm just messing with you. You did well. Those are tears of happiness. Now, can you help this old woman into the car? I've never missed a 4th of July celebration, and I won't miss this one."

"Oh yes, Mom and I will help."

Just as JD finished helping Grandma Sullivan in the car, he felt a tap on his shoulder. He turned and saw Kira standing behind him. She reached over, smiled, and kissed JD on his cheek.

"You might want to wipe that lipstick off before we're at the park," Kira said as she got into the car.

JD looked around. "Where's your mom?"

"Uncle Joe's picking her up. They're going to meet us there."

Kira sniffed the air. "That smells yummy. Aunt Susan, what did you bring?"

"I brought two of my home-made pecan pies," JD's mom said.

"And I found two watermelons from the garden that survived the flood," JD said.

"Both sound yummy to me," Kira said.

The usual roaming carnival couldn't make it that year. This year, the celebration had old home-style games of horseshoes, washers, and watermelon seed spitting. Some food-eating contests followed the baking contest. The weather cooperated with clear skies and mild temperatures. Laughter and excitement filled the air as a town let go of the stress from a historic storm and flood. It was a time of celebration and a time to be thankful to be alive. Everyone was invited, no matter where they lived in the town.

After the potluck dinner, the mayor gave a short speech and then gave the nod for the fireworks to start. Rockets red glared over the football field a short distance from the celebration. Kira sat next to JD on a grassy knoll behind the community center.

"Do they have fireworks in New Zealand?" JD said.

"Yeah, for New Year's Eve and Guy Fawkes Day in November."

"Guy Fawkes?"

"Don't know, something about a plot to overthrow the English Parliament in 1605."

"So, like the American Revolution?"

"I guess. I'm not a history buff. I just like the fireworks. What's after the fireworks?"

"There's a dance in the community center."

"Oh goody, so are you going to dance with your date?"

"My mom doesn't much like dancing, but I'll ask her if it's okay. She'll probably stay and talk with her friends."

"Come on, let's go find her now!"

"Wait, the finale is coming. You don't want to miss this."

"Oh, alright, but right after this finale, okay?"

"Agreed. I wouldn't want to keep my date waiting."

"Smart boy," Kira said, smiling as she reached over to hold JD's hand.

The finale battled with the stars over the football field, then silence and lingering smoke remained. A cloudless sky filled with stars provided the backdrop for a boy and a girl holding hands on a grassy knoll. Loud voices from below the knoll broke the silence and the ambiance of the setting. Kira and JD heard the taunts of several boys.

"Hey, isn't that Billy?" Kira said. "Who is he with? Is that Ben?"

"Let's go see."

"Who's your Negro friend, Billy?" a tall boy said. "Are you a Negro lover now? Are we going to have to beat that out of you?"

"He's my friend," Billy said. "Back off."

"Yeah, it's three against you and your little friend."

"Make that three against three," JD said. "You heard what he said. Back off!"

Kira stepped up. "Make it three against four."

"Hahaha, a girl, a Negro and two wimps. That doesn't add up to four to me."

Kira walked up to the tall boy eye to eye, "My friend said to back off. I suggest you do that now."

The tall boy pushed Kira aside to the ground. "I'm not fighting no girl, and no one tells me to back off."

JD stepped up and said, "No one touches my girl!"

The tall boy grabbed JD by the collar. "Shut up, punk, or I will shut you up."

JD kneed the tall boy in the groin. The tall boy crumbled to the ground in agony.

"You were warned," Kira said as the tall boy slumped to the ground.

Billy and Ben stepped forward as the other two boys approached.

"I think it's time for you boys to go home to mamma," Billy said. "And take this piece of trash with you."

Billy turned to JD. "Wow, where did that come from?"

"I don't know, it just happened," JD said.

Kira tugged on JD's arm. "Come on, hero, let's find your mom. Sorry, Billy and Ben, but JD and I are on a mission. Check you later?"

"Yeah, sure," Billy said.

JD turned and looked at Ben. Ben smiled back at JD. "Go on, you've been summoned by a higher power."

JD looked at Kira. She had dirt on her hands and some on her dress. "Are you alright? I'm sorry about that. Those were some of the kids Billy hangs out with at school. They are all bullies."

"I'm okay. I need to wash up a bit, but I'm fine. You did good back there. My handsome hero!"

JD blushed. "There are restrooms just inside the community center entrance. You can wash up there."

"And then we need to find your Mom. I still want that dance."

JD and Kira found his mother chatting with friends at one of the tables. She was smiling and laughing. A happy mother is the best kind when you need her approval. Uncle Joe walked up, still using the cane. He carefully delivered some punch to JD's mom. Kira's mom was helping him bring along some dessert.

"Hey, Sport, you two having fun on your date?" Uncle Joe said.

"I sure am," Kira said. "I got flowers, lost at horseshoes, saw fireworks, and now I'm hoping to…"

"Mom, is it okay if Kira and I dance?" JD interrupted.

JD's mother looked over at her fellow Baptist friends, who frowned. Uncle Joe tapped her foot with his cane, looking at her with a raised eyebrow.

"I guess, given the recent circumstances, a few friendly dances would be okay. Oh, and tomorrow evening, Uncle Joe and Aunt Sheila are coming for dinner. You two need to present your final plan for your, uhm, your trek to the canyon and the waterfall."

Kira and JD looked at each other with smiles. "Yes, ma'am, we will!"

JD smiled back at his mother and Uncle Joe as Kira pulled him to the dance floor.

"I have to warn you," JD said. "I don't know how to dance."

"Don't worry, just listen to the music, relax, and move to the beat. I'll show you. Remember the moves I showed you before."

"But what about the slow dancing? You didn't show me that. I'll probably step on your feet."

"Put your right hand around my waist, hold my right hand with your left hand, and pull me close. I'll put my head on your shoulder. You just shuffle your feet."

"Oh, I don't think Mom would like that."

"We'll go over on the other side of the dance floor. No one's going to see. Trust me, I won't embarrass you. You do want your date to have fun, right?"

"Yeah, but I don't know."

Kira pulled JD through the dance crowd. "You think too much, come on."

JD followed Kira's instructions. The music slowed. Kira pulled JD's arm around her waist, leaned in, and rested her head on his shoulder. He was now physically closer to a girl than he had ever been. He smelled her shampoo and felt her body against his. It was a new sensation, and he liked it.

"We're going back to the canyon," Kira whispered. "We've got planning to do. I'll come over to your house tomorrow after chores and schoolwork."

JD didn't answer. He just pulled Kira closer.

CANYON PLAN

After dinner the next day, Kira and JD presented their plan to JD's mom, Aunt Sheila, and Uncle Joe. They planned to repeat what they had done before, but head straight for the trail up the side of the hill and then down into the canyon.

"Your mother and I are okay with your plan, but we have one small change."

"Okay, what change?" JD said.

"Your Uncle is coming with you."

"What? Why? This is supposed to be a trek with me and Kira. No offense, Uncle Joe, but we don't want a babysitter along."

"Settle down, Sport," Uncle Joe said. "I'm just following you two to the top of the canyon. Your mother is concerned you will be out of reach if something happens. Besides, I want to check out that grotto cave you found. And I have a surprise."

"A surprise!" Kira said. "What is it?"

"I ordered some walkie-talkies."

"Walkie what?" Kira said.

"They're radios that let you talk to each other, JD said. "Big ones were used in the war. Uncle Joe, those were huge. Are we going to have to lug that up the trail?"

"The ones I ordered are new. They're not toys but are small and compact. I'll be using them for work and the disaster response team. They use the new solid-state transistors. The range should be enough to reach the canyon and the crossing. Your mother and I will have one, and you two will take one with you into the canyon."

JD was always up for new tech toys. The money he got from selling his home-grown strawberries and watermelons went to acquiring new science stuff like his microscope and shortwave radio kit.

"Cool, can we try them out?"

"They should be delivered this Friday. We can test them this Saturday morning. Also, the weather forecast has to be rain- and storm-free. I have a friend in the state weather office. He'll keep me posted. Are you okay with the conditions?"

"I guess," JD said. "How late can we stay? Can we stay long enough to see the Milky Way? Please!"

"Your mother said you can stay down in the canyon until sunset, then you have to move to where I'll be camping. You can then camp with me until the next morning. You'll be able to see the Milky Way from my campsite at the top of the canyon. All of this depends on whether Kira's mom also approves. So, what do you say?"

Kira looked at JD. JD looked at Kira.

"We agree!" they both said.

Kira anxiously looked at her mom.

"I approve," Kira's mom said. "During the storm and the flood, you proved capable and ready. This will be another time to prove yourselves. Safety first. No funny business. Understood?"

"Understood!" Kira and JD said.

"Come on, JD, we've got more planning to do."

JD and Kira went to JD's room to plan their return trip to the canyon. This time, they would investigate the entire canyon and the waterfall. They had to be prepared.

"How about some music while we plan?" Kira said. "Can you find that station with the rock and roll music?"

"Sure, give me a sec."

JD turned on the shortwave radio. A series of beeps and static came through the speakers.

"That's not music. What is it?"

"Sorry, it's Morse Code. I've been practicing reading it, because I want to pass the exam for my ham radio license."

"Okay, don't freak out, but that is nerdy."

"Yeah, I know, but I want to do it. My granddad was a radio operator in the Army. He's the one who got me interested in electronics. He got me this Morse Code learning kit, but it's harder than I expected."

"How does it work?"

"Do you really want to know, or are you just teasing me?"

"No, I really want to know. I might be a girl, but I can be just as nerdy as you."

JD grinned and grabbed the book. "I like that. Ok, so the tones represent dots and dashes. Letters are composed of these dots and dashes. Like the letter A is dot-dash. Dot-dot-dot-dash dash-dash-dot-dot-dot is SOS."

"You mean the 'we need help' signal."

"Yeah, something like that."

"Can I see that code chart?"

"Sure, what are you going to do?"

"You'll see."

Kira used the code chart and wrote a series of dots and dashes.

"What's that?"

"Decode it and you'll see."

JD took the code chart and carefully decoded the message. It read, "Bug Girl to Nerd Boy."

"Wow! I'm impressed. You figured that out fast."

"I get it, and I know you will get it," Kira said. "Hey, we'll probably need something more than a blanket if we are going to camp all night with Uncle Joe."

"We have plenty of sleeping bags. We have the two we used the other night."

"Ooh, cozy. I like the sound of that."

"Hopefully, we won't have any clouds so that we can observe the Milky Way and other stars."

"Under the stars. Yes, please!"

Kira smiled at JD as he kept listing everything they might need. "I don't want this summer to end. I don't want to go back to New Zealand. Remember the day you almost hit Grandma Sullivan's car? When I saw you looking back at me is when the best summer of my life began. I met Nerd Boy, and I want to stay with him."

JD touched Kira's arm. "I don't want you to go either. When you beat me to the park that day and said you wanted to go exploring is when the best time of my life began. I have never met anyone as cool as you, Bug Girl."

"Enough soppiness, or I will start crying," Kira said. "We need to keep making the list."

"Right, agreed. Suntan lotion! we can't forget the suntan lotion. My mom will add it if we don't include it. Hmm...I think that's everything. Do you have any suggestions?"

"What about swimsuits, a towel, and a change of clothes?" Kira said, still smiling at JD.

"Right, clever idea! I wish we could build a fire and roast marshmallows, but my mom won't allow that."

"That sounds heavenly. We can ask. The worst your mum could say is no. Come on, let's go ask."

JD looked up at Kira as she walked to the door. He never expected to feel this way about a girl and did not understand his feelings. He did not want Kira to go back to New Zealand. He wanted "Bug Girl" to stay here with him. He wanted to spend his high school days with this Kiwi.

"Coming," JD said with the list in hand.

In the living room, JD presented their plan to the adults. "We have our plan, but we have a question."

Kira blurted out, "We want to have a campfire."

"Oh, I don't know about that," JD's mom said. "What if it got out of hand and spread to the entire canyon?"

"Susan, I seemed to remember lots of campfires at the canyon when we were young," Kira's mom said.

"When JD goes to 4-H camp, they have a campfire," Uncle Joe said. "They are taught how to create one without matches. And they have to pass a fire safety lesson. If they create one near the water on one of the beaches..."

"There are beaches?" Kira exclaimed.

"Oops, spoilers," Uncle Joe said.

"Alright, alright, I am okay with the campfire on the beach by the water. But Uncle Joe will give both of you a refresher on fire safety and first aid. He can do it this weekend during the walkie-talkie demonstration. I will be there, so I'll ensure it's done."

"Thanks, Mom!" JD said.

"This Saturday is the current plan," JD's mom said. "Is that going to work for everyone? I'll come with everyone as far as the low-water crossing. Remember, Uncle Joe will camp out at the top close by. We can do the briefing and try the walkie-talkies at the crossing."

"I'm in," Kira said. "I have class in the morning at the university. Thursday, I will work on my studies. Friday, I will study for my exam on Monday. Yeah, that should work for me!"

"Fine by me," JD said. "Probably best if we do it sooner rather than later."

Uncle Joe added. "I'll have the weather report tomorrow and know if this weekend forecast is rain-free."

Kira's mother smiled at JD's mother and glanced at Uncle Joe. "Bring back any memories? I wish I were going too."

"Yes, it does," JD's mom said, smiling back. "Lots of fun times. I wish David were here. You would have to restrain him to keep him from going."

"The Four Amigos did have some fun adventures," Uncle Joe said. "Now these two can create some more."

"Agreed," Kira's mom said, smiling at Uncle Joe.

BACK AT THE CANYON

Saturday morning did not come soon enough for JD. He daydreamed through his chores. While plowing, he almost destroyed the back pasture fence, getting the pasture ready for fall planting. Uncle Joe called Friday morning with the weather report. No rain and mild temperatures in the forecast meant a green light.

His mother fixed breakfast and did an inventory of JD's backpack to make sure he had not forgotten anything. JD rushed through breakfast and scanned his list. The honk of Uncle Joe's car horn was the starting signal for what he imagined would be the adventure of his life. He hoped that, at the beginning of the summer, he would be going to the canyon, but he did not expect it to be with a girl.

"Did you check your list, Sport?" Uncle Joe said.

"Several times over. I got the essentials in my backpack."

"Let's pack it all in the back and pick up Kira. Susan, you can ride up front with me. Here's your walkie-talkie."

Kira and her mother were waiting on the porch as Uncle Joe drove up. Kira's mom approached Uncle Joe's side and asked, "Do you mind if I ride along?"

"Not at all," Uncle Joe said with a smile. "It will be like old times. Hop in the back with the two amigos. You can help Susan with the test of the walkie-talkie."

Only one person was missing from the original Four Amigos: JD's dad. JD sat looking out the window, remembering his granddad's stories about his dad. Now he was on his way to creating new stories. He wondered if he would tell his kids about this day.

At the crossing, Uncle Joe told everyone how to use the walkie-talkies. "Okay, everyone, please listen up. These are not toys. We got them for the county disaster response team, so please take care of them or my...well, you know. The first thing to do is turn the unit on. I have set them all to use the same channel. The unit is in standby mode until you press the talk button. You can receive but not talk until you press the talk button. These units are rated for several miles, and the battery should last overnight in standby mode. Does everyone follow me so far?"

"Roger that," Kira said while everyone else nodded yes.

Uncle Joe held up the walkie-talkie and pointed to the talk button. "When you press to talk, wait a second, then talk. After you talk, say 'over.' That lets the other person know you're finished speaking. It prevents talking over each other. Your unit cannot send and receive at the same time."

"Press to talk, wait, talk, say 'over,' got it," JD said.

"Alright, Kira and JD. Get your gear ready. Follow the same procedure as before. I'll take the rear."

"Watch your footing, Uncle Joe," Kira said, grinning. "We don't want a repeat showing of your falling."

"Hahaha, you and me both."

211

JD and Kira got hugs from their moms. Kira's mom hugged Uncle Joe and said, "Be safe and watch over them."

"I will. I promise."

The water level was back to where it was before the flood. The flood had carried debris downriver, collecting it into piles and dumping it along the riverbanks. The muddy flood waters were gone, replaced by clear spring water. Only a few puffy white clouds floated across the mostly clear sky. Kira and JD had pulled a perfect day for their adventure. With a moonless and cloudless night sky, a brilliant starry show was on the schedule.

The two moms waved as the three floated their inner tubes upriver to the island.

"How about you and I go to town?" Kira's mom said. "We can do some shopping and then have lunch."

"Sounds wonderful. I love that idea. Let's go as soon as I do the test with Joe."

Uncle Joe, Kira, and JD made it to the island's tip without incident. The flood had eroded the end of the island, allowing an easy landing. After a successful check to ensure the walkie-talkie was in range of the island, the two took Uncle Joe down to the cave.

"Wow, that's a lot of harvestmen. I remember this location. Sometimes, we camped here, but I don't remember it being inhabited with hundreds of these."

"Do you think it was used as a flint factory?" JD said.

"Maybe, I'll ask Kele. His tribe might know. Listen, this was not my idea, but I have to follow you into the canyon and see how you get down. This is just a precaution in case the walkie-talkies don't work, and I need to come help you for whatever reason."

"That's super," Kira said. "I want to know if it has changed since the Four Amigos explored it.

JD frowned. "Fine, but I feel like Mom still doesn't trust me. I'll be a freshman in high school. I plow, feed the livestock, and even bale the hay. Why doesn't she trust me to find a spot to set up camp?"

"Look, Sport, I understand. But that's how it has to be. We can test the walkie-talkies after I know where you will camp out. I will set up camp where I can be in contact with the crossing and where you guys will be. I am going to alter the agreement slightly. You guys can camp out down in the canyon. I will be nearby and within reach of the walkie-talkies. Don't you even hint to your moms about this!"

Kira and JD's eyes opened wide, and they shouted. "Wow! Thanks, Uncle Joe!"

Kira pulled her finger across her lips. "Our lips are sealed! Right, JD?"

"I agree, but what happens if the walkie-talkies don't work?" JD said.

"Well, it will be our secret, okay? I'm counting on you two being able to get help if you need it. But you two need to behave. It's my butt on the line too. No hanky-panky, got it?"

"No worries, I'll make sure JD behaves." Kira grinned.

Uncle Joe turned and winked at Kira. "It's not just JD I am worried about."

JD didn't catch Uncle Joe's wink at Kira. "Alright, it would be cool to know what you think about the canyon now."

"Well, let's press on," Uncle Joe said. "I'm excited to find out what it's like now."

The three walked through the shallows to the pond before the cave-in. The flood had piled some debris against the left side of the cave-in, but the pond was clear, with clean sand around it.

"Wow, lots of memories," Uncle Joe said. "This pond in front is new. It was shallow here, but I don't remember this pond in front. And I don't even remember water gushing out between the rocks. Back then, a trickle came through under the rocks and through the tunnel, but not like this waterfall."

JD pointed to the rocks on the right side. "Is that where the cave-in was?"

"Yes, but this is all different. Back when we came, it was more like a tunnel. If we crouched down, the tunnel was wide enough to squeeze through into the canyon. Flash flooding widened the opening and then weakened the rocks. We never thought about that. We just wanted to go back in the canyon to explore. We had made a fort inside near the waterfall. We imagined that the canyon was a magical land hidden from everyone else. Only the Four Amigos could visit the canyon. We were the lords of the canyon and masters of the waterfall."

Uncle Joe stood there, looking at the slabs of rock piled up on the right side of the opening. He didn't say anything for several minutes.

"Uncle Joe, are you okay?" JD said.

Uncle Joe didn't respond. Kira walked up and tapped him on the shoulder. "Uncle Joe, it was long ago. It wasn't your fault. You just acted on instinct."

"What? Yeah, yeah, right. You know, I can still hear the screams. I can still see the blood flowing out of my toe and ankle. So many happy times then that one incident. The four amigos were done. We never came back. We never went exploring again. Everything changed. It was like our childhood ended that day. We had to grow up. I wonder what would have happened if... Well, enough of that soppiness. Come on, let's check out the canyon. Lead the way."

"The path we found is over there, up along the side, just on the right side. It's steep; will you be able to walk it? What about your ankle?"

"Don't worry, my ankle is fine. So is my knee. And I have my walking stick."

"We'll go slow," Kira said.

"Thanks, the going up shouldn't be a problem."

At the top of the trail by the entrance to the canyon, Uncle Joe stood and looked out over the valley below. "This is an incredible view. We never came up here. I can see the crossing from here. I think I will camp here right by this sturdy oak."

Kira stood next to Uncle Joe, feeling the breeze against her face. "I fell in love with this spot when we came up before. It would be a wonderful spot for a house with the front porch in view of the valley below."

"I agree. It's too bad we four amigos missed it before. Let's press on to the trail down."

After a short hike, everyone stood by the pool at the top of the waterfall. The stream from the spring was flowing much faster, and the sound of the waterfall nearly drowned out any attempt to speak.

"Wow, the pool is twice the size now," JD said.

"I wouldn't know," Uncle Joe said. "We never came up here. This is all new to me. I have seen it from the aerial photos, but never in person. Where's the path down? I want to check out the waterfall."

"Over here," JD said. "It's a bit rough and rocky going down."

The trail down was eroded even more. The excessive rain had cut deeper grooves in the trail, leaving pieces of rock littering the trail.

"Wow, the trail looks rough," Uncle Joe said.

Kira looked at Uncle Joe. "Do you need help? We'll help. Won't we, JD?"

"Sure, right, we'll go slow."

"I'm fine. Stop treating me like an old man. The knee is fine and so is the ankle."

After a slow and careful trek down the trail, the three stood at the bottom, staring at the waterfall.

"That's not how I remember it," Uncle Joe said. "There's more water and lots more green. Our fort was right here by this tree, but it's gone–probably washed away long ago."

Water cascaded over the cliff above in several locations. A major part of the waterfall hit the moss-covered boulders below, then stair-stepped down over more rocks to a large pool below. On one side, water spray showered down over mounds of green moss. The mid-morning sun cast a bluish-purple shade through the spray.

"Wow, just wow," Kira said. "We only saw part of the waterfall through the trees before. This is fantastic. It's magical. It's so tall. How tall do you think it is?"

Uncle Joe walked around the pool and looked up. "I'm guessing it's sixty or more feet from the top to the pool here. It's amazing how it seems so much bigger now."

Kira kept asking questions. JD stood there, surveying everything. He felt his heart beating faster. His dream had come true; beyond anything he could have imagined. He walked over to the sandy beach along the pool below. A few rocks formed an open alcove.

"What about here for the camp?" JD said as he peered down into the clear pool of water. "There's no dead vegetation near the beach. We can build a fire pit in the sand. Uncle Joe, what do you think?"

Memories flooded through Uncle Joe's brain. He stood staring at the waterfall, thinking about when his world was less complicated yet filled with many more emotions. The details didn't come to mind, but the feelings did.

"Uncle Joe, are you crying?" Kira said.

"What? No, I think I got some sand in my eyes or the spray. Yeah, I think it was the spray. Okay, yes, JD, I approve of the campsite. We still need to figure out if it's within the range of walkie-talkies. Even if it isn't, I am certain it is at the top by the spring. It definitely should reach from there. Keep the unit on standby and the volume high."

"Roger that," JD said. "Do you need help getting back?"

"I can make it okay. There's no pain, and I will take it slow."

"Okay, we'll cross over, explore down the canyon, and come back up on this side."

"You two have fun. Make memories, but please be careful and behave. I don't want to experience the wrath of my sister."

"We will," Kira said. "I'm experienced in hiking places like this. I'll watch over JD."

"And I will take good care of Kira."

"I do have one more surprise for you two. Let me get it out of my backpack. Here…"

"Wow, it's a camp stove!" JD said.

"It's just a folding frame," Uncle Joe said. "You'll still need some small firewood, but it has a grill and hot plate on top. Oh, and this bag."

Kira peeked in the bag. "Marshmallows, graham crackers?"

"S'mores!" JD exclaimed. "Thank you, Uncle Joe!"

"What's a S'more?" Kira said.

"Oh, you will find out," JD said. "They're the best campfire food!"

Uncle Joe smiled. "Alright then. You guys are situated. I am going to head back."

Kira rushed over to Uncle Joe and hugged him. "Thank you so much!"

"You're welcome. JD, turn on your walkie-talkie. We can do a walkie-talkie test when I'm at the top."

"Already done and ready!"

At the top of the canyon, Uncle Joe transmitted his test message. "Uncle Joe to the two amigos, over."

"Two amigos here, over." JD responded.

"I'm receiving you loud and clear. One last thing: make memories that last a lifetime. I slipped a few things into JD's backpack that might help you remember. Over and out."

Kira grabbed the walkie-talkie. "Roger that, Uncle Joe, over and out."

JD looked in his backpack and pulled out a disposable camera, a notebook, and a pencil.

"You take the photos, and I will take notes," Kira said.

Exploring the Canyon

"What do you want to explore first?" JD said.

Kira crossed her arms and began to pull off her shirt.

"What are you doing?"

"I'm going for a dip in the pool. You can stand there staring or join me."

"But, but you're shirt. You're taking off your shirt!"

"Don't worry, I have my swimsuit under it."

"Right, me too," JD said as he pulled off his shirt and dropped his shorts.

Kira was already in the water, smiling at JD.

"Is the water cold?" JD said.

"It's perfect, come on, slowpoke."

JD inched into the water. Kira waded over and offered her hand. He took the offer. Kira pulled, and JD went head-first into the pool, sinking beneath the surface. Kira expected he would come up right away, but he didn't. Expectation turned to concern. Concern turned to fright. Kira dipped below the surface. She was face to face with a huge grin on JD's face.

"Gotcha!" JD said as they both popped up.

Kira splashed JD. "Don't do that. That scared me!"

"You're the one who pulled me in."

Kira laughed. "Yeah, that was funny. You nearly did a flip."

"I figured you were going to do that."

"Oh no, you didn't. I saw the surprised look as you planted your face on the water."

The two laughed as they dog-paddled in the deep part of the pool. Kira looked around to take in the view. Light splashed against the drops of water flying off the rocks below the waterfall. A green blanket of moss, bushes, and trees covered the rocks below, creating a jungle-like appearance. Birds flew above. A few stray clouds chased the sun to create momentary shade below.

Kira looked at JD. "I love this so much. Thank you for bringing me here."

"Thank you for helping me get here. I dreamed of coming here for years. It's totally awesome."

JD turned to survey the far end of the canyon. "Hey, the water is going down to a pool below this one. Let's check it out."

"Right behind you."

On the far side of the pool, water had found a weak spot in the rock, creating a smooth channel to a pool below.

"This is like a water slide," JD said. "Wanna give it a go?"

"You first."

JD positioned his body on the slide. He wiggled and inched his way forward until gravity took over. Kira smiled as he wiggled and inched his body.

JD landed with a splash in the pool below. "Come on, it's easy. Just put your body in the right position and inch forward."

Kira slid down and floated into JD's waiting arms. The two were face to face. JD looked into Kira's eyes, then felt her lips on his. He could feel her body close to his. JD closed his eyes. He wanted to stay in that moment forever. He opened his eyes to a smile on Kira's face. Her eyes were bright and wide open.

"Hello, Nerd Boy," Kira whispered.

"Hello, Bug Girl."

JD smiled and pulled her closer to kiss her again. They both wanted to stay in that moment, but they began to sink into the pool. They smiled at each other as they got lower in the water.

"That was nice."

"Yes, it was."

Kira felt something nibble on her leg. She pulled back. "Something's nibbling on my leg!"

JD looked down into the clear water of the pool. "Probably fish again. I can see them. Don't worry, they're not flesh-eating piranhas, only common perch. They're just looking for food or trying to get you to leave."

Kira looked down at the fish swimming around her legs. "Thank God they aren't people eaters. Where to next? Is there more to explore?"

"Let's just follow the water down the canyon."

Kira climbed out of the pool and offered JD a hand up. Predictably, JD pulled Kira back into the pool for another kiss.

"That's enough, Kissy Face," Kira said, smiling. "I want to, but remember, I promised Uncle Joe. Time to explore. Let's go."

"Yeah, okay, you're right."

Kira pulled on JD's arm. "I saw something blue down below before you pulled me back in. I want to check it out."

"Blue? Like a flower?"

"Yeah. Come on, there's a narrow trail down."

"Let me go grab the camera and the backpack first."

"Hurry up, there's so much to see!"

The canyon narrowed as it sloped down. The pools of water stretched out, connecting like a wide creek. Sometimes the water split around a pile of rocks exposing small sandy islands in the creek. A patch of blue flowers dotted the end of the island below the pool.

"Those are bluebells," JD said as he approached the patch of blue. "You can find them down by the creek by my house. I did not expect to find any here."

Bees were visiting the flowers on the bluebell plants. Kira kneeled, held out her hand, and whispered something. One bee flew up from a flower and landed on Kira's outstretched hand. Other bees followed.

"Wow, how are you doing that?" JD said.

"Doing what?"

"Letting bees land on your hand. Aren't you afraid of getting stung?"

"No, I have a secret to tell you. This is one way to show you. I can communicate with certain animals, especially insects. It is something my grandmother showed me. Her people have had this ability for thousands of years."

"So, you speak bee?"

"No, silly, bees don't have a language like humans, but they understand certain sounds. The sounds are like a language without words. I don't understand how it works. I just know how to do it."

"That's like some magic! What else can you do?"

"Grandmother was teaching me more, but she got ill. My mum knows some stuff too. Remember that time in the barn with the lamb?"

"Yeah, you were upset, but you wouldn't tell me what was wrong."

"I asked the lamb to wake up, and it did not. I thought I could keep it from dying. But it died. I did not understand why I failed."

"My mom keeps telling me these stories about Jesus healing people and raising this guy from the dead. Sounds like fairy tales to me. I don't understand why people believe that stuff. Something like that can be explained with science, or it just is made up."

"Really? Then explain this to me."

Kira spoke a few words in a language JD had never heard before, then held out both arms straight out. A butterfly appeared on one arm, then another on the other arm. More butterflies came. Soon, butterflies covered both of her arms.

Kira pointed to one of the butterflies, and it stopped in mid-air. "And how about this?"

"Wow! I can't explain that, but I believe you are Bug Girl! Can I take a picture?"

Kira laughed. "Sure, just don't spread it around."

"What else can you do?"

"A few other things. But that's not important right now. I'm not supposed to talk about it. Pride kills the ability."

Kira looked down. "Wow, are those catfish?"

JD looked down into the clear water between the rocks and saw the protruding whiskers as the catfish tried to hide.

"Yep, are there catfish in New Zealand?"

"Not native ones. They are found in some lakes, but I have never seen one."

"Some try to catch them with their bare hands," JD said.

"Just looking at them, that sounds dangerous."

"I tried it once and got stuck by those fins in front. I prefer using a fishing rod but getting them off the hook is tricky."

"Have you eaten catfish?"

"Yeah, I don't much like it. Has a real fishy taste. I have caught, cleaned, and fried perch before. They taste better, but they have way more bones."

"Let's keep going and see what else we can find."

Kira and JD approached the fallen rocks at the end of the canyon. The creek slowed and backed up into another pool with a sandy beach. Tall trees shaded both sides of the pool, and the water had cut channels through the fallen rocks.

"I'm a bit peckish," Kira said. "How about we stop for a snack? I don't suppose you brought any?"

"Sticky buns? Yep, I did."

"Choice! Let's break out those bad boys."

Kira and JD sat on the sandy beach under one of the trees. A gentle warm breeze flowed through the leaves, and sunlight danced through them. The sounds of birds competed with the gurgling of the water lapping on the sandy beach.

"This is heavenly," Kira said. "A warm breeze. I love the sound of water flowing over the rocks. Birds singing. I could stay here forever. This is where my soul can live forever."

"And shade from a tree," JD said. "I could take a nap here. In all the times I dreamed of coming here, I never imagined it would be a tropical paradise. When my granddad brought me to the rim above, trees blocked most of the view of the canyon. He told me the trees were a species of maple trees left here after the last ice age. They should turn color in the fall."

"I would love to be here when that happens."

"When do you have to go back to New Zealand?"

"When Nana gets better, I guess. My mum said we would stay as long as she needed us. She talked about staying and not going back."

"I hope she gets well, but I hope you can stay. You know, I saw you and your mom drive into Grandma Sullivan's."

"I know," Kira said. You almost ran into the car."

"I was, uhm…thinking about what I had to get at the store."

"What did you think when you saw me?"

"I uhm…uh…truth?"

"Always."

"Remember, I told you I wasn't happy to have another girl around. When I saw you, I wished you were a boy and not another girl. I wasn't happy when my mom said I had to show you around all summer."

"You're happy now, right?"

"Yes, I am happy you came. I feel different around you. I like being with you. I like you. I have never felt this way about anyone before. I uh, uhm…uh…can I ask you something?"

"Anything."

"Well, I was thinking since we like to do stuff together. I like you and...Well, I think you like me. Well, uh...Well, I wanted to know if you wanted to be?"

"Your girlfriend?"

"Yes, but we could just be best buds if that's what you would rather do."

Kira pulled JD close, face-to-face, and kissed him. "I'd rather be your girlfriend."

"Sweet as!"

"Hahaha, too funny. What took you so long to ask? I kept throwing out hints."

"Well, I'm not that good with girls."

"I noticed. No worries, I'll teach you. You teach me nerdy science stuff, and I will teach you how to be with a girl. Lesson one, help me up, we've got more exploring to do on the way back."

"My pleasure, ma'am."

Kira smiled. "Quick learner. Lesson two will be on kissing."

"What's wrong with my kissing?"

Kira grinned. "Nothing really. I have a few tips."

"Oh, okay. I am always willing to learn."

"And I am eager to teach."

The still water in the pond created a glass-like mirror effect. JD pointed to a spot in the pond near the edge. "Wait, come over here. What do you see?"

Kira saw their reflection in the still water. "It's us. Choice. Take a picture."

"Okay, it will be the first photograph of us as boy-friend and girlfriend."

"And we took it ourselves."

Kira and JD spent the rest of their afternoon steadily making their way back to the waterfall. They stopped often to examine rocks and plants. At one point, something scooted out from a bush.

"What was that?" Kia said.

"Looked like a roadrunner."

"Like the cartoon?"

"Yes! The roadrunner is the iconic bird of Texas."

"Cool, I love the cartoon."

Kira and JD walked on, talking as they went. They were just two kids getting to know each other and the world around them.

"Does Texas have a state flower?" Kira said. "I hope it's the sunflower."

"The bluebonnet is the state flower of Texas. Remember that meadow by the creek? The one with the sunflowers?"

"Yes, I loved that morning. You did well then. And then you remembered and brought me sunflowers for the 4th of July celebration. That was sweet. That was when I started wanting to be your girlfriend."

JD paused, trying not to blush. "My mother wishes the meadow were covered with bluebonnets instead of sunflowers. She loves bluebonnets."

"I love the sunflowers, but I bet the bluebonnets are lovely too."

"I'm not much into flowers. My mother is. She planted some bluebonnets in her flower garden. I do think it is interesting that I only find bees pollinating bluebonnets. I guess it makes sense. The bluebonnet flowers are shaped to make it easier for bees to pollinate them."

"Bees and bluebonnets are made for each other, then."

"You sound like my mom. She doesn't accept that species have evolved to be what each other needs. She believes God created it all like it says in Genesis."

"You don't believe in God then?"

"I don't know. I prefer to review the evidence and let the evidence lead me to a conclusion. Science is based on facts. A belief in God is based on faith without facts."

"Ah, that is why you were not impressed with my calling the butterflies. You don't believe something until you prove it with facts?"

"I thought it was cool and interesting, but there's probably an explanation. I need to experience it, then collect the facts."

"Do you believe New Zealand exists? I mean, you haven't been there. You have not gathered any facts about it."

"Yeah, okay. But that's different. I read about it. Others have seen it. I observe you, and for me, that's enough. I like being with you."

"Hahaha, good save, I like being with you, Nerd Boy. I like that we can explore together. I like that we can talk about anything."

"That's the thing I like the most, talking about anything. I know I am a nerd. I like other stuff, like sports, but I love exploring new things. You're the first person who likes to do that, too. I can talk to you about it and other stuff too."

Kira stopped walking, turned to face JD, and said, "You can tell me anything. I don't want to be your girlfriend only. I want to be your best friend, and you be mine."

"I want that too."

"Remember, I chose to come here to meet the nerdy kid from Texas. You be you. Come on, Nerd Boy, we need to set up camp for the night."

JD glanced up at the sky. "We're going to have a clear night. The moon will set early. We might even see the Milky Way."

"That'll be way cool. I'm so excited. I can't wait, but I don't want to miss a thing. Wait, what's that by those round flowers?"

JD stooped down to get a closer look. "That's a horny toad. Technically not a toad, but a lizard."

"They're super cute. And do you know what the flower is?"

"I'm not an expert on wildflowers, but this plant is called 'touch me not.' Touch the leaves. Don't worry, it won't sting you or anything."

Kira reached down and touched the leaves of the plant. "They curl up! That's weird and so cool. I love it!"

"Let's head back to the waterfall. I think we are going to see the stars tonight."

A STARRY NIGHT

Back at the pond below the waterfall, JD pulled out the folding frame from his backpack. "I'm setting up the camp stove. We're going to need some small firewood. Can you look around that tree for dead branches and dried leaves? And we'll need two straight twigs for the S'mores."

"I'm on it. This is like we are two survivors on a deserted island – like Robinson Crusoe."

JD had a look of surprise on his face.

Don't be so surprised. I do read books too."

"Or Swiss Family Robinson!" JD said. "I loved that movie."

"That's even better. I'm Roberta, of course."

"I guess I'm Fritz, because I want to stay here with you."

"That's sweet. And I choose to be with you. I think you are a mix of Francis and Fritz. Strong, brave, but curious about everything."

JD smiled. "I like that."

Kira searched around the tree looking for firewood. Behind the tree, hidden by some vines, was the opening to a cave. "JD, come here. I found a cave."

"What? Where?"

"Some vines hid it behind this tree."

Kira remembered what Uncle Joe's intern, Kele, had told them about the waterfall. She remembered what her grandmother said about waterfalls being doors to other worlds. Her grandmother said she had to show JD. She knew what she had to do: She had to take JD on a dream walk. Kira went over the word sequence needed to invoke the dream walk. Kira walked over and took JD's hand. "Come here, I want to share something with you."

"Okay. What?"

JD and Kira stood at the opening of the cave.

"Wow, there's a cave! Remember what Kele said? Let's explore it. I don't believe in ghosts, but maybe the outlaws left something behind when they abandoned the canyon."

"Remember what my grandmother said about waterfalls being doorways to other worlds. This could be the door."

"It's just a cave. I don't believe those stories about doors to other worlds. That's just not possible. Are you scared like the outlaws and Kele's tribe?"

"I'm not scared. I know something you don't know. I can show you if you stop being a nerd and open your mind."

"Okay, okay. Show me."

"Here's the thing, you can't tell anyone about this ever," Kira warned. "You physically will not be able to do it. It has to be a secret between you and me. Only I can make you recall it."

"I don't get it. How do I know if I don't remember? What?"

"Answer me. Are you okay with that?"

"Yeah, sure, I guess."

"Come over here and sit down facing me. Hold my hands."

JD smiled. "I like this part."

"No talking please. Now, close your eyes and clear your mind.

Kira held JD's hands and spoke a few words in the same strange language she used before.

Flashes of light and sounds rushed in. JD opened his eyes. Everything around him was fuzzy and blurry, like in a dream. Kira led JD through the cave below the waterfall. The cave led to a dark tunnel. The tunnel opened to a narrow ledge. JD found himself standing on the edge of a cliff looking out over a steep valley below. He stood next to Kira. Roaring water rushed over a protruding rock above them, splitting the water as it fell. A mist fell over them as they looked over the cliff. Below was a horseshoe-shaped valley surrounding a large body of water. Several other waterfalls flowed down the sides of the valley to the water below. JD felt sick, like he was going to throw up. The noise from the waterfall made it impossible to hear anyone speak. Kira pulled JD close, leaned over, and spoke into his ear. "Steady on there, I said it could be unsettling. I got you; I won't let go."

"I think I'm going to be sick," JD said.

And he was. Whatever was in his stomach was now headed down the side of the cliff.

"What you are experiencing right now is not real," Kira said. "You are in a dream walk. It's the closest thing to being here without actually being here. You can see, hear, smell, and feel like you are here."

"What am I seeing?"

"Kira pointed across the valley to the other side. "This is the eternal home of my people."

"Can we go down? I want to see more."

"Not this time. We will come back, and I will show you more then. Now you must wake up."

Kira spoke a few words and waved her hand over JD's head.

JD opened his eyes. "What was that?"

"What was what?"

"I can't describe it. It was like a weird light show, and I thought I was standing under a waterfall."

"What else did you see?"

"I'm trying to remember. It's like a dream fading."

"I took you on a dream walk. I shared with you the memory of a future event and put that memory in your brain. That memory is now like a dream you want to remember, but you can't. JD, listen to me, a storm is coming."

"What? Another storm? What are you talking about?"

"A storm is coming, unlike any before or ever will be. You and I are key players in this future struggle. I can't tell you more because I don't know anymore. But this I know. You and I were destined to be together, but powerful forces are trying to keep us apart. You are their main target. I don't know why."

"That is just freaky weird. How do you know this? How did you do that? What did you call it? A dream walk?"

"Nana's ancestors, and so my ancestors, are descendants from a race of people with supernatural abilities; some I have already shown you. I just took you on what is called a dream walk. I showed you something that will happen. Our connection is important. These powerful forces want to break that connection. Soon you will be tested, and I won't be here to help you. You have to stay strong."

JD looked shocked. "Wait, what do you mean you won't be here?"

Kira did not answer. Instead, she looked down and pulled up a dead branch next to the tree, uncovering a small metal box. "Hey, I think I found the buried treasure!"

"What? Let me see. That's an old cigar tin like the one my granddad had. It's old and rusty. Maybe there's money or jewels in it. Let's open it up!"

"It's stuck shut. Do you have something to pry open the lid?"

"I have a screwdriver blade on my pocketknife."

After a few failed attempts, JD pried the lid open from the metal box. Inside, they found a necklace and several sealed envelopes wrapped in wax paper addressed from Uncle Joe to Kira's mom.

Kira looked at the envelopes in wonder. "Uncle Joe and my mum? What does that mean? Did he like my mom? This is news to me. Did Uncle Joe ever tell you?"

"Uncle Joe never mentioned anything about your mom to me. My mom and your mom were best friends, but she never mentioned anything about Uncle Joe liking your mom. They did go together for the 4th of July thing. Do you think they were on a date?"

"My mum didn't say anything about a date. She just said Uncle Joe was taking her, so there would be more room in the car for the pies and stuff. This box was buried under the tree. It was left here on purpose. This is a mystery. We need to ask Uncle Joe about this."

"It's a mystery, but it was a buried mystery," JD said. "I don't think Uncle Joe wanted anyone to find it. Let's put it back."

"Don't you want to know?"

"Yes, and no. Some things are best left buried. Have you never heard the story about Pandora's box?"

"Yes, I have. So, you don't think we should keep the box and give it to Uncle Joe? He probably forgot it was here."

"I think we should bury it under the tree and not mention we found it to anyone. It will be our secret."

"Really? Okay. I'll put it back. It will be our secret then. I also found some twigs and dried leaves for the campfire. Come on, start the fire, and show me what S'mores are."

"You're going to love them. I'm surprised you've never had them before. I also brought stuff for cheese sandwiches. We'll grill them on the camp stove."

"We call those toasties, and I love them!"

"Alright, let's start cooking."

JD started the fire, and Kira helped prepare the sandwiches for grilling. A boy and a girl made fire and cooked on a sandy beach below a sixty-foot waterfall. Neither of them noticed the sunset. Light from the fire revealed the fascination and happiness on their faces as they ate the food they had cooked.

"Alright, time for the S'mores," JD said. "Hand me the straight twigs."

JD cleaned and sharpened the ends of the two twigs. He handed one of the twigs to Kira. "Stick a marshmallow on the end and hold it over the embers. Rotate it a bit. The trick is to melt the inside with the outside brown without burning it."

Kira put the marshmallow over the embers and rotated it. "It's on fire! My marshmallow is on fire!"

JD laughed. "No worries, just pull it out and blow out the flames."

"Stop laughing. It's not funny. My marshmallow is all burned."

"Yeah, it is funny. Look, it happens all the time. Here, just carefully pinch the burned part and pull it off. Now, put the marshmallow on a graham cracker. Put a piece of chocolate and another graham cracker on top. Press down and pull out the stick. Then squeeze the crackers together and enjoy."

"Wow, this is heavenly. It's a biscuit with a gooey, soft chocolate inside."

"Biscuit?"

"Oh, yeah. In New Zealand, we call cookies, biscuits. This is so yummy! I want some more. Hey, I just got why they are called, S'mores!"

JD opened his thermos and poured out a cup for Kira. "Try this strawberry tea my mom made. She made the tea. I grew the strawberries."

"It's delicious. Nerd boy scores again!"

JD laughed. "I would have been upset about being called a nerd a month ago."

"And now?"

"From you, Bug Girl, I like it."

Kira laughed. "Hahaha, touché."

"Come on, let's lay out the sleeping bags. The stars should be out soon."

Kira and JD lay on the beach, looking at the night sky.

"Look at all those stars," Kira said. "How many do you think have planets with people like us?"

"I don't know. It would be fun to travel the stars. At one time, I wanted to be an astronaut."

"But you don't want to now?"

"I have so many things I want to do. I can't decide. I do want to travel."

"Maybe you'll come to New Zealand one day?"

"It's on my list."

JD fixed Kira another S'more. "What do you want to do after school?"

"Haven't given it much thought. When I was little, I wanted to be an actor, then a teacher. I even held class with my dolls. When Nana came last year, I got into the nature stuff. I think studying biology or botany would be nice. You probably want to study science stuff, right?"

"I like building stuff like that shortwave radio kit. The articles I read in the science magazines are interesting. I like lots of things. I especially like being here with you. I have friends at school, and the Johnson twins have been buds. You are different. I like being with you. I don't know how to say it."

"Say what?"

"Well, I've never felt like this with anyone before. I think about you when you are not with me. I enjoy stuff more when you are with me than when you aren't."

JD looked up at the stars. The Milky Way was rising. He saw Kira look up. The soft light from the campfire embers made her eyes and hair glow. He wanted to tell her how he felt. He mustered up the courage and started to say to her.

The walkie-talkie squelching interrupted JD. "Hey guys, can you hear me? Over."

"That's Uncle Joe," Kira said. "We'd better answer that."

JD was disappointed he didn't have a chance to tell Kira how he felt about her. He reached for the walkie-talkie. "You're right."

JD pressed the talk button. "What's up, Uncle Joe? Over."

"Sorry, but you two need to come up now. I'll tell you more when you're here. Be careful. Just leave the stuff there. We'll come back for it later."

"Is there a problem? Over."

"Just come, right now. Over."

"Okay, coming. Over."

JD put out the fire and picked up his flashlight. "I guess we have to go. Grab your hiking stick. I'll lead the way."

"No worries, I'm right behind you."

"Put your hand on my shoulder and just watch your step."

"Roger that."

After a slow and careful trek up, Kira and JD made it to Uncle Joe's camp.

THE CALL HOME

Uncle Joe was packed and waiting for them when they arrived. "Sorry to interrupt you guys, but it's important. I got a call on the walkie-talkie from Aunt Susan. Kira, your grandmother has been taken to the local hospital. Don't worry, she's okay. Aunt Susan is there, and the doctor is running a few tests."

"Let's go!" Kira said.

"Look, it's dark. This is not going to be easy. We'll follow the leader, okay? I'll lead. JD, you follow in the back. Take it slow and careful. We'll be fine."

All the negative thoughts about her grandmother's condition flooded out anything else. She just wanted to be with her grandmother and not at the top of a canyon. "Got it, please let's just go."

"I have another flashlight for you, Kira. JD, give me a check from the rear as we go. Let's go slow."

It was slow going down the path to the island. With flashlights and care, the three made it back to the crossing. During the ride to the hospital, Kira stared out the window silently. JD touched her hand. "It's going to be alright. My mom's great. She'll make sure your grandmother gets the best care."

Kira didn't respond. She knew this day would come, but knowing is not experiencing. She tried to think about the good times, but the thought of losing her grandmother would not go away. She wanted to be strong, and her grandmother would want that. At that moment, she did not feel strong.

JD's mother met them in the hospital's waiting room. "Kira, your grandmother is doing fine. She is stable right now. The doctor has requested some tests to be conducted in the city."

Kira's mother came out to the waiting room. "Kira, Nana has to have some tests done. I am going to take her early in the morning. You can stay over at Aunt Susan's tonight."

"No, I'm coming with you," Kira said.

Uncle Joe stepped up and touched Sheila's arm. "I will take you both. I know the city better than you. You're not going to do this by yourself. That's final."

Kira's mother hugged Uncle Joe. "Thank you. It would be so much better if you could help. Kira, Nana would like to speak with you."

Kira turned to JD. "I'll come visit you tomorrow. We can talk then."

JD hugged Kira. "Take care of you and your grandmother."

Later the next day, Kira biked over to JD's house. JD's mother answered the door.

"Good afternoon, Aunt Susan."

"How's your grandmother?"

"She's about the same. We just got back from the city."

"Are you okay?

"Not really, but I will be okay. I need to talk with JD."

"Sure, he's out back in the barn."

Kira found JD carrying the milk bucket to wash it out. "Hey, JD. Sorry to bother you. Can we talk?"

JD set the milk bucket down, walked to Kira, and hugged her. "Sure. How're you doing? How's Grandma Sullivan?"

"I'm okay. I spent the night at the hospital. I look like a mess and feel like one. Nana is okay. We just got back from the city."

JD took Kira's hand. "Let's take a walk to the meadow. We can talk there."

Kira and JD walked hand in hand down the path to the meadow. They sat together on the bluff overlooking the meadow below.

JD picked up a rock and tossed it over the bluff. "I love this view. It has so many wonderful memories attached to it. When my granddad and I would come here, he would go on and on with so many stories. I wish I had written them down."

"I love it too. I will always remember that morning with the moon setting and the sunrise. I feel...I feel anchored here. Like I'm supposed to be here. This is where I want to be. But I...I...I can't."

"What's the matter? I don't care what it is. You can share it with me. We're best friends, remember."

Tears filled Kira's eyes. She put her head down and sobbed. "I have to go back to New Zealand. I don't want to, but I have to."

"When? Why?"

"The specialist in the city confirmed what the doctor feared. Nana has cancer. It's spreading. They think she has a year at most."

"I'm sorry. You must be hurting. Why go back to New Zealand? Shouldn't she stay here and get treated?"

"Nana wants to go. She wants to go back to New Zealand. She doesn't want to die here. She's refused treatment."

"I don't want you to go. I want you to stay, but if it were my granddad, I would want to be with him as long as he was alive. You have to go. I'll still be here."

Kira's crying turned to bawling. Tears flowed down her cheeks. Her chest rose and fell.

"This is so hard. I feel like I am losing either way. I can't breathe. I hate crying."

JD offered Kira his handkerchief and put his arm around her. "Cry all you want. And you are not going to lose me."

Kira eventually settled down in JD's arms. She looked up at him. "You are my rock."

"I'll be here. We can write. I might even be able to arrange a HAM radio phone patch to you."

"A what?"

"There are ham radio operators you can call locally. They patch the call through to another operator, who patches the call to the other person through the telephone. I bet Uncle Joe knows someone."

"Nerd boy to the rescue again. I'm going to miss you so much."

"You're coming back from New Zealand, right?"

Kira placed her hand on JD's heart. "You must remember this. Sometimes, people don't come back, but they are never truly separated. Even though I am not with you in person, I will never truly leave you. Remember that."

"What are you talking about? You are coming back. We're going to go to high school together."

"That's what I want more than anything, but we don't always get what we want. Sometimes we have to wait."

A worried look came over JD's face. "Are you feeling okay? You're freaking me out."

Kira caressed JD's temple, whispered something, and kissed him softly. "Yeah, I'm fine."

JD instantly calmed down and looked back at Kira. "So, when do you have to leave?"

"In about ten days. Mum has to book the tickets. Nana wants to ensure the ranch is cared for, so she is meeting with the foreman."

"Hey, how about we get our bikes and go to the drugstore. I think you still owe me an ice cream float."

"Nice try. We had those already, remember? I remember seeing a theater in town. How about you take me to a movie?"

"You mean a date?"

"Well, I am your girlfriend."

"Okay, what do you want to see?"

"How about a comedy or a nerdy sci-fi flick? You pick."

"Are you sure you're up for a movie?"

"Yeah, there's nothing I can do right now. I want to be with Nerd Boy as long as I can. Besides, it will take my mind off stuff."

"I hope there's a movie about bugs."

"Or people shipwrecked on an island," Kira said. "So, what do you think our moms will say when we tell them we are girlfriend and boyfriend?"

"That will be more of a shock to my mother than yours. I don't think she wants me to meet anyone ever. So, it has to be dinner and a movie, huh?"

"What? You don't think I'm worth dinner and a movie?"

JD checked his pockets. "Hmm. How about lunch and a movie?"

"Works for me!"

THE BIG REVEAL

Everyone gathered at Grandma Sullivan's house the next morning for the news. Grandma Sullivan walked into the living room where everyone was seated quietly. "Feels like a funeral in here. Yes, I'm going to die. No surprise to me. We're all going to die at some point. I just happened to have a better idea about when."

"We're sad," Kira's mom said. "We have a right to be sad. We love you."

"Fine, be sad, but be sad somewhere else. I'm alive right now. I have living to do right now. And we've got planning to do. I'm going home and be buried with my ancestors."

"Mom, do you have to be so blunt and morbid? You're talking about you dying. I don't want to think about that."

"Yes, I do have to be blunt and to the point. This is my time to arrange everything. We'll be rushed and teary-eyed when the time comes to leave. We also need to call and purchase the airline tickets."

The Big Reveal

"I'm going to help with that," JD's mom said. "The doctor has cleared you for air travel. He wrote a medical urgency order to help you schedule a flight within two weeks."

"I can also help with the tickets," Uncle Joe said. "I have a friend who is an executive at one of the airlines at the airport in the city. I think I can arrange for a flight within 10 days."

Grandma Sullivan motioned to Uncle Joe to come into the parlor. She handed him an envelope and whispered. "This is a copy of my will. My lawyer in town is the executor of my estate. Go visit him. Don't say anything right now. Just smile and take the envelope."

Grandma Sullivan walked back into the living room. "Please, everyone, listen up. I want to go over a few things. JD, would you please take care of the house, lawn, and garden? You know what to do. Do you still have the spare key?"

JD glanced at his mom, who nodded yes. JD's sad eyes betrayed his emotions. "Yes, ma'am, I do. I will check on it every day."

Grandma Sullivan turned to JD and Kira. "Now tell me, have you two tied the knot yet?"

JD's mom stood up. Her shocked face said it all. "Grandma Sullivan! They're just kids! They're not old enough!"

"Good Lord, I'm not talking about them getting married. And you and Sheila can stop the charade. I know what you two had planned all along! But I suspect these two have something to announce, don't you, JD?"

"Well, uhm…we are…hmm…" JD stammered.

"We're boyfriend and girlfriend," Kira announced.

"Congratulations," Grandma Sullivan said.

Grandma Sullivan turned to JD. "What do you have planned for a celebration with my granddaughter?"

"JD is taking me to lunch, and then we are going to a movie."

"Poppycock, you two are going on a date, and I'm paying for it. I don't want to hear any objections."

"But I want to pay my own way," JD said. "I only have enough for lunch and a matinee."

"I think that's honorable that you want to pay your way. But this is my one and only granddaughter. Sheila, hand me my purse, please. Here's the money I owe you and Kira for the help with the lambs and other chores. Take it and give my granddaughter the date she deserves. Let's plan for tomorrow. That'll give everyone time enough to get all prettied up."

"Yes, ma'am. Thank you, ma'am." JD replied.

"There. Let that be an example to the rest of you amigos. That's how you answer the request of an old sick woman."

JD reached for Kira's hand. "Kira, would you go on a date with me?"

Kira smiled at JD. "Yes, please!"

"Kira, we need to go shopping," Kira's mom said. "What time should Kira be ready tomorrow?"

"How about five, I guess," JD's mom said. "I'll make the reservations at the café. The owner owes me a favor. I'll also call and check showtimes.:

Uncle Joe put his arm around JD. "You and I are going to take a trip to the clothing store and the barbershop."

"Why the barbershop? I just got a haircut."

"You'll see."

A Date to Remember

That afternoon, JD and Uncle Joe arrived back from their outing. JD's mom presented the bad news. "The theater is having a movie festival. They are showing reruns of old movies. Sorry, JD, but I don't think any of those movies would be something Kira would want to see."

"What are they showing?"

"Some movie about a shipwrecked family and an island with giant animals. I don't understand why the theater would even show such trash. My word!"

JD exclaimed. "Swiss Family Robinson! And Mysterious Island! That's brilliant! I'm calling Kira right now."

JD picked up the phone handset in the living room. The phone line to JD's house was on a party line. Someone could be using the phone when you wanted to make a call. "Mrs. Wilson, I'm sorry to interrupt your call. May I please make a call? It's important. Thanks."

JD placed a call to Grandma Sullivan's number. "Hello, Aunt Sheila? This is JD. May I speak with Kira? It's about tomorrow."

JD explained the situation to Kira. He held the phone receiver in one hand, and shouted, "Kira wants to go to both movies. Can we? We could go to the afternoon shows and have dinner afterwards."

Uncle Joe looked at JD's mom with a go-ahead nod.

"Oh, alright, if Kira's mother and Kira are okay with that."

"Kira, both it is!" JD said. "Mom, what time?"

"The first movie is at 2 pm, so I guess 1:15 if you want to be there for the previews and cartoon. I'll make the dinner reservations for six."

"We'll pick you up tomorrow at 1:15."

JD rushed through his supper and then called Kira again. The two talked for two hours. Several times, they were interrupted by someone on the party line wanting to make a call.

"JD, please get off that phone. Other people need to use that line. You might as well have gone to Grandma's Sullivan's and talked in person."

"Sorry, Mom, we're almost done."

"What on earth could you be talking about for two hours?"

"We're talking about the movies tomorrow."

"For heaven's sake, you will be with her tomorrow. I don't remember talking to a boy on the phone for hours."

"Kira, I gotta go. I'll talk to you tomorrow. Okay, mom, I'm off the phone."

Before his mother could answer, JD rushed off to his room. His mother washed and pressed his new clothes for the big day tomorrow. He never got new clothes in the summer. Just before the start of school in September, his mother would take him into town to buy clothes and new shoes for school. Summer was spent wearing out what was bought the previous year. He never felt like he was poor, but his mom struggled to make ends meet. He hadn't been to a movie in several years. Eating out was buying lunch in the school cafeteria once in a while. JD and his mother didn't have much, but they had enough.

JD lay in bed, thinking about Kira and him. He never expected to meet someone like her and be able to go to the canyon in one summer. He didn't want the summer to end. The one person who brought new joy into his life was leaving, and that was sad. He wished his mother were rich so he could go to New Zealand with Kira.

JD prayed for the first time in a long time: "God, please keep Kira and her family safe as they fly to New Zealand and bring Kira and her mother back safely. Amen."

After chores in the morning, JD did something he had never done in the middle of the week. He took a bath. His mother was shocked that she did not have to prod him.

JD's mother was also worried. She was worried her son would experience the pain she felt when his dad was killed. She wanted her son to experience love, but without the loss of love. She felt helpless to keep the loss from him, but she did not want love to pass him by.

"JD, you barely touched your lunch," JD's mom said.

"I'm not hungry. I'm too excited. Besides, we'll get something at the movies."

"Don't fill up on popcorn and candy at the movies. Remember, I have dinner arranged for you two at the café."

"Thanks, Mom. We'll probably be enjoying the movies too much. Did you know Kira studies bugs? We talked about that and the movie Swiss Family Robinson when we were hiking the canyon. It's cool, we can watch it together again. I'm sorry I gave you a hard time about showing Kira around. Boy was I wrong. She is so fun to be with. She makes me laugh, and she's super smart. She never once said no to anything, but if she believes in something, boy, she stands by her belief. I like that. The coolest part is that she doesn't care that I'm a nerd. She's like a boy, but better. She has pretty eyes, a beautiful smile, and I love her hair. She's strong too. Did I tell you she's smart?"

JD rambled on and on while his mom just looked at him. She understood what was happening. Her little boy didn't know it, but he was in love.

"You'd best start getting ready," JD's mom said. "It's almost time."

"I'm mostly ready."

"I think a wash rag needs to find your face, and a comb needs to find your hair. And don't forget to brush your teeth!"

JD did not resist this time. The last thing he wanted was to show up and not be presentable to Kira. He carefully washed his face and hands. He had already washed everything else in the bath earlier. He decided to go with a mostly combed but wild look for the hair. Uncle Joe paid for JD to have his first shave. There wasn't much more than peach fuzz to shave off, but JD's face was now smoother than a baby's bottom.

JD's mother knocked on the bathroom door. "JD, I have something for you."

JD opened the bathroom door. "What's that for?"

"It's deodorant for under your arms. Just roll it on. Trust me, you will thank me later."

251

JD reluctantly did as his mother said. The barber had splashed some awful smelly stuff on his face after the shave, which he successfully washed off during his bath. JD's preferred scent was 15-year-old farm boy au naturel. His mother preferred that he smell more like a human than a farm animal for his date.

JD finished dressing and went downstairs to present himself to his mom. Uncle Joe had bought him a new collared shirt, slacks, boots and felt cowboy hat.

His mother fought back the tears as she looked at her boy dressed as a young man. She did not want to think about him leaving home soon to start his own family. "You look handsome. You know, I think that outfit is suitable for going to church. Are you ready for this?"

"I think so. I am feeling nervous. I hope Kira doesn't think I'm dressed too fancy."

JD's mother remembered the first date she had with his dad. A tear rolled down her cheek. "Oh, I'm sure she won't."

"Mom, are you crying?"

"No, no...simply happy and proud of you. I'm sad that my little boy is growing up so fast. Soon you'll have your own family."

"Mom, I'll always be here for you. That will never change."

"I know, I know...well, let's go before I start crying. We don't want to be late. I have something else for you. I put together a small bouquet. A boy should always bring flowers to his girl."

JD hugged his mom. "Thank you, you're the best."

On the ride over, JD realized how important the deodorant was. He was nervous in a completely different way. He wasn't anxious like he was when he first met Kira. He had biked over to visit her several times, never giving it a second thought. Now lots of second thoughts flowed through his mind.

JD knocked on the door. Kira's mom answered.

"Hi, Aunt Sheila, is Kira ready?"

"She's just finishing up," Kira's mom said. "Please come in, you can wait in the parlor. Grandma Sullivan would like a word with you."

"Come on in, JD," Grandma Sullivan said. "Let me have a look at you."

JD removed his hat and hung it on the coat rack by the door. He cautiously walked into the parlor. Since this was his first date as Kira's boyfriend, he didn't know what to expect. The hallway to the parlor seemed to stretch to infinity. Now he was extremely thankful for the deodorant.

"Stop looking so anxious and scared," Grandma Sullivan said. "My, my, my, so handsome and grown up. Come sit here next to me."

"Yes, ma'am."

"How're you doing? Feeling okay?"

"Yes, ma'am. A little nervous, I guess."

"I have known you since you were just a baby. I have watched you grow up into a fine young man. And now you are taking my one and only granddaughter on a date."

"Yes, but Kira and I did go on a date for the 4th of July celebration," JD interjected.

"That was a chaperoned group date. This will be a one-on-one date—your first official date as boyfriend and girlfriend.

"You should know, not much gets past me. I have people everywhere telling me stuff. You two have grown to be close friends. I have seen how responsible you are with my own eyes. I know you two have declared you are boyfriend and girlfriend, but that is just the start of what can be something more. I want to be sure you understand a few things."

JD sat twirling the bouquet of flowers with his hands, trying to keep from fidgeting. "Yes, ma'am. I always respect what you have to say."

"I know you do, and I appreciate that. What I have to say now is what I would say to any young man who wants to take my granddaughter on a date. I want you to treat her with respect and as your equal. Some holding of hands and a little kiss, especially a goodnight kiss, is okay, but nothing more than that. Do you understand? You be good to her."

"Oh yes, ma'am. She's like a sister to me, but better. I mean…I'm glad she's not my sister. She's my best friend. I would never want to hurt her in any way ever."

"Yes, I know. I heard about you defending her honor at the drugstore. Love is a precious thing. It takes time to grow. Don't rush it."

JD looked bewildered, wondering how Grandma Sullivan had learned about the drugstore incident, but he agreed. "Like the plants in my mom's garden. They need caring for."

"Yes."

Kira walked into the parlor. "Hi, JD. I'm ready to go."

JD was thankful he was sitting down but worried he would not be able to stand up. He had seen Kira in a dress before and with makeup on when they came for dinner and for the 4th of July celebration. Both times, it reverberated through him like a wave of emotions. Now he was in shock.

Kira stood wearing a flowery dress that went down to her knees. The front was cut out just below her shoulders. Her long, copper-red hair hung softly down in front. Her eyes sparkled like diamonds. Her lips formed a smile that would have calmed a bear."

JD swallowed hard. He tried to say something. His brain could not find the words. It wouldn't have mattered because he couldn't speak. He uttered something that only he could hear.

Grandma Sullivan stood up, leaned on her cane, and said, "Here, JD, let me help you up."

Still staring at Kira, he took Grandma Sullivan's hand and slowly got up.

All JD could say was. "Wow."

"Did you bring me flowers?" Kira said.

JD thought. "Flowers, what flowers?" JD had forgotten about the flowers. He looked down at the flowers. He looked at Grandma Sullivan. She nodded in Kira's direction.

Miraculously, JD's brain rebooted, and he regained the ability to speak. "Yes, flowers. These are from my mom's garden."

"They're lovely. Let me go put them in a vase, then we can go."

JD took one step, then another. Thankfully, his legs worked. "I'll be waiting by the door."

JD's mother and Kira's mother had been standing in the parlor doorway and heard everything Grandma Sullivan had said. They both looked at Grandma Sullivan and mouthed the words. "Thank you."

Grandma Sullivan winked. "Sometimes a few words can slow things down to a safe speed. But those are two exceptionally fine kids. I don't have a worry in the world about them."

Kira came back and grabbed JD's hand. "Come on, JD. Let's go. I don't want to miss the coming attractions and the cartoon."

JD grabbed his hat. He thought. "And that's why she's my girlfriend."

Uncle Joe was outside, standing by a fancy luxury car. It look like a limousine. Uncle Joe was wearing his black suit.

"Uncle Joe, where did you get this car?" Kira said. "It's gorgeous. And nice suit. I feel like a movie star being taken to a premiere."

"Oh, I know a few friends who have some money. It's just a loan, so be careful."

"Uncle Joe, you sure do have lots of friends in high places," Kira said.

Uncle Joe winked and smiled. "It helps to be the Civil Defense Chief and the head geologist for the county."

"You look amazing," JD said as he opened the car door for Kira.

"And you look so handsome," Kira smiled. "Love the cowboy hat. I could get used to that look."

Uncle Joe chauffeured Kira and JD to the theater in time for the previews and cartoon. Several college kids walked by and whistled at Kira when she exited the car.

"That's annoying and rude," JD said. "Whistling at my girl!"

"Ignore them. I'm with you and not with them."

"Their actions prove their lack of culture," Uncle Joe said. "Okay, you two, I will pick you up after the second feature and take you to the café."

"Thanks, Uncle Joe, we'll be right here outside."

JD walked to the ticket office and bought the tickets for both shows. Kira stood looking at the billboard posters outside. "I'm so excited. I've never seen Mysterious Island. This is going to be so much fun."

"What do you want to drink? I'm getting popcorn and a cherry limeade for sure."

"Ditto for me. And a bag of peanuts, please. Can we sit down front, but not too close?"

"That's where I like to sit."

Only a few people were in the theater for the first show, so Kira and JD had their choice of where to sit. The usher escorted them to their seats.

During both shows, JD glanced over to look at Kira's reactions. She never flinched once and only squeezed JD's hand once. It was the giant bee scene in "Mysterious Island." Kira pulled JD's arm around her and leaned into his shoulder.

When the theater lights came back on, Kira said. "I don't want to move from this spot. Thank you for suggesting we see both movies."

"I especially loved seeing Swiss Family Robinson with you. But the night is not over. We'd better go."

"Yeah, okay. We don't want to keep Uncle Joe waiting."

JD and Kira walked out of the theater hand in hand. Uncle Joe drove up in the fancy luxury car. It was like having a chauffeur come pick them up.

"Did you guys like the movies?" Uncle Joe said as he opened the door for Kira and JD.

"They were super awesome!" JD said.

"It was so cool to see Swiss Family Robinson," Kira said. "We talked about that movie when we were hiking the canyon. What a coincidence."

"Sounds like fun. I hope you left room for dinner. Aunt Susan told me what the chef has fixed for you."

"We only had a bag of popcorn, some peanuts, and two drinks," JD said.

JD hopped out first at the café to help Kira out. Kira offered her hand to JD. "Thank you, sir."

"I'll come back around 7:30 to pick you two up."

JD walked over to Uncle Joe and whispered. "Could you pick us up at the town square around 8:30? I want to take Kira to the ice cream parlor for ice cream and show her the swing in the gazebo."

"How about nine thirty? I will call your moms so that they won't worry."

"Thank you, you're the best uncle a guy could have."

"Ha, well, I'm your only uncle, but I do try."

The café in town was not a fancy restaurant. Up front was just a diner, but a dinner section was in the back for those who wanted more than a burger and fries. A waiter met JD and Kira at the door and escorted them to a private table.

"Welcome. Tonight, the chef has prepared an Italian-style dinner for you. We will start with a bubbly citrus drink to whet your appetites and cleanse your palates. Then I will bring out a cheese platter, followed by the pasta dish. Tonight, the pasta will be spaghetti marinara. For dessert, we have."

JD interrupted. "Can we skip the dessert?"

"As you wish."

"Why are we skipping dessert?" Kira said.

"I want to take you to the ice cream parlor on the square. We can get some ice cream cones, then go swing in the gazebo by the courthouse."

"Oh wow! That sounds fun and romantic. Yes, please!"

The waiter brought the bubbly citrus drinks in wine glasses and lit the candle on the table. "Here is some Italian bread. And there's some olive oil mixed with salt, pepper, and herbs. You can dip the bread in it. Enjoy."

"Would you look at this," Kira said. "Wine glasses and a candle. I feel so grown up."

"My mom arranged it all."

"She did well. I have dreamed about going to Italy and having a candlelit dinner in a small café. You said you wanted to travel, right?"

"Yes, very much. Don't laugh. Sometimes I fall asleep listening to broadcasts from around the world on my short-wave radio. Some are in English, but most are not. I imagine I can understand their language. That's what confuses me. I want to do so much."

"You'll figure it out. I would love to travel too. I want to hike the Swiss mountains, walk the beaches of the South Pacific, and ride across the Serengeti."

"Would you go on a safari hunt?"

"With a camera, not a gun. I don't like killing things. If I were attacked, I would, I guess. To me, life is precious."

"One of my aunts gave me a subscription to National Geographic. Every issue has some amazing photographs. I don't know how they do it, but I would love to learn."

"What did you think about the movies?" Kira said. "What a coincidence both movies were showing. This has been the best summer of my life. I don't want it to end."

"I know. It's almost like a divine plan that is if I believed in such things. I loved both movies, too. I don't think I can choose. Swiss Family Robinson made me think of us wading through the river and camping. I read a lot, but I don't always have the words to express how I feel. I want you to know how happy I have been this summer. In the past, my granddad would take me places. My uncle did too, but he's been so busy in the past two years with the Civil Defense duties and his regular job. I had this hole in my life. You filled that hole. I wish we had more time."

"We have some time before I leave. How about we do something? I do need to pack and do extra studies, but I bet I can find a few days."

"Yeah, I'll be busy too. Mom wants me to repair the garden and get it ready for the fall planting."

"I would love to come help. Would you show me how?"

"Are you sure? It's not something most girls would want to do. It's hard work and you will be dirty."

Kira leaned over and looked JD in the eyes. "I'm not like most girls. You should know that by now."

JD laughed. "No, you certainly are not. You're the best. Hey, we could explore the park. We can even swim there."

"That's a plan, man," Kira smiled.

The waiter returned. "Are you two ready for the next course?"

Kira and JD smiled at each other. Together they replied, "Yes, we are."

During the spaghetti dish, JD remarked. "Did you see the movie, 'Lady and the Tramp'?"

"Yes, it was cute, but oh no, we aren't doing that with the spaghetti!"

"Oh, come on, let's try it."

Kira relented. "Okay, but I'm going to hold my napkin under my chin. My mom will kill me if I get this dress stained with spaghetti marinara sauce."

The spaghetti was long enough to repeat the Lady and the Tramp scene. They both got marinara sauce on their noses. JD laughed. Kira laughed as she wiped the sauce off her nose.

JD looked at Kira, laughing. The candlelight painted a soft glow across her face. Her eyes sparkled as the light bounced off them. He wanted to tell her how he felt, how she made him feel, but only small talk came out. "What did you think about the movies?"

"I loved both of them. Bug Girl liked the giant bugs in Mysterious Island, but I loved Swiss Family Robinson the most."

"Me too!"

Kira framed her face with her hands and batted her eyes. "So, do you think I am like Roberta?"

"I think you are so much more than Roberta. You are just as smart and brave, but so much prettier. Who do you think I am like? And don't say the monkey!"

"I see the childlike spirit of Francis, the brave strength of Fritz, and the intelligence of Ernst all in you. I like you, Nerd Boy, just the way you are. I would go anywhere with you."

JD blushed. This was the moment. He needed to tell her now.

Once again, only small talk came out. "Did you notice they had a waterslide too? That was cool. I will never forget when you slid into my arms, and we kissed. I don't know how to say this, but I am so happy you came. I'm sorry about your grandmother. I wish I could go with you. I don't want you to leave. I would go anywhere with you."

261

"I know. Nana told me something. She said, 'You have to walk the path before you know where you are going.'"

"What does that mean?"

"I think it means we don't know what life will bring. She also said you and I being together was important. After being with you, I know you are important to me."

"Ditto, so you think I am like Francis? Francis was all over the place, chasing elephants, ostriches, and monkeys. Am I like that?"

"In a way, your desire to explore and learn anything reminds me of Francis and Ernst. Francis was the comic relief, but remember, he did catch a tiger."

"True, there were so many great scenes in both movies. Sometimes, I want to be a writer and create stories that will take people away in their imagination to far-off worlds."

"Maybe one day you will write about our adventures. You'll figure it out. I believe in you, Nerd Boy."

JD smiled. "I will never forget this summer."

Kira grinned. "You better not!"

After more conversation and laughs, the meal was over—but the night was not. JD thanked the waiter, left a nice tip, and paid for the dinner. Kira kept looking at JD. Here was a nerdy boy becoming a young man.

"Are you okay with a short walk?" JD said. "The ice cream parlor is just around the square. They have many things like sundaes, cones, and fancy ice cream dishes."

"I am okay walking if you hold my hand."

Without hesitation or reservation, JD smiled and said. "My pleasure."

At the ice cream parlor, JD ordered two scoops of strawberry ice cream in a waffle cone.

"I'll have the same thing," Kira said. "Where's this gazebo and swing?"

"Just on the other side of the courthouse. I'll grab some napkins."

Time seemed to slow down as the two walked to the gazebo, trying to keep the ice cream from melting down the sides of the cones. People saw a teenage boy and a teenage girl walking together.

Kira and JD looked at each other and saw a friend. A friend who did not care if ice cream was covering their lips and running down their hands. They walked as if they were the only ones on the sidewalk that summer night.

A boy from Texas and a girl from New Zealand had created memories that would last forever. They sat in the swing talking about everything and nothing. It was a date to remember, but time does not stop for anyone.

Right at 9:30, Uncle Joe pulled up in front of the gazebo. It was time to go, but neither JD nor Kira wanted to go.

"You two love birds ready?" Uncle Joe said.

"Not really, but I guess we have to," Kira said.

Kira and JD sat quietly in the back during the ride back to Grandma Sullivan's. They held hands all the way, stealing glances at each other.

Uncle Joe waited in the car while JD escorted Kira to the door. JD stood in front of Kira, trying to find the words. He and Kira had been on a chaperoned date for the 4th of July celebration. There was no goodnight kiss then. Once again, his brain failed him. JD stepped forward and said, "I had a great time."

Kira walked up to JD. Her fingers played with the buttons on his shirt. She looked up. "Aren't you going to kiss me goodnight?"

JD would not have been able to account for what happened next even if he had been called to testify in a trial. He had kissed Kira before at the canyon. He wanted to kiss her again. He remembered getting the word goodnight out of his mouth, then all he could remember was feeling like he was floating. He opened his eyes and saw Kira staring back at him. JD felt anchored to that moment at that spot. He tried to say the words. He wanted to tell Kira how he felt but could only say goodnight.

He walked back to the car, turned back, waved, and said. "See you tomorrow."

Planting Memories

"Good morning, Aunt Susan. Is JD here?"

"Good morning, Kira, how're you doing? How was the date last night?"

"I'm fine. The date was fantastic. Thank you so much for arranging everything. JD did well. You would have been so proud of him."

"That's wonderful and always something a mother likes to hear. JD is out back of the barn. He's getting ready to work on the garden."

"He said I could come help. Is that okay with you?"

"Did you tell your mom about this?"

"Yes, ma'am. She wasn't too excited about it, but she said okay."

"If you don't mind getting dirty, it's okay with me."

"I don't mind. I'm looking forward to it."

"Well then, I might have to arrange another date for you two. There are other dirty chores…"

Kira didn't hear what JD's mom said. She was focused on finding JD. She did not want to miss a thing. JD was gathering what he needed to repair the flooded garden in the barn.

"Hey, JD. What do we need to do to start working on the garden?"

"Hey Kira, are you sure you're ready for hot, sweaty, dirty work? Nice overalls by the way."

"They're my mom's from when she was my age. I prefer jeans and a shirt, but overalls are better than a stupid dress."

"You look great in anything. You look amazing in a dress, but that wouldn't work today."

"Hahaha. So, you like how I look, huh?"

JD smiled and reached for Kira's hand. "I like everything about you."

"Right back at ya. I'm ready to get dirty! Just tell me what I need to do."

"Alright. Here are some work gloves. Grab the wheelbarrow. I'll bring the shovel, digging fork, and rake. Let's go. The garden is a mess from the flood. We're going to have to rebuild most of the beds."

"Let's get started."

JD surveyed the damage to the garden. Flood waters had rushed through the entire garden. The rock walls of some beds had collapsed, spilling dirt out and covering the paths with mud. "Let's clear the paths first. Then we will have to repair the walls. After that, we will need to turn the soil. That was the part Dolly loved the most. She would stand in front, waiting for me to press the fork into the ground. She danced back and forth on her legs, getting ready to pounce. As soon as I lifted and turned the dirt over, her eyes would spot a grub. She snatched that grub and chomped it down before I had sidestepped to the next part of the row."

"I wish I could have seen that," Kira said. "I've never had a dog or any pet. We live in an apartment in Auckland with no yard. Still, I wish."

"Dolly was part of my life. She was more like family. My uncle got her for me."

"It must have been hard to lose her."

"Yeah, it was."

"I remember someone recently telling me that loss is part of life," Kira smiled. "Do you believe there's a heaven?"

"I don't know. There's no scientific evidence for it. No one has come back to tell us about it."

"So, you don't believe Jesus rose from the dead?"

"My mother does. My granddad did, but he didn't come back. It's a lot to believe without facts, without some evidence. What do you believe?"

"Nana has told me stories that were passed down from her ancestors. They believe humans came from a place beyond this world. They are just stories and no facts, but thousands of people over thousands of years have believed those stories. How can so many people believe a lie for so many years? I don't know. I don't believe this is all there is."

"I hope heaven, or something like it, exists beyond this life. I would love to have Dolly run to me when I die, jumping up and licking my face. I read an article that said energy and matter cannot be destroyed. So maybe something survives. Right now, I see dirt and lots of work right."

"I love working with you," Kira said. "I love that we can talk about anything."

"Hey, can you stay for lunch? If we can finish this today, how about we go to the park tomorrow?"

"I'll call my mum when we are back at the house. I do have to work on my studies tomorrow and help pack. How about this Saturday? We can spend the entire day at the park."

"Super. I'd like that. And if heaven does exist. I want to be there with you."

"Ditto. What next?"

"We need to turn the soil over in the beds."

"Okay, but what do we do with the grubs? I'm not going to eat them!"

"We have to remove them, or they will destroy the new seedlings. We'll just put them in a bucket as fish food. Hey, how about we go fishing Saturday?"

"I guess, but do we have to keep the fish? I'm not wanting to kill anything right now."

"Nah, we can just toss them back. I have hooks with no barbs, so they come right out. Or we can toss the grubs to the fish."

"I'll try fishing, but I want to swim and explore."

JD looked at Kira. She had dirt on her from head to toe. Splotches of dirt dotted her face, above and below her eyes. He leaned on the digging fork and smiled at Kira.

"What? Why are you smiling?"

"You'll find out when you look in a mirror," JD said. "I think we have done enough for today. How about lunch, before you go home?"

Kira picked up some of the mud, formed a ball, and tossed it at JD.

JD unsuccessfully tried to dodge the mudball. "Hey, why did you do that?"

"You don't look muddy enough. Your mother might think you were letting me do all the work."

JD picked up some dirt, formed a mud ball, and tossed it at Kira. "Hahaha, I'm not buying that."

Kira threw up her hands. "Alright, alright. I call 'uncle!' Let's get some lunch. I'm going to need to use the outdoor faucet to wash up. I don't want to track mud in your mom's house."

FOREVER FRIENDS

JD was at Grandma Sullivan's door early on Saturday morning. He brought two fishing poles and a box of grubs. He also packed two deflated inner tubes and an air pump.

"Morning, Aunt Sheila, is Kira ready?"

"She's just about," Kira's mom said. So, you two are going to the park today?"

"Yes, ma'am. I hope that's okay."

"It's more than okay. Kira told me all about your date the other day. Thank you for being a gentleman and treating her right."

"I had a wonderful time. I wish she weren't leaving so soon. I'm so sorry about Grandma Sullivan."

"We all are, but you're helping Kira keep her mind off it. Thank you for that."

Kira walked up while JD was talking to her mom. "Hey, JD, I'm ready. I need to grab my bike."

"Cool, I packed us a lunch," JD said.

"Sweet as, we can have a picnic like before."

Kira and JD rode their bikes down the dirt road where they had had their race before. A swift summer breeze sent Kira's ponytail flying behind her head. So much had happened since JD and Kira raced to the park that first day. There was no racing this time, but a dust cloud followed behind them as they pumped their pedals. They stopped at the crest of the hill above the park.

"I love this park," Kira said. "It's so wild and open."

"We usually have our 4-H camp here, over there in the open field near the community center."

"How about we camp out here sometime? I mean when I...when I come back."

"Sure. Come on, we can fish by the dam," JD said, trying to stop Kira from thinking about what would happen before she came back.

"Right behind you."

Kira and JD leaned their bikes against a tall oak tree. They sat down in the shade of the oak tree, their legs hanging over the side of the riverbank. JD opened the box of grubs and pulled one out.

Kira took the grub from JD and carefully examined it. "They look so weird with white bodies and hard heads. And they squirm so much."

"Getting them on the hook is tricky. Here, let me show you."

"Do we have to?"

JD picked up on Kira's tone. "No, we can just use these plastic worms."

An intermittent breeze flowed around the trees. The breeze traveled across the water, creating tiny ripples. During the still moments of that summer morning, a splash was heard, then another as fish attempted to jump out to catch some flying critter. The ripples in the water caused the float on the fishing line to bob up and down. Aside from the breeze and ripples in the water, nothing happened. A few birds came by to offer their song, but otherwise it was just two friends sitting on the riverbank patiently waiting for some fish to take the bait.

"So, this is fishing," Kira said. "It's so peaceful here. I want to lie back and watch the wind play with the leaves."

"Wow, Bug Girl loves nature and is poetic too!"

"Haha, well, I feel what I feel, and nature brings out more of what I feel. I don't always have the words."

"I like sitting here. My brain stops thinking about stuff. I do get ideas, but they don't all rush in at once when I am sitting holding a fishing pole. My granddad would take me fishing all the time. We rarely ever caught anything. It was more about being there together."

"I wish I had met your granddad. It must have been hard to lose him."

"My granddad was more like a father to me, and my Uncle has been like a big brother. They both have always been there to help me through stuff."

"They have been your anchor, your rock."

"Yeah, I guess so. Granddad taught me lots of stuff about farming and nature. He and I could talk about all sorts of things. Uncle Joe got me into science. Yeah, they both were there for me."

"I love my mom. She's a rock for me, too, but Nana is my wind. My love of nature comes from her. The Māori have a name, pounamu, or greenstone. It can mean many things, but mostly peace and connection to the natural world. When Nana came last year, she bought me a greenstone necklace. She said it connects me to my ancestors and creates a bond. That is the bond I have with her. That is why this is going to be so difficult for me."

"I wish I had the power to keep you from this. Don't you have power that you can use?"

"I'm just a child in the eyes of my people. I am like a minnow. And what power I have is not mine to use as I wish. It's complicated. I don't understand it all myself."

"I wish I believed more like you. My granddad did. He said all life is connected and all life should be respected. But then science says what is real is what can be measured."

"I believe in you, Nerd Boy. I can't explain it, but I believe it. I don't believe this is all there is. This life is wonderful, and being here makes it like heaven, but I believe there is more. You don't believe there's life after death, do you?"

"It's not that I don't believe. I hope there is, but there's no proof. I know I am alive right now. How can I be certain there is something after I die? What would be the purpose?"

"Maybe the purpose is something we cannot understand until we die? I believe we were destined to find each other."

JD looked perplexed. "So, you think we are soulmates? I don't think soulmates exist. I think two people meet and they sorta click. They spend time together and build on that. They decide to be together; it's not planned that way by destiny or God."

"Do you think we click?"

"Yeah, I do. I want you to come back, and we can build on that. We can go to school together and have other adventures."

"What if I don't come back? What if my mom decides to stay in New Zealand?"

JD looked down at his fishing rod. "I'd be sad. That wouldn't mean we were or were not meant to be together. We met because my mom and your mom are friends. It was likely that your grandmother would eventually need help. You all could have stayed in New Zealand, then you and I would not have met. There are several ways that life could have been different. I am happy it happened the way it did. I got to meet Bug Girl and go on the adventure of my life. I look forward to more."

JD paused and looked at Kira. "I want more. I want to be with you and have more adventures."

"I do, too, but we might have to wait. I can't say anymore. It's not easy to explain. We are meant to be together, even if you don't believe that."

"Either way, I'm happy you're here now. Right now, I don't believe these fish are going to bite. How about we go swimming and wading, then have some lunch?"

"Let's go for it."

As Kira stood up, she gently touched JD's shoulder and whispered, "Don't forget."

"What'd you say?"

"Nothing important. Last one in the water is a grub!"

Kira stripped to her bathing suit and jumped into the water before JD could put away the fishing poles.

"Hey, no fair!"

JD jumped into the water and was immediately greeted with several splashes from Kira. He returned the splashes. "Now you're going to get it!"

JD fought through the rapid-fire splashes coming his way, pulled Kira up out of the water by her waist, and tossed her back. Kira sank below the surface, swam around JD, and jumped out of the water onto his back. They both went over and into the water.

The two rose out of the water in an embrace. JD pulled Kira close and gave her a passionate kiss. Kira felt herself losing control again. She pulled back and said, "Alright, Kissy Face, let's go explore the river."

"Okay, if we must. I have a surprise. I brought two inner tubes. I have to inflate them."

"Why the inner tubes?"

"You'll see."

JD pulled the inner tubes from his bike basket and inflated both with the air pump. "Here, this one is for you. We'll go down to the river below the dam."

The water from the springs filled the river until it flowed over the dam through culverts just below the road. Below the dam, the water fell in a long shower of tiny waterfalls, then snaked around and through piles of rocks. Stairs led down from the road to the water below. JD led the way down the stairs.

Kira tiptoed into the shallow water. "This is so cool! Not one, but many tiny waterfalls."

"Let's wade down. We might find something you will like."

"I like this so much. I love being here with you, exploring."

"Me too. You're not just my girlfriend but my best friend, forever."

"I want to go everywhere we can and explore everything. I want to see those bluebonnets and all the fields covered with wildflowers."

"I want to show you all that, but right now, look over there on that rock below that tree."

Kira walked over to JD, leaned over his shoulder, and looked in the direction JD pointed. "What is it? Is that a frog?"

"Yeah, I don't know what kind, but remember the tadpoles and the tiny frogs from the springs?"

"Yes, that could be a frog from one of those."

"Maybe. Either way, it's pretty cool."

"We need to get a journal and document everything we discover. When I come back, can we do that?"

"We can take science courses together in school. I mean, I assume you will go to school here."

"Yeah, I guess. Wow, we'll be best friends in school together. Are you okay with that?"

"Are you kidding? I'm excited about. You'll be like my sister."

"Whoa, wait a minute. I don't want to be your sister. I want to be your girlfriend. But I know what you mean."

"No matter what. Best friends forever, right?"

Kira grinned with a side look at JD. "Agreed, and more."

JD set his inner tube down, picked up a flat, smooth rock, looked at Kira, and smiled. "I hope so. Hey, have you skipped rocks before? My granddad was the expert."

JD leaned to one side and tossed the rock, skipping it almost across the river to the other shore.

Kira set her inner tube down, picked up a rock and tossed it, but it sank immediately. "Rats, mine just sank like a rock. Hahaha!"

"Here, I'll pick out a rock for you."

JD put his arms around Kira to help her position her arms.

"Whatcha doing, Nerd Boy?"

"I'm just showing you how to throw the rock so it will skip."

"Yeah, right. Here, I think I got the idea."

Kira leaned over and tossed the rock, skipping it to the other side.

"Wow! Quick learner!"

Kira turned to face JD and kissed him. "Thank you for teaching me."

JD picked up his inner tube and walked to the deep water. "Grab your inner tube and come over to the deep water."

"Okay, then what?"

"Sit back on top of the inner tube and push off with your feet."

"River tubing! I've heard of people doing it but never had the chance."

"When you come back, we can float down to our island."

"Sounds lovely. I hate to cut this short, but I have to get back and help with the packing."

"Do you need any help?"

"No, but thanks. You'll come by in the morning, right?"

JD held his head low. "You bet, let's get you home."

Kira lifted JD's chin and kissed him again. "Cheer up, Nerd Boy, this isn't over."

JD wanted to tell Kira what he felt. He had tried that night in the canyon. The words were there, but the courage was not. He took Kira's hand, and they walked back to their bikes.

The next day, JD arrived early at Grandma Sullivan's house to say goodbye to Kira. This was going to be difficult, but he had to, or he would regret not doing it.

Kira's mom opened the door. "Good morning, JD. Kira is finishing packing her suitcase. Come on in. You can wait in the parlor."

"Thank you, Aunt Sheila. "I don't know what to say to her. I'm going to miss her a lot."

"Just be honest with her and tell her how you feel."

Kira walked in while JD was talking with Kira's mom. "Hey, JD."

"Hey, Kira. So, are you all packed?"

"Yep, I just had a suitcase to pack."

JD handed Kira an envelope. "Cool, so, I uhm. I got some photos developed. You know the ones we took on the island. I had a copy made for you. The canyon ones are still in my backpack there."

"Sweet as! Thanks. I have something for you, too."

Kira handed JD a small box. Inside was a necklace. "The necklace is the greenstone Nana bought me when she came to New Zealand. I want you to keep it safe."

"Of course, I'll keep it safe. Are you sure you don't want to take it with you?"

"No, it will keep us connected no matter what happens. Look, I don't much like long goodbyes."

"I don't either."

JD turned to walk to the front door. Kira grabbed him. "I do like long kisses goodbye."

The sound of a car pulling into the driveway and Kira's mom's "ahem" shortened the long kiss.

"That's probably Joe," Kira's mom said. "He's going to give us a ride to the airport."

"I'll help with the luggage and Grandma Sullivan," JD said.

"Thank you, JD. That would be helpful."

"Did I hear my name?" Grandma Sullivan said as she walked down the hallway. "I'm coming. I don't need help getting into the car but would greatly appreciate help with the luggage."

"You're going to get help with both," Kira's mom said. "I'm going to start carrying out the suitcases. Uncle Joe and JD can help with the steamer trunk."

"Hello, JD," Grandma Sullivan said.

Then she winked and said, "I suspect your objective was to visit Kira, but I appreciate your offer of help and your taking care of the house. Come here and give us a hug."

Grandma Sullivan said something in Māori to herself. Then, looking at JD, she whispered, "Stay strong. Dark times are coming. Be the light. All will be well."

JD didn't understand what Grandma Sullivan said, but felt a deep sadness, like an impending doom. He gave Grandma Sullivan a tender hug. "I'm going to miss you."

Grandma Sullivan held JD at arm's length and smiled at him. "You've been like the son I never had. I've lived a long and happy life. I have no regrets. My greatest pleasure has been seeing you and Kira find each other. The time will come when you will need her and she you. Be good to her."

JD tried hard to hold back the tears. "I will, I promise. I will."

"I know you will. Now let's go. We don't want to keep Joe waiting."

Uncle Joe and Kira's mom were standing by the car, talking. Uncle Joe handed Kira's mom something. She said something, then hugged him and kissed him on the cheek.

JD straddled his bike and waved as Uncle Joe drove off, taking the one girl he loved to the airport. He turned and rode his bike home.

NOW AND FOREVER

It was several days before JD heard anything about Kira's flight home. Uncle Joe was coming this morning with a telegram. He hoped they all got there safely, but deep down, he felt nervous and afraid. JD sat at the kitchen table after breakfast, looking at the photos of him and Kira. He hoped to return to the canyon soon and retrieve the camera with the photos they took exploring that day.

Uncle Joe knocked on the kitchen door. From Uncle Joe's face, JD could tell immediately that the news was not good. Uncle Joe sat down at the table, holding the telegram. JD remembered his mother telling him about the telegram Uncle Joe gave her after he was born. Now, Uncle Joe had another telegram. He held the telegram in his hands, folding it and unfolding it over and over again. He tried several times to find the words.

JD dropped the photo he was looking at and said, "Just tell me!"

"Their plane was hit by severe turbulence from a cyclonic storm system. The plane crashed. There were no survivors."

JD's eyes did not blink. He sat there staring at Uncle Joe. His mind was blank. He couldn't feel anything.

"I'm so sorry, JD," Uncle Joe said.

JD's mother grasped her mouth. "Oh my god! This is horrible!"

JD got up from the table, ran up the stairs to his room, and slammed the door behind him. A few minutes later, his mother came up.

"I don't know what to say," JD's mom said.

"I hate your God! This is not fair. She was the only person who understood me; now she is gone. She is never coming back. I'm never going to see her again. This is wrong!"

The anger erupting inside JD turned to tears, then sobbing. "I even prayed! I didn't do anything wrong! This is not fair! I hurt so much. I want to die."

"I know. I felt the same way when I got the telegram about your father. I don't have any answers. It hurts because you loved her."

"I never told her I loved her. Now I, I, I can't!"

JD's chest rose and fell as tears gushed down his face. His mother put her arms around him, holding him close to her chest. He cried for several minutes before falling to sleep. His mother gently put him on the bed and covered him with a blanket. Uncle Joe was waiting outside the bedroom door.

"How's he doing?" Uncle Joe said.

"He's sleeping right now. I'll keep an eye on him tonight. How are you doing?"

"I had my cry on the way here. I won't lie, it's tough. I lost her twice."

"I know. I lost my best friend again, and the town has lost a rough and tough loving advocate. We all lost love today. This will be tough, but we will get through this together. Come back in the morning and have breakfast with us. JD will need us both, but I think you will be able to help the most."

"Will do. I love you, Sis."

JD slept through supper and into the night. Early the next morning, Uncle Joe knocked on JD's bedroom door.

"Hey, Sport, can I come in?"

"What?" JD said as he turned over, trying to wake up.

"I said, can I come in?"

JD stumbled to the door, opened it, and returned to the bed. He sat on the edge of the bed with his head staring at the floor.

"Come on down and have some breakfast. I need your help today with something."

"I'm not hungry. I'm too tired to do anything today."

"Yeah, but you need to, and you will. Put your boots on."

JD put on his boots and reluctantly followed Uncle Joe to the kitchen. He sat at the table, holding a spoon and staring at his bowl of cereal.

"Have some coffee, it will help wake you up," JD's mom said.

"I don't like coffee. I'm not hungry. I want to go back to bed."

"You can't and you won't. Drink the coffee, or I will take you to the clinic for tests."

"Fine, whatever."

"After breakfast, I need you to help me with something," Uncle Joe said.

"Do I have to? I don't feel like it. Why are you even here? To bring more bad news?"

"John David Jayson! Don't be disrespectful to your uncle. I understand you are hurting, but that doesn't mean you can take it out on others. I will be cleaning the house today, so I need you out of the house anyway."

"Fine, whatever. I don't care."

Despondent, JD lumbered out the kitchen door. He stood on the back steps. "Why are we taking Granddad's truck?"

"It has 4-wheel drive, and where we are going, there are no roads. It's more rugged and will handle the terrain better."

It was a quiet drive down the back road from the ranch. JD leaned back in the seat, staring at the road going by. Uncle Joe slowed down to cross the low-water bridge.

"Where are we going?" JD said as he looked up.

"We're taking the long way around the canyon. We need to get the stuff you and Kira left behind."

"I never want to go back there. I can't. You don't understand."

"I understand more than you think."

"Uncle Joe, it hurts so much. Just the thought of going back there makes it worse."

"I know, trust me, I know. But you have to go back. You have to face this before it destroys you inside."

JD had no energy to resist. He put his head back against the seat. With no road, it was a long, bumpy ride in silence. Uncle Joe parked the truck close to the tree by the spring pond above the waterfall. He stumbled out. He was a walking ghost following without emotion. His chest hurt. Kira was gone. All he had left was a hole in his heart and no will to go on. He lumbered on like a heavy boulder and floated like a feather simultaneously. Time slowed for him while the world whirled around him. He was in a dark, lonely tunnel.

JD struggled down the trail behind Uncle Joe to the campsite. Everything was still there where he had left it that night.

"I hate this canyon. I wish I'd never come here."

"No, you don't. You and Kira made memories here. Don't hate those memories because you are hurting."

"You're not the only one hurting, you know. Your mother lost her best friend. And I. Well, I."

"I know about you and Aunt Sheila."

"How? I never told you. Only your mother knows. Did she tell you?"

"She didn't have to."

JD walked over to the tree and dug up the box.

"Kira found this buried by the tree. We opened it and saw the letters."

"Did you read them?"

"No, we didn't. We buried the box again where Kira found it. Were you and Aunt Sheila in love?"

"I don't know. I think I was. I never gave Sheila the letters. I felt we were close. I wanted to tell her many times, but it never seemed to be the right time. After the accident, things changed. Your mother and father fell in love and later got married. Sheila was different around me.

"After the war, there was talk about Korea. Your dad went off to join the MASH unit. Sheila talked about going to New Zealand to help with the post-war effort. I wanted her to stay, but I didn't want to stand in her way. I wish I had said something. One day, we were kids exploring our canyon kingdom. The next day, World War II broke out. We weren't old enough to go to war, but too old to rule our canyon kingdom.

"I was never good at talking to girls, so I wrote the letters. I never had the courage to give them to Sheila. One day, I went to ask Sheila to stay. I was going to tell her I loved her and to please give me a chance. She was so excited about going to New Zealand to help her mom's people recover. I stood there looking at how happy she was. I couldn't keep her from that. So, I took the letters, put them in the box, and buried them by the tree. It was our favorite spot."

"Were you going to give her the necklace?"

"What necklace?"

"We saw a necklace in the box. We figured you were going to give it to Aunt Sheila."

Uncle Joe pulled the necklace from the box. A note was attached to it. It read. "I love you, always. -Sheila."

Tears dripped down Uncle Joe's face.

JD put his hand on Uncle Joe's shoulder. "That's a greenstone necklace like the one Kira gave me."

Uncle Joe stared at the necklace, reading the note over and over. "I never told her I loved her. When she came back with Kira, I should have reached out. I was a stupid, proud fool."

"I never told Kira I loved her, either. That hurts the most. She died not knowing."

"I am certain she knew. Sometimes actions are the only words needed. You experienced what love is. Don't bury it under a tree like I did. Keep it in your memories and find a way to continue."

"It's hard. I keep thinking about everything I wanted to show Kira and experience with her. I wanted to show her where the bluebonnets bloom in the spring."

"Trust me, I know it's hard. I hurt too. I feel like I missed out on so much. We'll get through this. It'll take time, but we'll do it. Let's gather all this stuff and go back to the house."

Uncle Joe kept the necklace but took the box and buried it again by the tree. JD grabbed his backpack but left the Graham crackers and marshmallows behind for the ants and other bugs to enjoy.

"Did you guys ever explore the cave?"

"What cave? We never found a cave here. Where is it?"

JD walked over behind the tree and pulled back the hanging vines. "Right here."

"I don't see a cave. Just rock covered in moss."

JD turned and looked at the face of the cliff. The cave was gone. "What? I swear there was a cave here. I'm pretty sure there was one."

"I believe you, Sport, but maybe you're remembering a dream. You've been through a stressful time. The mind does some strange things."

"Yeah, maybe. It does feel like a dream, but almost a real memory. Let's go home."

On the way up the trail, JD turned to look back at the waterfall. "I will never sell this land. One day, I will donate it to become a park as a memorial to Kira. It will be our place now and forever. Others will come and experience the beauty we did. Kira would love that."

"I agree," Uncle Joe said. "That's a great idea. Next year, we can come back and camp out. Just you and me."

"I'd like that."

On the trip back to the house, Uncle Joe told JD more stories about the Four Amigos.

"Did you guys slide down the rock?"

"Oh, yes, every time we went. One time, I slipped and fell right on my butt. I was sore for weeks."

JD laughed. "I wish I had seen that. Kira and I found some bluebells. She liked nature and especially bugs. She loved the wildflowers, the bees, and stuff."

"Her mother loved nature too. She was always collecting rocks and flowers to press in books. She kept a record of everything she found."

"I want to do that. You and I could do a study of the canyon."

"You got it, Sport. I'd like that."

"Oh no. I think…"

"What?"

JD rummaged through his backpack and found what he wanted.

"Never mind, I found it."

"What is it?"

"The disposable camera you gave us. I hope the film is okay."

JD felt better that night, but a dull pain persisted. He did not have problems sleeping, but he woke up when his shortwave radio turned on in the middle of the night. A Morse Code message kept repeating over and over again. "What the hell?" JD thought.

He sat at the desk and copied the code letter by letter, translating each combination of dots and dashes. The message read.

"BUG GIRL TO NERD BOY NEVER FORGET"

He rubbed his eyes and carefully copied the code as it repeated. The message was the same each time:

"BUG GIRL TO NERD BOY NEVER FORGET"

The message repeated several more times and stopped. JD didn't know what to think. What did this mean? Who sent the message? Bug Girl and Nerd Boy was a secret between him and Kira. He stared at the decoded message. He couldn't tell anyone. No one would believe him. He figured people would say he heard some coded message and wrote down what he wanted it to read.

JD got up the next morning, finished his chores early, and sat at the kitchen table, smiling at the photos he had taken with Kira.

"Good morning, I didn't expect you to be up so early. How are you feeling?"

"Good morning, Mom. I'm feeling fine. I finished all my chores."

"Well then, I'm going to fix you breakfast."

"Can you make some pancakes?"

"Sure, and how about some scrambled eggs. Did you collect any eggs this morning?"

"Yes, ma'am, I did."

"Good. I need to talk to you about something."

"Sure, Mom. What?"

"Uncle Joe and I have been talking with Grandma Sullivan's friends and ranch hands. The African American Church wants to hold a memorial service. The church loved Grandma Sullivan. You are welcome to attend, but I understand if it would be too much for you."

"No, I want to come. I can put some photos in an album for everyone to see. I bet Grandma Sullivan has some of her and Aunt Sheila at her house. She put me in charge of the house, so I have the key."

"I think that's a lovely idea. After the service, we must visit Grandma Sullivan's lawyer to settle her estate. You and Uncle Joe are mentioned in Grandma Sullivan's will."

"What does that mean?"

"I don't know. I guess we will find out."

The memorial service was solemn but filled with joyful moments. The church was overflowing, with standing room only. So many people signed the photo album and guestbook that JD needed extra paper from the pastor.

Grandma Sullivan impacted so many lives. She never boasted about her work with the African American community. JD's mom knew, as they often worked together. That consistent quiet love came back in loud, joyful music. Even JD gave in. He sang and clapped to the music. After getting the Morse code message, JD wasn't sure what he believed. He wasn't even certain he hadn't just imagined the message. Deep down, he felt it was real. It was a comfort.

Following the memorial service, JD, his uncle, and his mother gathered at the lawyer's office that afternoon. It was another solemn moment.

The lawyer walked in, holding the will. "Good afternoon, I am so sorry we must meet under these circumstances. I will be out of the office for several weeks in two months. I wanted to start the process now."

"It's quite alright," JD's mom said. "I don't understand why we were mentioned in Grandma Sullivan's will. We loved her dearly, but we are not her kin."

"Yes, well, apparently, she considered you her closest friends and as if you were her family. Her immediate family has passed away."

"Surely, there are cousins and other relatives," JD's mom said.

"None of her side of the family remains. She was hoping to be buried where her ancestors were buried. That has been arranged. She specifically gave a copy of her will to Mr. Hayden and me, whom she designated as the executor of her estate. I believe that establishes her intentions along with her will. Once I go over the will's contents, I will start the probate process before leaving. The inventory of all assets and accounts has already been done, and there are no outstanding debts. I expect the probate process to be quick."

"That sounds like Grandma Sullivan," JD's mom said. "I will miss her so much."

"I agree," Uncle Joe said. "Even as kids, we would gather at her house for lemonade and cookies. She would give us all a penny for some treat at the drugstore. But we all had to earn that penny first by doing some chore or task, which we gladly did and would have without being paid. She was like a grandmother to all of us kids."

"Yes, she had a significant impact on the entire community. May I continue?"

"Yes, of course," JD's mom said.

"My secretary will witness and record that the will has been read. Now, beginning with the estate.

Except as mentioned below, the house and five hundred acres, to include the barn and other buildings, go to Mr. Joseph Hayden. Mrs. Sullivan wishes that Mr. Hayden reside at the house and manage that part of the ranch. The sum of 10,000 dollars is to be donated to the African American Church. The remainder of her estate, which includes another five hundred acres and other assets, is to be held in trust for Master John David Jayson until he reaches eighteen. Until then, Mrs. David Jayson (birth name, Susan Marie Hayden), Master Jayson's mother, will be the guardian. In addition, this book of Māori legends and myths, along with all of her other books, is willed to Master John David Jayson. Mrs. Sullivan wishes that Master Jayson would enjoy reading and benefit from her books. Mrs. Sullivan's daughter also left a will. It specifies her mother and daughter as equal heirs to her assets. Those assets will be split accordingly as specified in Mrs. Sullivan's will, except that the bicycle belonging to Kira is to be given to Master Jayson."

"I don't understand why her daughter wasn't mentioned in Grandma Sullivan's will?" JD's mom asked.

"She was in the original will, but that was changed. She came to my office a week before they left for New Zealand and changed the will at that time. At that time, I had the new will notarized. She gave Mr. Hayden a copy before they left for the airport. He brought his copy to me. It matched word for word to the one she gave me."

"Wait," Uncle Joe said. "So, you're saying she knew they would not make it to New Zealand?"

"I'm not saying that at all. I am just recording that the will was changed. That is all I know. Are there any other questions?"

Uncle Joe and JD's mother both said, "No."

"Good. I will submit the will to the court this afternoon. Given that there are no outstanding bills and all assets have been inventoried, I fully expect the probate process to be completed before I leave. I will notify you when that happens. Thank you all for coming. Please accept my heartfelt condolences on your loss."

"That was unexpected," Uncle Joe said as they all stood outside the lawyer's office.

"Yes, it was," JD's mom said. "I don't know what to make of it. What do we do now?"

"I don't know," Uncle Joe said. "I'm kind of in shock. Can we go back to your house? I'm getting hungry, but don't want to eat right now."

JD opened the Māori book of legends. Inside was an inscription from Grandma Sullivan to him: "Never stop believing in yourself." Below that was a note from Kira, "Bug Girl to Nerd Boy, Never Forget."

JD stood there looking at the inscriptions in disbelief. "I can't believe this."

"What?" JD's mom said.

He showed the inscriptions to his mom. "Last night I heard a Morse Code message from my shortwave radio. It repeated over and over again. I wrote down the code and got it decoded just as the message disappeared."

"What did the message say?" Uncle Joe said.

"I put it in my pocket this morning before we left for the church."

JD and his mother read the message, "Bug Girl to Nerd Boy Never Forget, " and compared it to the inscription in the book.

"Kira called me 'Nerd Boy,' and I called her 'Bug Girl.' No one else knew about this. How could a message come over my shortwave radio and be the same in the journal? What does it mean?"

JD's mother put her arm around him. "There are some things beyond our understanding, but to me, it means this life is not the end. Let's go home and have lunch. We can share stories and memories."

"I'd like that," Uncle Joe said.

"I'm saying grace," JD said.

"Sport, I'm going to need help around the ranch," Uncle Joe said. "Are you up for helping out? I will help you get your learner's permit and official driver's license."

"You got a deal!" JD said.

JD's mother frowned. She knew she had to let go but did not enjoy the process.

That night, JD walked over to his shortwave radio, wondering if he should leave it on. In the back of his mind, he did not want to let go, yet he knew he had to at some point. He looked down at the on/off switch and switched it to the off position. Then, he unplugged the power cord from the wall socket. JD went to bed, still feeling the loss but taking the first steps to accepting it.

In the middle of the night, the shortwave radio powered up and started broadcasting Morse Code again.

"-... ..- --. / --. .. .-. .-.. / - --- / -. . . .-. -.. / -... --- -.-- -.-.--
/ - .... / .. ... / -. . --- - / --- ...- . .-. -.-.--"

JD woke up, turned over, and stared at the shortwave radio. He got up, went to his desk, and picked up the power cord to the radio. He stood there looking at the plug. It was not plugged into the wall socket. The on/off switch was still in the off position, but the dots and dashes of Morse Code kept broadcasting through the speakers over and over. "What the hell?" JD mumbled.

He sat down at the desk and started copying the message, which repeated over and over again. Once he had copied the entire message, it stopped broadcasting.

JD grabbed his Morse Code book and translated the code to English text. It read:

"BUG GIRL TO NERD BOY! THIS IS NOT OVER!"

EPILOGUE

Every week, JD, Mark, Ben, and Billy got together for poker and general gossip about the previous week – "the who did what or why that trade?" JD and Mark met in college, then served together in the military during the Vietnam War. Mark and JD swapped each week as each other's wingman in college. JD was responsible for Mark meeting his wife, Mary. This Friday, it was just Mark and JD. Ben and Billy were off on their respective honeymoons. Billy had been Ben's best man, and Ben had been Billy's best man. Their wives agreed to having the weddings together but said no to joint honeymoons.

"Mark, I am not joking. There is something out there and it's been tracking me," JD said.

"It was just the wind. You know how it is in the canyon," Mark said.

"It was a foggy morning. No wind at all," JD said.

"Then what do you think it was? Sasquatch? A mountain lion?"

Epilogue

"Sasquatch in Texas? Too funny. And I don't think it is a mountain lion. I know that property very well. I have never seen the tracks of a mountain lion. As far as I know, they are as scared of us as we are of them. No, I don't know, but I will find out."

"Have another beer before Mary shuts us down. Sit back and enjoy the sounds of the evening. I'm certain it was nothing. Are you okay? It's been 15 years. You need to get back out there. You know, Mary has a cousin who wants to meet you."

"I'm fine. Yeah, it still hurts at times, but I'm fine. I don't want to get back into dating right now. Every time I tried, it ended badly."

"That's because you keep putting Kira up as the standard. No one is ever going to replace the first love. Look, have dinner with Marjorie and us. Nothing else, okay?"

"Fine, whatever. Geez, you can be a nag at times!"

"Great, how about next Saturday evening? Now, go home and get some rest. You're getting obsessed with this spooky action. It's probably nothing. Just some wild animal or the wind."

"Mark, I know what I felt was not the wind. I am going to find out what it was."

"Well, how about you grab your fancy camera and take a hike tomorrow morning. Document this thing of fantasy. I think you've been working too many extra shifts since Ben and Billy have been away. You should have hired some temp help while they are gone."

"I'll be fine. We scheduled jobs around their absence. And I always have my camera with me. I'll see you next week with proof!"

This will be continued in the sequel, "Beyond the Falls."

296

About the Author

Hi, I'm Rich (RichO is my nickname). Writing a novel has been a lifelong dream. For years, I have published short stories, poems and articles online. For over twenty-five years, my focus has been on my wildflower photography. I am the author of several nonfiction books about Texas Wildflowers. This novel is from my heart. It is a work of fiction but based on my experiences growing up in Texas on a small farm. It is my love story about Texas.

https://www.facebook.com/RichOCreative/
https://www.instagram.com/richo_creative/
Website: https://www.richo.org/
(Visit the website to sign up for bonus material.)

The Map

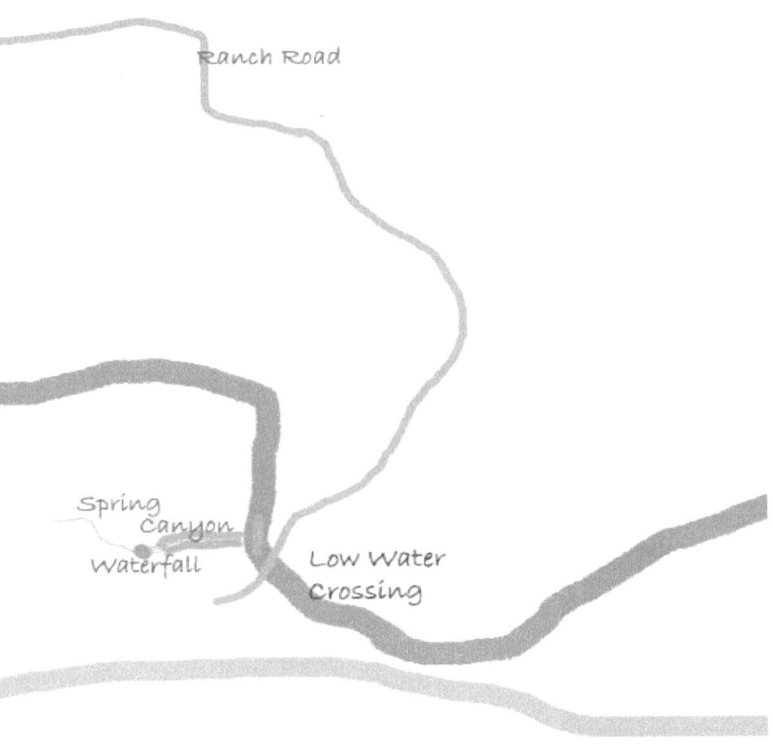